"You really think this is the end for Eagle Springs, Nash?" Helen stared up at him, looking like she needed reassurance. "I keep hoping for a Christmas miracle."

"Me, too." Nash shrugged deeper into his coat, having no reassurance to give her. In fact, it was the opposite. Having her by his side gave him a sense of optimism that had been lacking these past few months. "But the rest of the town? They've given up hope. To them, this is the last Christmas parade. The last lighting of the town Christmas tree. And no one wants to miss the last anything in Eagle Springs."

Helen sighed. "Unless something changes, it will be the end. Next year, we'll all be somewhere else."

He hoped her somewhere else would also be his.

"Only if you give up before the challenge really starts," he said softly.

A small smile blossomed on her beautiful face.

Dear Reader,

I come from a large extended family and have developed a large extended writing family. So, when it came time to decide if I was going to explore another branch of the Blackwells with my Blackwell author sisters, how could I say no? Especially when given the opportunity to write a Blackwell Christmas!

Family is also important to cutting horse trainer Nash Blackwell. This holiday season, it's up to him to raise the final chunk of money to save the family ranch. He doesn't want to let his Blackwell siblings down. He also wants to do right by his ex-wife, Helen, whom he still loves. But intentions sometimes run into roadblocks and for the simplest of reasons. In short, Nash finds himself in a pickle, and suddenly, saving the ranch is on Helen's shoulders, too. Is she up to it? You'll have to read on to find out.

I hope you enjoy this installment of The Blackwells of Eagle Springs and the other Blackwell books—as of this writing, there are fifteen! Although each book stands alone, there is one character that binds the series together—Big E Blackwell. I like to think he's watching over the Blackwell series the same way he's watching over his family in Eagle Springs.

Happy reading!

Melinda

HEARTWARMING

Wyoming Christmas Reunion

Melinda Curtis

HARLEQUIN®
HEARTWARMING™

Recycling programs for this product may not exist in your area.

ISBN-13: 978-1-335-58474-8

Wyoming Christmas Reunion

For questions and comments about the quality of this book, please contact us at CustomerService@Harlequin.com.

Harlequin Enterprises ULC
22 Adelaide St. West, 41st Floor
Toronto, Ontario M5H 4E3, Canada
www.Harlequin.com

Printed in U.S.A.

Award-winning *USA TODAY* bestselling author **Melinda Curtis**, when not writing romance, can be found working on a fixer-upper she and her husband purchased in Oregon's Willamette Valley. Although this is the third home they've lived in and renovated (in three different states), it's not a job for the faint of heart. But it's been a good metaphor for book writing, as sometimes you have to tear things down to the bare bones to find the core beauty and potential. In between, and during, renovations, Melinda has written over thirty books for Harlequin, including her Heartwarming book *Dandelion Wishes*, which is now a TV movie, *Love in Harmony Valley*, starring Amber Marshall.

Brenda Novak says *Season of Change* "found a place on my keeper shelf."

Jayne Ann Krentz says of *Can't Hurry Love*, "Nobody does emotional, heartwarming small-town romance like Melinda Curtis."

Sheila Roberts says *Can't Hurry Love* is "a page turner filled with wit and charm."

Books by Melinda Curtis

The Mountain Monroes

Charmed by the Cook's Kids
The Littlest Cowgirls
A Cowgirl's Secret
Caught by the Cowboy Dad
Healing the Rancher
A Cowboy Thanksgiving

Return of the Blackwell Brothers

The Rancher's Redemption

The Blackwell Sisters

Montana Welcome

Visit the Author Profile page at Harlequin.com for more titles.

To Carol Ross, Cari Lynn Webb, Amy Vastine and Anna J. Stewart for taking this writing journey with me. And to our editor Kathryn Lye for watching over us in a way Big E would approve of. Love you, ladies!

CHAPTER ONE

"I CAN'T MARRY YOU, PHIL." Helen Blackwell tested out the line in the cab of her blacksmithing van as she left Eagle Springs and headed toward nearby Carson, Wyoming.

Her declaration felt argumentative. And Phil Mitchell had been nothing but kind to her this past year.

Helen tried again. "I can't *marry* you, Phil."

That felt too glib. And Phil deserved her heartfelt sincerity.

The miles ticked by without revealing the best way to break her engagement.

Helen slowed, taking the turn to the Mitchell Ranch on a gravel drive that had a sprinkling of snow. "Keep calm. Just don't tell him you're still in love with Nash." Her ex-husband and the father of their five-year-old son, Luke.

The van's chassis rattled as she crossed the metal cattle guard and passed beneath the grand arch welcoming her to the Mitchell Ranch, predictably, the dashboard display flickered. She hoped she was still welcome after she returned Phil's engagement ring.

"I'd like for us to still be friends," she said, practicing her warm, yet neutral, smile in the rearview mirror. She pulled up to the barn and got out, her cowboy boots crunching on a thin layer of crisp snow.

Each step heralding the end of Phil's dreams of a happy life with me.

Helen drew a deep breath of cold winter air, reminding herself not to be overly dramatic. She'd been brash and boisterous through the first half of her twenties.

And look where that got me.

No. It was best to be reasonable and diplomatic, even if she had to bite the inside of her cheek.

"There's my best girl." Phil emerged from the barn, walking beneath a beribboned and snow-dusted holiday wreath. He was everything a gal was *supposed* to want in a fiancé—taller than she was, more financially stable than she was, more settled all around than she was. He was also prettier than she was.

Truth.

Phil had the blond, dimpled, all-American good looks of models pretending to be ranchers and cowboys. His boots were always as polished as a new set of horseshoes. Helen, on the other hand, always looked like she'd been tossed around by a bull. Not just once, either, but several times. Adding to that, her frame was too lean, a casualty of long days spent shoeing horses. What she wouldn't give to have some curves.

"Hey, Phil."

Do you have to sound like the bearer of bad news?

Helen shrugged deeper into her jacket, suddenly feeling the bite of the early December wind.

Phil was no dummy. He stopped a few feet away from her instead of sweeping her off her feet the way he usually did. "You look like you just spent the last hour stuck in a ditch. Anything I can do?"

"No. Phil, I've been thinking..."

He tipped back his gray felt cowboy hat.

All the words she'd practiced stuck in her throat. How was she going to break their engagement?

The simplest ways are the best.

Those were her father's words. He'd been dead more than six years now, a welder who'd been happy to share his pearls of wisdom, while she, rejected as too soft by her mother, had been eager to listen to him.

Simple. Right.

Helen worked the platinum band with its solitary diamond free from her finger and extended it to Phil.

"Helen..." Phil's blue eyes softened, creating lines that emanated across his cheeks. "I thought we agreed not to overthink this." That's what he'd said last month when he'd proposed, possibly because she'd hesitated to answer.

Show them your backbone, dove.

That was her mother's voice, bracing and unwelcome.

Helen took Phil's hand, along with her resolve, and pressed her engagement ring into his palm, curling his fingers around the diamond. "You deserve someone who'll work this ranch by your side."

Phil's arm wound around her shoulders, trying to draw her closer. "Marry me and you don't have to work. You can spoil Luke with time and anything his little cowboy heart desires."

"You know me, Phil. I have to carry my own weight." That was something her mother had been adamant about.

"We can table the wedding for now, Helen. And continue our engagement indefinitely." Phil tried to open his fist, tried to offer her the ring again.

Helen kept her fingers clasped over his.

Even their hands were different. His were the

unblemished hands of a man with a stableful of hired cowboys. Hers were scarred, bruised and colorful from shoeing horses.

"Helen, we have a good thing here," Phil said softly, smoothly, temptingly.

And maybe that was what Helen found wrong with Phil. Everything was too good, even her promised life with him. Phil had no rough edges. He may have owned a ranch and competed in cutting horse competitions, but he wasn't a worker the way her father or her mother had been.

The way Nash is.

If they had a good thing, Phil would respect Helen's need to work for a living. If they had a good thing, she wouldn't look twice at his starting-to-be-prominent wrinkles and think about their fifteen-year age difference and how the gossips loved to say she was only marrying Phil for his money. If they had a good thing, she wouldn't have kissed her ex-husband two weeks ago while wearing Phil's engagement ring.

To be honest, Nash had initiated that kiss. But she'd kissed him back. And truth be told, she'd wanted that kiss more than a woman engaged to another man should.

"Being with you helped me to see things more clearly, Phil." To realize she had to pull herself up by her bootstraps and be honest with herself about what made her happy. "And I appreciate it, I really do. But if we continue to date, Nora Peachtree will never get her shot at you."

"Nora Peachtree?" Phil shook his head, smiling a little.

"You know you love her cooking." Nora cooked for Phil more often than Helen did. "And she's had her eye on you for I don't know how long." Decades, maybe.

Snow began to fall. Someone in the barn turned up the volume on Bing Crosby singing "White Christmas." The weight on Helen's shoulders lifted. This was going to be a civilized break-up. She'd lost sleep since she'd decided to end their engagement and worried all the way over here for nothing.

"We can still be friends." Helen took a step away from Phil. And then another. "Now, which horses am I shoeing today?"

Phil shifted on his feet, boots erasing his tracks in the snow as if he were wiping a slate clean. Something shifted in his eyes as well. He shook his head. "I can't be your friend, Helen. And I can't have you here, as a reminder of what might have been, either."

Helen's heart leapfrogged up her throat, making her croak, "What are you saying?"

"I'm saying I no longer require your blacksmithing services." His gaze turned as flinty as his words, a clear indication that she'd wounded his pride and would suffer for it.

"But..." She'd been relying on his business to buy Luke a horse for Christmas. "You've been a client of mine since I moved back to Eagle Springs." Six years ago. And he was one of her most lucrative accounts.

"I'm sorry." Phil settled his hat more firmly on his head. "It's too soon for me to let you back in, even as far as the barn."

And by too soon, it sounded like he meant forever.

NASH BLACKWELL CLUCKED at the fine piece of horseflesh circling him on a lunge line.

The ebony filly was eager to do his bidding and didn't care about the mistakes Nash had made in the past.

Nash cared. His sister Adele would probably say he cared too much. But she was a softy when it came to mistakes and forgiveness. For her, his descent into binge drinking for two years was firmly in the past. Two years past, to be exact. But the causes of his drinking and the drink itself had cost him his marriage. Today, he had more regrets than a thirty-three-year-old man should have.

Nash swung the training flag in the opposite

direction, signaling to the filly to turn and head the other way. And then he did it again, keeping Rose executing tight turns back and forth in the covered round pen.

Ears forward, Rose did as he asked with a toss of her head. She was a clever, well-behaved three-year-old that enjoyed cutting horse training. With the right rider, she had a shot at being a champion one day.

Like Jet.

Nash felt the familiar wave of cold wash over him as memories of the accident four years ago funneled past. The crunch of metal. The squeal of tires. The tumble into rocks and trees. The blood. His blood and… He shied away from the brutal images in the horse trailer.

Nash's fingers clenched on the lunge line just as they used to close around a whiskey glass.

He drew a deep breath, focusing on the sound of hooves on loamy soil and a gust of cold winter wind on his face. He'd been sober two years and didn't plan on falling for whiskey ever again. He didn't want whiskey. He wanted…

Helen.

Her sweet face swam before him. He wanted Helen.

But I'm not good enough for her.

"Daddy." A small hand tugged on Nash's shearling coat, a small hand belonging to his son.

"Whoa." Nash made sure Rose came to a full stop before kneeling to talk to Luke, smiling.

His son had haystack blond hair and a sturdy build, and he wore a gray felt cowboy hat that was too fancy for his mother to have purchased.

Phil.

Irritation tried to coil around his chest. Phil Mitchell got to Nash on too many levels.

Nash took a deep breath to keep irritation at bay. "Hey, buddy. You're not supposed to come into the round pen when I'm working horses." A quick glance revealed the gate behind him was a few inches ajar. "And if you do come in, you close the gate."

"Yes, Daddy." Luke nodded as if he'd done just that.

Rose ambled forward. Luke was one of her favorite people. Heck, Luke was a favorite to all the horses in the stable, primarily because he snuck them handfuls of oats and loved on them as if they were his pets. The kid was a natural horseman in-the-making.

"I was good at school today. We wrote Santa letters." Luke leaned into Nash, all warmth and wheedling smiles, smelling of candy canes and Christmas wishes. "I want a turn with Rose. She likes me. And you said I'll make a good horse trainer someday, like you."

Nash wasn't just a good horse trainer. He was

an elite horse trainer. Nationally renowned. His cutting horses commanded a premium. Cutting horse competitions had deep roots in ranching. Sometimes cows needed to be separated from the herd. A good cutting horse could take cues from its rider as to which cow to isolate. Once locked on a cow, a well-trained cutting horse could point it away from the others and keep it there-—all with little to no direction from its rider.

He'd be proud if his son followed in his footsteps. But he hadn't gotten there alone. Gran had a way with horses, too. And she'd trained Nash in her approach from an early age, principles she'd learned from her fiancé Cal before he died.

"Okay." Nash relented, acknowledging the importance of the family legacy. "You can hold the flag and I'll hold you and the lunge line."

"Daddy." Luke placed his small hands on either side of Nash's face and whispered, "I'm a big boy now. I rode the school bus here. I can do it by myself."

Nash's heart swelled with love and pride, feelings that slowly erased the weight he'd been carrying the last four months. A weight that was caused by his family's ranch toe-tapping on the edge of financial ruin.

Luke pressed Nash's cheeks with his little

palms until Nash's lips undoubtedly resembled those of a fish. "I'm older than Rose." The filly Nash was currently training.

Luke's statement was true. Nash grinned. How he loved his clever little boy.

And his mother.

The pressure in his chest returned. Nash might still love Helen, but she was better off without him, which was why that kiss before Thanksgiving had been a mistake.

If only she'd gotten engaged to someone other than Phil.

Nash drew a labored breath.

"Daddy," Luke said impatiently.

"Rose is too big for you to hold by yourself." Sadly, there were no more ponies at the Flying Spur.

Luke's pony hadn't survived the sickness that had raced through their stables over a year ago, taking down several horses owned by the Flying Spur as well as those Nash had been training for others. They were only now getting back on their feet.

Or they would be if Nash could finish training four blue-blooded fillies and sell them for top dollar before year's end.

"Daddy," Luke said a third time, just as stubborn as his mother, unwilling to let go of an idea or Nash, even when they should. "How am

I gonna train horses and help save the ranch if you don't let me work?" Luke tipped his cowboy hat back and tilted his head as he looked directly into Nash's eyes.

Just the way Helen did during a disagreement.

Nash's heart caught in his throat. He never should have kissed Helen. Her engagement to Phil Mitchell had come out of the blue and knocked him for a loop. She deserved a man who wouldn't mess things up. Nash was going to tell Helen as much when she came by to shoe horses and pick up Luke today.

It was just… *Why did it have to be Phil?* The rancher had a way of ruining cutting horses with his heavy-handed riding style. Nash refused to work with him or to sell him stock.

"Daddy." Luke used his commanding voice.

Rose perked her ears.

And Nash bit back a grin. If he let Luke, he'd run roughshod over him and all the livestock on the Flying Spur.

Nash wasn't going to let him.

He stood and swung Luke onto his hip. "Young man, when you're in this corral, there's only one boss. And who's that?"

"You." Luke giggled, relenting. "But when I'm older, I'm gonna be the boss."

Nash could only hope the Blackwells still owned the Flying Spur when Luke was older.

Four months ago, the bank had called in a second mortgage on the family ranch, a loan taken to buy out Nash's parents when they retired to Arizona a few years back. Turns out, the valley the Flying Spur and Eagle Springs sat in was prime real estate for a developer to create a man-made lake and surround it with fancy homes, a golf course and a luxury town called Mountain Ridge. The Blackwells had discovered that a development company had strong-armed the bank to call in the Flying Spur's loan, as well as other mortgages in the area, for just that purpose. Recently, the town council had authorized the sale of the fairgrounds. If the Flying Spur fell, the development company would complete its buyout of the town next.

Merry Christmas! Happy New Year!

Worry tried to lasso Nash's chest again.

Also, among the newest revelations, the founder of the development company, Frank Wesson, was Nash's grand-uncle and had a vendetta with Gran, who'd jilted him to run off with his younger brother, Cal. And who else was in on this dastardly plan to submerge the town? Frank had assembled a pack of money-hungry investors, a group fronted by the slick Xavier Howard that included one Phil Mitchell.

Nash gritted his teeth.

Thankfully, Nash's siblings had banded together to raise the money to pay every penny of their outstanding second mortgage to save their inheritance. Three of them—Wyatt, Levi, and Adele—had helped raise or save the ranch close to sixty thousand dollars. The last forty thousand fell on Corliss and Nash. Last summer, they'd invested in four fillies with impeccable cutting-horse breeding lines that had been through a year of education. But Nash had to condense another year of cutting horse training into five months. And then he had to sell them for top dollar before New Year's Eve in order to earn back their investment and make a forty thousand dollar profit.

No pressure.

Nash ground his back molars. He couldn't let his son see he was afraid of losing the ranch or afraid of breaking down and picking up a drink again. "How old are you going to be when you're the boss?"

"Six?" Luke was five now.

"Ha! You need to be at least seven," Nash joked.

"Nash." His sister Corliss came through the gate, closing it behind her. She wore a thick blue jacket that was buttoned up tight against the cold. She settled her straw cowboy hat more firmly on her golden brown hair and tromped over with purpose. "There's a problem."

"Why do you always have to say that?" Nash sighed, plunking Luke down and setting a hand on his son's shoulder to hold him in place and out of trouble. "What is it this time?"

"Adele found a potential buyer for Queenie." Corliss referred to their auction yard-running sister and another one of the highly pedigreed cutting horses Nash was training. "The buyer is an amateur rider. He wants to compete in the Holiday Showcase Levi's hosting in two weeks." Their brother Levi was making a go of running events at the indoor rodeo facility he'd purchased in town. "He's hot to buy one of your horses." She picked up Luke and the pair stroked Rose's neck.

"Before Christmas?" Nash scoffed. "Impossible." Queenie was no Rose. The roan had all the physical attributes to make a successful cutting horse. She was quick and had a muscular build. But Queenie hadn't taken to the sport the way the other fillies had and would need a competent rider. "A novice might ruin her."

"Listen to me, Nash." Corliss set Luke back on the ground. "This guy is willing to pay top dollar." Her words came out as cold and hard as hail. "If we can't provide him a cutting horse, we'll lose a sale."

"I don't wanna lose the ranch," Luke said, leaning against Rose's front leg.

Rose reached her head around and nibbled at Luke's hat.

Nash wouldn't mind if the filly ruined the brim. He was going to take great pleasure tossing that hat in the trash bin someday.

"Don't you worry about the ranch, Luke." Corliss stared at Nash, eyebrows arched. "Your dad and me are going to do our best to save it."

Nash matched Corliss's arched eyebrows and raised her a pair of arms crossed over the chest. It was true that his oldest sister carried the heaviest of loads when it came to the Flying Spur. She managed everything, including Gran, so that all Nash had to do was train horses. But it was his reputation at stake, too.

"Tell Adele..." Nash began slowly, fighting the urge to reject the offer. "Tell Adele that Queenie needs at least another eight weeks of training, if not more. We need a buyer who's willing to let me at least try to finish her. If he's willing to pay now and work with me into the new year, it's a deal."

"I'll buy her," Luke piped up. "I've got money in my piggy bank."

"I wish you could buy her, Spud, but Queenie is a grown-up's horse." Corliss drew Luke a step back from Rose before giving Nash another meaningful look. "Your counter-offer is risky. We only have four weeks until the money is due."

Oh, I know.

But it was hard to sell a horse that wasn't up to his standards. "Tell Adele to contact the buyer and ask him if he's willing to let me train him and Queenie for up to two months. I'll give him free sessions."

"Free?" Corliss looked like she might faint. "Now isn't the time for free anything."

"I'll cover the buyer's training fee." Somehow. Nash bent his knees to drop to Luke's level and lowered the boy's hat brim, something Nash did when he meant business. "A Blackwell cutting horse is always the best horse in the arena. Right, Luke?"

"Right." Mirroring Nash, Luke lowered his hat brim. "Our horses are the best."

Corliss stomped off, muttering, "This is no time for perfection."

"It's always that time." Nash might not have been a good role model to Luke after his accident, but he was going to make sure that his son understood the importance of standing for something.

In this case, the Blackwell name.

CHAPTER TWO

HELEN PULLED INTO the Flying Spur ranch yard, nerves aflutter.

Up until three years ago, this had been her home. She, Nash, and Luke had lived in a small mobile home permanently situated behind the barn.

Since Helen had left Nash, she'd been telling herself that her husband had stopped loving her when he'd chosen alcohol over their marriage. She'd given him an ultimatum: *It's me or the whiskey, Nash.*

She'd been crushed when he hadn't picked her.

Up until two weeks ago, she'd been resolved to the fact that she'd carry unrequited love for Nash in her heart until the day she died.

And then he kissed me.

She hadn't seen Nash since. He'd been conspicuously absent when she dropped off or picked up Luke at the ranch.

Avoiding me, more like.

But no more.

Helen backed her blacksmithing van up to the

barn so her tools, including her portable forge and anvil, would be handy while she worked. She glanced about and in her mirrors, trying to locate Nash or Luke. Neither were to be found.

Bow and Arrow, the two ranch dogs, trotted over the inch or so of fresh snow from the main house where Nash's youngest brother Wyatt was stringing outdoor Christmas lights. The dogs were followed at a much slower pace by Denny Blackwell, Nash's grandmother. The old woman could be as hard as nails or as comforting as a well-loved family quilt. Today, Denny was bundled up in a thick black jacket with a burgundy scarf wrapped around her neck. She seemed intent upon talking to Helen, since she gave her a friendly wave.

Helen waved back, smiling a little.

That was the thing about the Blackwells. They still treated Helen as if she were a member of the family.

Maybe that was because Helen had divorced Nash due to his drinking. Or maybe that was because Nash hadn't dated anyone else, at least to her knowledge. And maybe that was because, like her, the Blackwells held on to the hope that she and Nash would get back together. That was too many maybes and helped explain the reason she'd spent the past few years subdued in her interactions with Nash and...well, everybody.

Don't apologize for protecting yourself, dove.

Chasing memories of her mother out of her head, Helen hopped down from the van and slipped a puffy blue coat over her holiday sweatshirt. "How are you feeling, Denny?" She greeted Bow, the chocolate Labrador, and Arrow, the smaller Jack Russell terrier, and then moved to hug Denny, who felt frail beneath her layers of clothing. She'd been battling kidney disease and it seemed to be wearing on her.

"I'm still kicking up trouble." Denny held Helen at arm's length, gaze assessing. "I hear congratulations are in order."

Ugh. Awkward. "Actually, things didn't work out between me and Phil. There's no longer anything to congratulate." Without meaning to, Helen glanced toward the barn.

Denny followed the direction of her gaze. "I see there's something positive to be found in the mess we're in." Denny chuckled, heading to the barn. "I came to find Luke. He promised to help make biscuits. The sooner a man learns to cook, the happier the woman in his life will be."

"I can't disagree with that." Helen helped Denny open the heavy barn door, closing it behind them.

Nash was leading a big, prancing roan into the barn from the other side where the round pen and arena were located.

Their eyes met.

Helen's steps slowed even as her heart pounded erratically in her chest, as if trying to break free and fly toward the man she still loved.

Nash Blackwell was a proud, caring person. He walked tall, his broad shoulders square, as alert and ready for action as the quick-striding horse he led. And like the filly, Nash carried his head high. But there was no hint of that near-lopsided smile she loved so much. His dark whiskers indicated it had been days since his last shave and his brown hair was shaggy beneath his straw cowboy hat, in need of a cut. And his eyes… They were brown and deep, filled with emotions he kept tightly locked away. Even when they'd been married, he'd been a man of few words.

I love you, she'd say in her soft, young voice.

I feel the same, he'd answer slowly, as if even that much was a risk for him to admit.

If she wanted answers about that kiss, none were forthcoming and wouldn't be, especially not with Denny present. And if she wanted to talk about a reconciliation…

Without a word of greeting, Nash led the roan into a stall.

…she'd have to do the heavy lifting. She'd been good at talking and living life to the fullest before Nash started drinking. Now, she was more reserved.

Or should I say timid?

Her mother would hate what she'd become.

"Luke, where are you?" Denny called. "Time to make biscuits."

Helen's little boy poked his head over a stall door, having climbed it halfway up from the inside. He glowed with happiness. "Great Gran, cookin' isn't what I do best."

"That may be, but it's what you'll learn to do." Denny's gait was slower and more deliberate than it had been last December, as if each step took a lot of concentration. "Folks should learn how to cook. Or else how are they going to eat when they grow up?"

"I don't need to cook. I'm gonna live here, Great Gran." Luke beamed, waving at Helen. "You and Mason will feed me." Mason was Corliss's teenage son and a professional chef in the making.

"Young boys and their ideas," Denny scoffed, coming to a stop on the other side of the stall door.

A black horse appeared behind Luke and knocked his hat to the ground.

"Rose. Cut it out." Luke dangled his hand over the door. "Help, somebody. I can't reach my hat."

Denny picked it up for him, dusting off the

gray felt. “This is a mighty fine hat, but it’s not a ranch hat. A hat like this is for Sundays and show days.”

“Phil gave that to him.” Helen rushed forward, regretting the gift, especially when Nash emerged from the next stall down, frowning at it. She took the slightly too large hat from Denny, placed it on Luke’s head, then lifted him over the stall door and set him on the ground.

“I’ve seen worse parting gifts.” Denny turned back the way she’d come. “Giddyap, Luke. Those biscuits aren’t going to make themselves.”

Whinnying, Luke galloped after Denny, grabbing her hand. “But I don’t like all the hot stuff.”

“Mark my words, young man. You’ll love jalapenos one day. It’s tradition around here.” Denny led Luke and the dogs out the door, closing it behind her.

And leaving Helen alone with her ex-husband. At least, in theory. He’d disappeared.

She went to chase him down, finding him in a stall across from the roan. “Hey.” Inwardly, Helen grimaced. That one word proved she’d become just as bad at communication as he was.

“Hey.” Nash slid a halter on a pretty, little bay. “We’ve got four horses scheduled for shoes today, all board and train.” Meaning they were being boarded here while Nash trained them in cutting. “First four stalls. They’re all good about having their hooves handled but be careful just the same.”

That’s all you’ve got to say to me? What about that kiss?

Nash’s gaze cut her way, brown eyes widening slightly.

“Oh.” Cheeks heating, Helen realized what had happened. “I said that out loud.”

He nodded, reaching for a curry comb, and giving the filly a quick brushing. “Not much to explain except to apologize for my behavior when I… It’s not right to kiss another man’s intended.”

This all sounded very rehearsed. And Helen should know, having rehearsed so many lines to say to Phil. But she’d rehearsed none for Nash.

Why didn’t I rehearse anything to say to Nash?

She stood outside the stall, waiting for him to say something more.

And of course, he said nothing.

Something inside Helen shifted. Something that had been off its axis for nearly four years. Before she’d met Nash, she hadn’t waited on a man to lead the courtship dance. Before Nash, if she’d seen something she wanted, she’d gone after it.

She looked at Nash. She wanted Nash.

"I gave Phil his ring back." *I'm free.* She couldn't say those last two words. Something may have shifted inside, but she was still afraid there was more at stake now than when she'd been young and single and had sung to a handsome stranger—*him*—across a crowded bar—*the Cranky Crow.*

Nash's strokes of the curry comb slowed. "I didn't mean for that to happen with Phil. Sorry."

This man...

Helen's shoulders tensed. "I didn't break up with Phil because of you." *Liar, liar, pants on fire.* "Not everything in my life is about you, Nash Blackwell. I have my own friends, my own place and my own problems." Helen frowned. It was one thing to stop being a timid field mouse and another to saunter around sounding off like a well-fed barn cat. "Never mind."

She stalked toward the other end of the barn.

"You have problems?" Nash emerged from the stall, leading the bay.

"Nothing I can't shoulder alone, *handsome.*" That last bit was added by Helen of Old, teasing because he'd riled her, and she wanted a reaction in turn.

She hadn't seen the man since before Thanksgiving, not since his lips had brushed against hers. And now, instead of showing so much as a glimmer of happiness at her broken engagement, Nash was still the reticent man he must have always been.

"Handsome..." He chuckled, sounding the way he had when he'd courted her, back before they'd discovered their buckets of confidence had leaks.

Why was he acting this way now?

Helen whirled. "Oh, no. Don't you go being charming now." She should have stopped there. But the emotional tap had been turned on by the events of the past few weeks and words flowed out full blast. "After that drive-by kiss of yours, you should be explaining your feelings and intentions, not giving me the silent treatment. I am your—" *Shoot.* "—*was* your wife. And if you have any hope of winning me back, you will move those lips of yours out of the satisfied-from-kissing-you position and into explain-yourself mode."

Nash stilled, humor visibly evaporating from his features.

Double shoot. She'd scared him worse than a deer startled in the woods during hunting season.

She needed a moment—better yet, a day—to reconcile the turmoil inside her.

Nash opened his mouth, but words were a long time coming. “I…uh…”

It was taking him too long to fill the void between them. And a discombobulated Helen still had things to say. “If you play your cards right, *handsome*, I’ll consider taking you back. But I’m a woman with options. I’m not waiting around forever for you to return to your senses.”

You’ve pushed him too far, Helen.

His brows drew together. “Helen—”

“Too late.” She held up a hand, marveling at her nerve, but needing to escape. “I’m not listening. I have work to do.”

“Hang on.” Nash wore a determined look on his face. “First off, I have always been charming.”

Prove it, she wanted to say. Instead, she countered, “Not true. One hundred percent not true.” A dare, plain and simple.

“Now, Helen…” He wasn’t taking the bait.

“No—no.” She’d let him lead the tone of their relationship for years. That hadn’t gotten him back. She’d tried some of her old bluntness of character. That didn’t seem to be working either. It was time to retreat. “I’m a single mom. A business owner. And a woman of principle. I don’t need a man to complete me.”

But she wanted one. *Him.*

His lips twitched. Likely because he knew what she wanted.

He's still rejecting you. Do not smile.

"I said no charm." Helen spun around and told herself to breathe. She stepped into the nearest stall, one marked with a nameplate that read: *Beanie, owned by Sylvie*. An older, plain brown gelding stared at her with a bit of suspicion. She dug a mini carrot from her pocket and then extended a hand toward Beanie. "You're right," she whispered. "I've upset you and I need to take a chill pill."

Beanie ambled forward, extending his nose until his lips gummed her palm.

"You, my friend, are more charming than my ex," she told the horse.

"I heard that." Nash stood on the other side of the stall door, having followed her. "Never enter a horse's space in anger, honey. It could be dangerous."

Helen rolled her eyes.

"Bad day at the office?" He stared at her ringless left hand.

She scoffed. It was either that or crumple into the straw, death by a combination of unrequited love and mortifying embarrassment.

"Ah. I guess Phil didn't take your friend speech very well." Nash turned away, leading the bay toward the training arena. "Beanie doesn't need shoes, by the way. It's the first four stalls, remember?"

"Thanks for that explanation about the kiss, *handsome*." Her words shook, darn it. "Your communication skills are why we aren't married anymore." Helen exited the stall, but not before Beanie nudged her backside with his nose. "Hey!"

Nash paused in the breezeway, staring at her over his shoulder. "That's not why we aren't married."

"Well, it should have been."

WHEN NASH RETURNED to the barn after working with Java, he heard Helen's voice before he could make out what she was saying.

She's calm now.

He could tell by her tone. Calm was Helen's status quo. Or at least, it had been the past few years. Her calm settled him.

On those rare occasions when Helen was visibly frustrated, the very air around her was charged the way it was during a summer thunderstorm. Noise, huffing, words flung about looking for a dramatic crash landing. And then the clouds moved on as quickly as they'd blown in. And she'd be even-keeled and easy-going, like a clear cloudless day where you'd feel recharged beneath her rays of sunshine.

She was humming something off-key now, tune falling off as she nailed a shoe to one of Cinder's rear hooves and picking back up as she twisted off the excess nail ends.

Nash smiled, remembering the first time he'd seen Helen at the Cranky Crow. He'd just returned to Eagle Springs after delivering a cutting horse to a client in Montana. All he'd wanted to do was sleep. But Jake Gallagher had convinced him to head into town for a beer. Nash and his ranch hand had taken up stools at the bar.

Helen had been sitting in a corner booth with her friends, who'd gathered for a bachelorette party. She was wearing a yellow sundress, cowboy boots and a purple feather boa. She'd gotten up to do karaoke and, man, had she been awful. She couldn't carry a tune. Not that she'd seemed to know it or care if she did. She belted out the love song and performed for the audience as if she were a talented, veteran pop star performer. And during the song…

It was as if she'd sung it to him.

Afterward, he'd taken up that off-key invitation and gone over to talk to her, thinking that she was new to town. He would have remembered that pert nose, those green eyes, that dark blond hair.

Helen took a rasp to Cinder's hoof, filing

back protruding nails and momentarily interrupting his reverie.

He'd been surprised to discover she'd graduated high school in Eagle Springs the same year as his sister Adele, four years behind him. After graduation, Helen had gone to Cheyenne to attend farrier school, followed by a year of apprenticeship in Canada, another year in Ireland and a final year in Kentucky. She'd followed her heart and her muse, training with the best blacksmiths she could find. Only the death of her father had brought her back to town, where she'd started her own business. She had drive, like Nash. And she had a sense of humor, like Nash. And instead of belonging to a big, meddlesome family, like Nash, she was an only child.

The more he got to know Helen, the harder he'd fallen. She was worldly, yet down to earth. Sometimes, he'd felt tongue-tied, at a loss as to what to say to her.

Which is why I couldn't talk to her after the accident.

He'd had no problems talking to alcohol. Yeah, he and whiskey had a good rapport. At least, they had until he'd looked around and realized Helen and Luke were gone, and that he much preferred their company over whiskey's.

"Good girl, Cinder." Helen set down the

mare's hoof and moved the hoof jack a few feet to one side. She'd put on her blacksmithing chaps and had hung her cowboy hat on a nearby wall hook. Her blond hair was in a short, thick braid. "If you wash out as a cutting horse, I know a little boy who'd love to ride you on the daily."

Nash put Java back in her stall, taking a few minutes to stroke and praise the overly-affectionate bay.

After the blight last year, the ranch had let all their paid ranch hands, like his good friend Jake Gallagher, go. Since they'd been cleared to operate again, Nash had spent most of his afternoons alone with the horses. Sure, Corliss helped in the morning with feeding and mucking out the stalls. But nothing went on in the afternoon except training, which he mostly did by himself. And now, listening to Helen work, Nash realized he was lonely.

"Back to your stall, sweet thing," Helen crooned.

It was nice to hear someone else's voice, especially the voice of his special someone.

Whoa. Nash brought himself up short. He'd broken Helen's heart once. He didn't need to cause her any trouble again.

But she called me charming and handsome.

Pride urged him to respond. But pride had

also kept him from talking to her after the mountain accident that had taken the life of Jet, his prize cutting horse. Pride had made him reach for a drink instead of his wife. Pride had a way of ruining everything. Too bad, pride was something the Blackwells had too much of.

The filly rubbed her face against Nash's chest, demanding more affection. And since he was hiding out from Helen, he gave it to her.

At the other end of the barn, Helen opened and shut stall doors.

There was a burnt smell in the air, a by-product of Helen's work. It reminded him of her and the feeling of home. She used to elbow off his embrace after work until she'd had a chance to shower, as if he wasn't used to the smell of all aspects of raising and training horses. Now, he spent as little time as possible in the double-wide mobile home they'd shared behind the barn. Because Helen and Luke weren't there, it was less home than a place to lay his head at night. Most nights, he slept on the couch.

"Starling, you are in desperate need of a pedicure." Helen's teasing voice tugged at him. "You need some bling-bling to match those shiny dapples of yours. I've got some glitter in the van."

Glitter?

No self-respecting cowboy rode a glittery horse.

Nash left Java's stall and walked the length of the barn. "Starling's owner is not the kind of guy to appreciate bling."

Leading the dapple gray out of the stall, Helen blushed. She'd removed her jacket and pushed up the sleeves of her deep green hoodie. The lettering emblazoned across the front was cracked, but the message was still legible: *Santa, I've been really good this year.*

He'd given her that sweatshirt the first Christmas they'd been together. Helen loved everything about Christmas—decorating, buying gifts, filling stockings, kissing under the mistletoe.

Nash glanced up at the rafters, but none of the mistletoe sprigs he'd put up there in years past remained.

"You know better than to pay attention to what I'm saying to a horse." Helen clipped Starling to the cross-ties in the breezeway.

I pay attention to everything you say and do.

He closed the stall door once Starling was clear of it. Safety was important, and that included safe conversations with Helen, ones with guardrails so the topics didn't touch upon his mistakes, especially that kiss she'd wanted to know about. "Are you still planning to get Luke a horse for Christmas?"

Her brow furrowed as she did a quick cleaning of Starling's hoof. "I'm not sure that's wise."

"Hang on. You've been talking about buying him a horse since September." Not that they'd had a lot of talks recently, but that topic he remembered.

"There are two problems with that gift." Helen reached into a deep pocket in her chaps for a rasp. She positioned Starling's hoof on the metal hoof jack, which was set on the ground between her legs to alleviate the need for Helen to support the horse herself. She quickly worked to remove the nail clenches. "The first reason is that the Flying Spur, and Eagle Springs, might not be around next year. Who knows where you or I will be living? And if we go our separate ways, I may not be able to afford keeping a horse."

"We are not going our separate ways." Still, her words were like a punch in the gut. Nash didn't need another reminder that a lot hinged on him training and selling four cutting horses for a premium fee. "And the second reason?"

"I had a lot of cancellations today." She tucked the rasp back in its pocket and grabbed her shoe pullers. She clamped on the shoe to loosen the nails at the rear, banged it to further release the shoe and then pried out nails as the heads came up. As always, her work was efficient.

But something about the jerkiness of her movements bothered him. What had she been saying? "Cancellations…as in rescheduling?"

She shook her head. "Cancellations as in services no longer needed. Thank you, Phil, for blackballing me with your friends."

A growl of disapproval rumbled in Nash's throat. But he knew better than to argue with Helen about her ex-fiancé. "Back to the horse… When Luke's out here, he's constantly climbing on a stall door and then slipping onto a horse's back. It's time for him to have a mount of his own again." But it wasn't like Nash could buy his son a horse on credit. Every penny he had needed to go to saving the ranch.

A different kind of growl collected deep inside him, the frustrated kind. If not for the likes of Frank, Xavier and Phil, Nash would have the funds to buy his son a horse.

"You sound upset." Helen cast him a wary glance. "I know Luke is headstrong but… You don't have any dangerous mounts in here, do you?"

"No." Nash paused, reminded that Helen was deathly afraid of riding. "I'm choosy about the horses I train."

"Good. Because Luke has no fear, unlike me." Helen removed a horseshoe and tossed it into a plastic bin. She switched out tools for a nipper, trimming Starling's hoof as confidently as Nash cut his own nails. "Listen, it's not wise to buy Luke a horse when neither of us knows for certain where we'll be this time next year."

"I'm not going anywhere," Nash said in a hard voice. "The Blackwells have been on this ranch for three generations."

"Life doesn't always work out the way you want it to, Nash." Helen moved the hoof jack aside and then set the gray's hoof down. She straightened and looked him in the eye. "It would be different if…"

If we were back together, he silently finished for her, gut knotting.

She deserved better than Nash, who, admittedly, was a step up from Phil. But still… "You deserve a prince," Nash told her hoarsely. "Not a man like me."

"Really? I hear princes are hard to come by in Wyoming." Helen gave a weary sigh and walked to the barn door, opening it wide enough to slip through. The anvil and portable forge were extended off the back of her work van and propped on metal support legs. She stepped between them and rummaged in a box of horseshoes in the back. "I don't think Santa is delivering princes in stockings either. Sometimes a girl could be happy with a frog."

A chill wind swept through the barn. But the

wind wasn't as chilly as Helen's demeanor. She was still upset, presumably because he wasn't welcoming her back with open arms. Didn't she realize he was damaged goods?

Nash knew he should get back to work and train the next filly, but he waited near Starling all the same. Right or wrong, Nash was pining for Helen.

Maybe it was because his four siblings had somehow managed to find love these past few months, eking out a positive in the shadow of disaster.

Helen returned with a horseshoe, drawing the barn door nearly closed behind her. She lifted Starling's hoof and briefly checked the fit of the shoe she'd selected before heading back outside where she heated up the shoe in the forge and then banged on it against the anvil. Several swings of the hammer later, she returned to check the shoe fit again. The shoe was hot and sizzled against the mare's hoof, sending up a plume of smoke.

"What are we doing here?" Helen asked without looking at Nash. She set the mare's hoof down again and walked back to her anvil and forge as if she hadn't left a question on the table.

He waited until she'd heated and hammered the horseshoe into a shape she was happier with and returned. "What we're doing is being friendly while we talk through important parenting choices. Luke needs a horse and he's going to keep it here. I'll spread the word that we're looking for a good mount." They'd figure out how to pay for it once they found the right horse for their son.

"What you're doing is risky." Helen fitted the hot shoe to Starling's hoof, creating another plume of smoke. "Why can't Denny just ask this Big E fella for a loan? He's Denny's brother and people are saying he's well-off. If the Flying Spur folds, the rest of the town is going to fold with it."

"I know, but..." It was bad enough that Corliss had approached Big E, otherwise known as Elias Blackwell, to finance the purchase of the four fillies, using their sole remaining cutting horse stud Skyfire as collateral. "Denny built this ranch by herself. It's a matter of pride that she doesn't ask her brother for a loan."

"Pride goeth before a fall," Helen quipped gently.

"We've all got lines we won't cross. I won't fault Gran for her decision."

The barn door slammed shut, as if someone had tried to get in but didn't have the strength to open the door all the way. They both pressed pause on their argument, waiting for whoever was outside to join them. But no one came in.

Bending back to her task, Helen sighed.

"I should let you get to work." And yet, Nash hesitated.

"We've still got an unexplained kiss hanging between us." Helen tapped nails into the shoe. "Do you remember when we were first dating? We'd talk for hours. What happened?"

"Things happened, Helen," he said gruffly. Bad things. "It's always been easier to talk about the other stuff. The stuff that doesn't eat you up inside."

"Is that stuff you talk to your family about?" She examined her work. "You're supposed to talk *more* with your spouse and family when things are bad, not less."

He disagreed.

Nash glanced at a photo on the wall of him competing in a cutting horse competition on Jet. But a different memory came to mind. He relived the feeling of blood trickling down his temple and his heart pounding in his ears as he opened the horse trailer. And then there was the jolt of the recoil of the gun in his hand when he'd made the decision to end Jet's suffering.

A part of him wanted to replace that feeling with a glass of whiskey.

And another wanted Helen to wrap her arms around him and kiss the bad memories away.

That's enough of that.

Nash turned on his boot heel.

"That's exactly what I'm talking about," Helen said as he walked away. "The bad things that just replayed in your head need to be said out loud. If not to me, then to someone else, like Corliss or Denny. Or those bad things will chase you 'til the day you die."

Nash stopped, half glancing at her over his shoulder. "You can't know what's going through my mind." She couldn't even see his face.

"You were thinking about the night of your accident and how you had to put Jet down because of his injuries."

Was he that transparent? He swallowed thickly, unable to speak.

"You did the right thing, Nash. We both know that sometimes the right thing is the hardest thing."

She was correct about that. The worst thing he could do was be selfish and let Helen back into his life. "I've got another horse to train."

She didn't say another word, not to console or to argue.

And oddly enough, he was disappointed.

CHAPTER THREE

"WHY ARE WE headed into town?" Elias drove Denny's truck toward the gates of the Flying Spur. "Dinner's going to be ready soon. Mason said we should come to the table in about an hour. Delaney, you need to take better care of yourself. I'd rather not visit you in the hospital again so soon after you were released."

"I've got stuff to do," Denny grumped, keeping her affairs to herself. "Time is running out."

"If it's gifts you need, there are still plenty of days until Christmas." Elias slowed. Like her, he was bundled against the cold in a thick brown jacket. Since he'd learned of her illness, he'd barged into her life after a nearly sixty-year estrangement and parked his motorhome in the ranch yard, refusing to leave. "I'll take you Christmas shopping this weekend. There's not enough time to browse right now."

"Keep driving."

"But—"

"Can we not argue?" Denny sank deeper into the passenger seat and stared out the window, feeling the frailty of age and disease and fear-ing it. "For once, Elias, can you drive and not ask questions?"

She'd overheard Helen asking Nash why Denny couldn't just accept her older brother's help to save the ranch and possibly, the town. And she'd heard Nash's answer: *pride.*

Pride. It gnawed on Denny's heart just then, making it ache.

Pride was the reason she hadn't run back to her family in Falcon Creek, Montana, after Cal died. She'd been pregnant with twins and hadn't wanted to hear her father say, *"I told you so."*

I told you Cal was a caution, Delaney.

A gambler who couldn't hold his liquor, he'd meant.

Yes, Cal had a weakness for alcohol. Of all the grandkids, only Nash had acquired that same trait. Funny, he was also like his grandfather in other ways. Nash was the spitting image of Cal and had also inherited his horse-whispering talent.

Cal...

Cal had shared Denny's love of horses and her talent for training them. As a young girl growing up on the Blackwell Ranch in Montana, Denny's role was clear—train the horses and be content as the second fiddle to Elias, who'd been groomed to run ranch operations.

Frank Wesson is the better choice, Delaney.

A man with a head for business, her father had meant, hoping their marriage would lead to a merger of the Blackwell and Wesson ranches. He'd envisioned Elias eventually running everything with Frank as his second-in-command. And Denny? Well, back then her "horse habit" as her father called it was considered a hobby she'd eventually outgrow. Denny had told her father she could never be the sweet little lady Frank wanted as a wife. She hated high heels, fancy dresses and make-up.

That charmer and your horses won't provide you more than two nickels to rub together, Delaney.

How many times had her father told her that in the weeks before she and Cal had run off?

Despite his faults, everyone had been enchanted by Cal. His family had doted on him. Her family had doted on him. He was quick with a smile and a funny line so his fascination with drink and gambling tolerated, as long as he won cutting horse events, showed up at family gatherings and didn't elope with the woman his family and hers had pushed his older brother to marry.

And now, Cal's only brother, Frank, was reveling in the fact that he was close to destroying everything Denny had built, everything she and

Cal had dreamed of when they'd decided their families would never accept their love.

And nothing had changed. It was still pride that Denny clung to.

"I'm an old fool," Denny muttered. And everyone knew, old fools didn't change.

"Delaney, you're no fool." Behind the wheel, her brother chuckled. "We Blackwells are more stubborn than a tick on an exposed ankle. But we're not fools."

"I'm thinking about our meeting with Frank on Thanksgiving Day." Where she'd apologized for jilting him and he'd laughed in her face. Just remembering that encounter had frustration and embarrassment churning inside her.

"Frank caught us flat-footed." Elias spared her a glance. "I bought the Wesson ranch from Frank after Cal's parents passed away, never imagining he'd use that money to build a real estate development business that would eventually target you and yours."

"I suppose I should be flattered that I'm not forgettable. Do you think if I proposed to Frank, he'd forget all this?"

"Nah," Big E teased. "It's not unrequited love motivating Frank. He and his family blamed you for Cal's death. He wants his revenge."

And she was determined he wouldn't get it.

"Much as I loved Cal… Much as I miss

him..." Denny hugged herself. "Whiskey was going to take Cal one way or another." Whiskey and horses didn't mix.

They passed by a large grove of pine trees in the southern pasture, a grove beautifully blanketed with a layer of snow above and below. Out of habit, Denny scanned the trees for wild horses.

Something moved in the shadows, something that looked like—

"Stop. Stop, I say." Denny thrust a hand toward Elias even as she pressed her nose against the cold window glass. "There's a horse out there."

"Well, this is a horse ranch, after all." Elias slowed the truck to a halt. "And your pasture, too, I take it."

"Do you see it?" She pointed into the trees. "There's a white horse back there."

Elias dutifully leaned forward to look. "I don't see a thing."

Denny experienced a moment of doubt. Was it a horse?

She sat back in her seat, demoralized. "After we eloped, Cal and I caught and trained wild horses to sell." It was why she always looked for them, especially now. Wild horses had saved her once. Foolishly, she thought they might save her again. "Wild horses... That was long before the Bureau of Land Management began rounding them up for auction."

"You taking them was probably illegal back then," Elias mused, still looking toward the trees.

"What folks don't know won't hurt them." Denny couldn't see the horse anymore. A white horse. The first wild horse she and Cal had captured and trained together had been white. Denny was good at gentling horses, earning their trust. Cal had been a cutting horse genius, much like Nash was now. "Is this horse a sign from Cal?" Her hands trembled. "Is it gone? It was right there...wasn't it?"

"It might have been," Elias allowed gently. "It could have been a deer. Or an elk."

"An elk?" Denny jerked around to face him, suddenly angry, suddenly certain. "That was a horse. A white horse. I know that I'm not at my best, but I'm not seeing things."

"All right. There was a horse." Her brother eased back into his seat, tipping his hat brim up. "What do we do about it?"

"We tell Cal. He'll catch it."

"Cal?" Elias frowned. "Delaney, Cal is dead."

Denny sucked in a breath, suddenly cold. "I mean... I mean Nash. We tell Nash. He'll track it down."

"All right," Elias said again, putting the truck in reverse, backing toward the ranch proper.

"Not now," Denny bit back, shaken to her very core but determined to follow through with her trip to town. "I'm sorry, I… I need to talk to Harriet at the Cranky Crow." The town's most popular bar and grill. "She's been gone since before Thanksgiving."

"And when we tracked Frank down on Thanksgiving, he told you there was trouble at the Cranky Crow," Elias surmised. He could be annoying, but he wasn't slow on the uptake. "That's your urgent business in town? You think she sold to the developer group? To Frank?"

Denny nodded. "But I hope not." Harriet was her oldest and dearest friend and had been out of town until today.

"At least you're still snapping and hoping, Delaney. If we lose hope, we might just as well close up shop here."

"Bite your tongue, old man. Now drive."

Several minutes later and they were entering the Cranky Crow. The large, Western-themed bar and grill was an institution in Eagle Springs. It had everything one needed when looking for a distraction—friendly customers, good food and drink, a pool table, video games and the occasional karaoke night.

Lately, however, there'd been more fights in the Cranky Crow than was normal. Tempers were flaring between those who had opted to sell to the developers and those who were defending Eagle Springs until the end.

Harriet stood behind the bar, fiddling with a small Christmas tree on a shelf in front of the mirror. Harriet's reflected gaze lit on Denny and she blanched, the way best friends did when they were caught betraying their best friends.

Denny's steps slowed to a halt. Her heart felt heavy. "It's true." She pushed herself forward and climbed on a bar stool, heedless of Elias taking a seat next to her. "You sold us out—me and the rest of the town."

Harriet turned, visibly gathering herself for a fight. "Yes, I agreed to sell the Cranky Crow. It's all conditional on whether or not the Flying Spur folds. I'm sorry, Denny."

She waved off the apology. "And you couldn't tell me this? I had to learn it from Frank?"

"I thought…" Harriet scrubbed a hand over her forehead. "I went to visit my daughter for Thanksgiving. There was no time to tell you beforehand."

"No time to call either, I imagine," Denny murmured. It turned out there were fewer and fewer folk in Eagle Springs with the nerve to stand up for what was right. "You'd have them demolish the town? Wipe out our history? Dam it up and create a lake for hoity-toity people like my brother here to recreate on?"

Elias heaved a put-upon sigh.

Harriet placed her hands on the bar. "Denny, I'm not getting any younger. And none of my kin wants to take over the Crow. This fight has made one thing clear to me. I don't have a retirement strategy."

"Our retirement strategy has always been to be taken out feet first," Denny countered, trying to hold back the tears.

"With your boots on," Elias murmured.

"Yes, gosh darn you." Denny swatted his arm with the back of her hand. But given her illness, she couldn't have killed a fly with that swat.

"I can match their offer," Elias said to Harriet.

"You'll do no such thing." Denny carefully slid off the bar stool and headed toward the door. "This has always been my fight. And me and my kin are going to ruin everyone's retirement plans."

Her money—and her pride—were riding with Nash.

CHAPTER FOUR

"MAMA, WHY DIDN'T we stay at the Flying Spur for dinner?" Luke sat in the front of the blacksmithing van strapped into his car seat. Christmas music played on the radio just loud enough to be heard over the road noise. "I made biscuits and they didn't have holly-peenoes."

"Jalapenos." Helen handed him the bag with two of the biscuits he'd made. "There'll be other dinners at the ranch, honey." That felt like wishful thinking. Eagle Springs wasn't going to survive long into the new year. She'd just received an email from her landlord, notifying her that the small duplex she was renting had been sold to the development group. Helen had ninety days to vacate the premises. "We couldn't stay for dinner. Remember that I have to take jobs when they come." And someone had called her after their horse threw a shoe. Someone who wasn't part of Phil's social circle.

"No work means no money." Luke bit into a biscuit. Crumbs cascaded into his lap. "Lucy Goosey is a good horse." That was the name of the horse that had thrown a shoe.

"I like good horses." They made her job easier. Helen turned on Lander, which was a little-traveled shortcut back to Eagle Springs proper. The chassis creaked and her dashboard lights flickered the way they sometimes did. Helen hardly paid heed. The road was dark and there weren't any lights on the country road, but it would save them a good fifteen minutes in getting home, especially since it had been plowed. "A good horse usually means there's a good cowboy owner."

"I want a horse," Luke said wistfully. "And I want to move back to the Flying Spur so I can be with my horse day and night."

"Wouldn't that be nice," Helen murmured just as her engine went *boom.*

Luke shrieked, dropping the biscuit bag. "What was that?"

The engine coughed and sputtered, then died.

"It's the motor, honey." Helen pulled over onto the snowy shoulder. She tried to restart the engine.

Nothing happened. Not even the grind of the starter.

"If this was a horse, we'd be home by now," Luke said solemnly. His little face was illuminated by the dashboard and tinged with fear.

And then the dashboard lights and headlights went out.

Helen had a few choice words about engines

and electronics that failed in all the wrong places, but since Luke was with her, she voiced nothing of the sort. Instead, she turned on the hazard lights and said, "Let's call Daddy."

"Daddy to the rescue!" Luke perked up.

Nash didn't answer Helen's call, which probably meant he was in the middle of training a horse. So much was riding on those fillies. She didn't want to pull him away. But she left a message. "Nash, we broke down on Lander and it's dark. But don't worry. We're okay. We'll call Marvin for a tow." Marvin ran the service station in town.

Except Marvin didn't answer, perhaps because he'd sold out to the developers and was keeping banker's hours now.

The snow started falling thicker, and the cold was beginning to seep in, nipping at her fingers and toes.

Helen tossed a spare blanket over Luke and tried Nash again.

Still no answer.

So, she called the next most reliable man in her life.

Her former fiancé.

NASH SPED DOWN snowy Lander, frantic after having received Helen's message over an hour after she'd left it.

A breakdown. At night. On a deserted road. It was pitch black. The moon and stars were hidden behind thick snow clouds. His windshield wipers were busy brushing off snowflakes. Memories of his crash plagued him, making Nash drive too fast in the snow.

It's not the same. They're okay.

Helen had said as much in her message.

If only Helen would answer her phone now.

Nash's hands were sweaty on the wheel.

And then his headlights illuminated her work van. He pulled up behind it, practically sagging with relief.

Bundled up in her heavy blue jacket, Helen stepped out from in front of the van and waved.

Only then did he realize there was a truck parked in front of her. It didn't look like a tow truck.

Nash hopped out, ruing the fact that he didn't keep his cell phone with him when he was training for fear of startling a horse. Helen was being taken care of by a passerby, possibly a stranger. He lengthened his stride.

"Yeah, it's not starting. Sorry." That masculine voice… Was it familiar? A man climbed out of the van's driver seat and closed the door.

Phil.

An overwhelming feeling of jealousy pounded in Nash's temples to the beat of the flashing yellow and orange hazard lights from his and Phil's trucks.

"Hey, reinforcements are here." Nash came to stand next to Helen, draping his arm over her shoulders. "What seems to be the trouble?"

"It went boom." Helen eyed his hand on her shoulder, and moved a little away from Nash, as if considering shrugging him off.

He held on despite her cold shoulder and the icy clumps of snowflakes landing heavily on his bare hand.

"The electrical shut down," Phil said frostily, keeping his gaze on Helen. "And it doesn't seem to want to start, not even with a jump."

"I thought you were calling Marvin." Nash tried to stay calm, tried to keep a close rein on his emotions.

"Marvin has no need to work long hours anymore," Phil answered for Helen.

Nash huffed like an impatient horse on a too short lead. "No need to come to the aid of stranded motorists, you mean? He'd still be available if he hadn't sold out to you and your buddies, Phil." Nash wasn't normally a sneering man. He sneered anyway. "Your greed has made life in Eagle Springs more dangerous."

"And your short-sightedness is holding back progress that will benefit everyone," Phil snapped back, eyes narrowing.

"Everyone," Nash scoffed. "Everyone who sells out early, you mean."

"Can we not do this now?" Helen pleaded, slipping from beneath Nash's arm, boots sinking in inches of fresh snow. "Luke is right there." Bundled up in the passenger seat, a phone resting on his chest and his eyes closed.

"He's asleep and not paying attention to anything." Assuming that was Helen's phone, not even Nash's calls had awakened him, of which there had been several. Although to be fair, they might have come after Phil arrived.

"I hear you've got some cutting horses for sale." Phil shut the van's hood. The flashing orange and red hazards shadowed his face deeply, as if revealing his true, dark nature. "I've always wanted to have a Nash Blackwell cutting horse. Or two."

"And I've always turned you down," Nash said automatically, quickly putting that idea to rest. "Even before you started dating my wife."

"*Ex*-wife." Helen frowned.

"This does make things interesting, doesn't it?" Phil chuckled as the high plains wind blew past. "If you sell a few horses to me, I could help you save the Flying Spur and Eagle Springs. And perhaps you'd win your wife back."

"*Ex*-wife." Helen's frown deepened. "You

undercut my business, Phil. I'd appreciate you leaving me out of this fight."

Phil tsked. "And yet, you called me in your hour of need."

Helen crossed her arms over her chest and gave Phil a look that said he was in the doghouse.

Nash hoped his rival would stay there permanently. "I've got chains in the back of my truck," he said to Helen, done with Phil's games. It was getting late. He needed to get his family home. "I can tow the van to the Flying Spur. Wyatt can repair it for you." His youngest brother could fix anything.

"I'll pay top dollar for two of your horses," Phil, Mr. One Track Mind, said.

"They aren't for sale to you," Nash said coldly.

"Not even if the fate of the Flying Spur rests in your hands?" The older man's smile came across as craggy and menacing. "Not to mention the fate of Eagle Springs?"

"Not even," Nash confirmed, as snow fell in thick sheets.

"Nash." Helen moved closer to him and lowered her voice. "We had this discussion earlier. About *pride*."

Nash knew what she meant, that there were bigger things at stake here than his pride. But until December thirty-first, he could afford to put his pride first.

"There are good riders and bad riders, Helen," Nash said loud enough for Phil to hear. "And then there are riders, like Phil, who rein their horses with a heavy hand that breaks their desire to compete." Not to mention, costs him competition points. Good cutting horses did the work with little to no guidance from their rider once a cow was chosen to separate from the herd. Phil couldn't seem to let his horses do the job themselves.

Phil clenched his fists and took a step forward. "Why you—"

"Stop it." Helen stepped between them. "Both of you." She held Nash's gaze. *"Please."*

"I will have two of your horses," Phil said fiercely. He pointed at Helen. "And one day, she will be my wife."

Nash swore.

Helen gasped and then ground out, "How dare you say that."

Phil looked contrite, but it only lasted a second. He glared at Nash. "How about a friendly wager?"

Nash had a bad feeling in his gut, but he'd never backed down from a bully. "I'm listening."

"This is a terrible idea," Helen said, none too softly.

"If Helen competes in the Holiday Showcase on one of your horses and places—" Phil grinned "—I'll pay you top dollar for two horses, but you can keep them both."

Oh, Corliss would like that.

"Come on, Phil. You know I don't ride." Helen rolled her eyes, but the glance that landed on Nash was painted in nerves and a clear message: *Do not take this bet.*

"And if she loses?" Nash had to know what Phil had in that twisted mind of his.

"If Helen doesn't place first, second or third—"

"Which I won't," Helen interjected.

"—I'll pay half of what you're asking and claim both horses as mine." Phil puffed out his chest.

Helen recoiled.

The odds were against Nash, but the prize—beating Phil and saving the ranch—was too tempting to pass up.

"That's a bet." Nash thrust his hand forward to shake on it.

Their frozen handshake was brief, a single pump between enemies.

"It doesn't matter what you two agree on—" Helen practically howled her objection "—I will *not* be party to this wager. All bets are off!"

Phil didn't take his gaze from Nash. If he'd

ever truly cared for Helen, he wasn't showing it now.

"Best get on home, Phil, and count those unhatched chickens of yours." Nash followed Helen, who'd already started walking back toward his truck. "Because this cracked idea is going to cost you."

Phil laughed. But mission accomplished, he got in his truck and drove off.

Leaving Nash with a new problem: *getting Helen on horseback.*

"HOW COULD YOU agree to that?" Helen put her hands on her hips as Phil pulled away, shaking from a combination of cold, disbelief and anger. "You know I'm scared in the saddle. Why would you wager everything on me?"

Forget being happy to see Nash when he pulled up. Now Helen was furious.

"We have two full weeks to train." Nash moved to the truck bed, putting his cell phone in flashlight mode. He removed some chains from the back. "We'll start tomorrow. We'll work night and day."

"No." Helen hugged herself to keep out the chill of the wind and the foolish gambles of her ex-husband. "I have a business to run."

"You and I are backed into a corner, Helen." He carried the chains to the front of the van and then handed her his straw cowboy hat. Heedless of the snow, he crawled underneath her van, shining his phone at the undercarriage where he found a place to attach the chains. "I can't save my family's ranch without a big payday on those horses. And you can't shoe any horses if your van doesn't run. I'll cover the cost of the van's repair bill if you do this for me."

"You want me to ride?" Anger evaporated, replaced by fear. In her mind's eye, Helen relived the bone-breaking snap when a hoof struck her and the taste of dirt where she landed. Her arm twinged in all the places it had been injured. "I don't want any part of this."

"But you can do it." Nash scooted out from under the bumper. He came to his feet and faced her. "You're the strongest woman I know."

"Stronger than Denny? Or Corliss?" Helen didn't feel strong. She felt small and frightened.

He nodded.

Fear was momentarily elbowed aside by a sure sense of pride.

And then reality kicked in because pride didn't pay the rent or hospital bills. "What makes you think I can do this?"

"You aren't scared of horses, Helen. You love them, despite that one bad experience."

Her body throbbed in every place she'd been kicked, stomped on, bitten and head-butted by horses in her lifetime. "This is wrong. I'm not strong. I wasn't tough enough to stand by *you* during your darkest times."

"Some things a person has to do alone." Nash sighed, hands dropping to his sides. "And you had to leave me, I always understood that. Because of your mother, you needed to be in an alcohol-free environment."

Helen shivered, unable to argue. When Nash hadn't stopped drinking, she'd wanted to leave him before history repeated itself and he left her, the way Mom had. But now, everything she'd said and done two years ago just felt cowardly. "I'm not a good bet."

"You let me be the judge of that. Come on. We need to get you and Luke home and warm." Nash walked back toward his truck, putting the issue of the bet on the backburner.

The snow continued to fall. There'd be a foot or more by morning.

In short order, he'd pulled around and backed into the space Phil had occupied before. He got out and returned to where she was standing, too shell-shocked to move. "And by home and warm, I mean back at the Flying Spur."

Helen's mouth dropped open. But she didn't refuse because it was what she wanted—to go home with him. If only riding a horse didn't figure into the equation of getting him back.

Forty-five minutes later, they pulled up to the Flying Spur.

Helen had driven Nash's truck with a still-sleeping Luke in his car seat in the back. Towed behind her, Nash had driven Helen's vehicle, braking whenever she slowed or came to a stop. His had been the more stressful job since he lacked power brakes or power steering in the van. But it was Helen who was a nervous wreck when they arrived.

He expects me to ride.

Nash must have called ahead because the Blackwells living on the ranch came out in force to greet them. Wyatt helped Nash remove the towing chains. The pair put up the engine hood and began talking through different diagnoses, poking around despite the snow and the dim ranch yard light.

"We kept dinner warm for you." Corliss freed and lifted a groggy Luke into her arms. She marched toward the main house. "Spud, you did such a good job on the biscuits that we almost ate them all."

A stylish blonde approached Helen, introducing herself as Wyatt's wife, Harper. "Are you really a blacksmith?"

"Yes, a farrier. I shoe horses," Helen corrected automatically, grabbing her backpack, which had her wallet, cell phone and a change of clothes. She headed after Corliss toward the house outlined in brightly colored Christmas lights. "I'm kind of like a horse foot specialist."

"A podiatrist for horses. That's cool." Harper fell into step beside her. "I have an audience for that kind of thing, if you're interested."

"I'm not entirely sure what you mean," Helen said, suddenly confused, not to mention self-conscious.

They may have both been blond and wearing cowboy boots, but there the similarities ended. Harper was a city cowgirl. Everything from her cowboy boots to her fringed blue leather jacket was statement-making style. And everything about Helen's attire was serviceable Western wear, not to mention she was covered in stable muck and sweat.

"My social media audience enjoys the unique and unusual," Harper said in an excited voice. "I'd like to take some photographs of you at work and post them. Think of it as a more visual interview than you'd see in a magazine."

"And what purpose would that serve, exactly?" Helen hurried up the porch steps, veering around toward the mudroom entrance that led directly to the kitchen.

"Besides opening a discussion about women in a traditionally male role?" Harper matched Helen step-for-step. "And perhaps even becoming a role model for little girls? I suppose you might get some business out of it. Others have."

"More business? I'm in." Helen spared Harper a smile before entering the mudroom and removing her boots, coat and cowboy hat.

Harper remained outside, while Helen entered the kitchen.

The warmth and comfort of the Flying Spur's large kitchen enveloped her like a hug. The noise—it was always full of people. The warm yellow walls and smell of baked goods—it was always spirit-lifting and cheerful. The full plates of food—no one ever went hungry here.

Helen washed up at the kitchen sink, greeting Corliss's teenage son, Mason, who was scrolling through his cell phone while leaning against the kitchen counter.

"I added some shredded jack cheese on top of your stew, Helen," Mason said without looking up. "You always did like cheese on everything."

"I could survive on cheese," Helen admitted, smiling. "And bread. And your chocolate cake." Honestly, the kid was destined for great things off the ranch.

Maybe he won't mind if Nash loses the bet.

Helen bit her lip at the disloyal thought. The Flying Spur was home base for every Blackwell. No one wanted it to be flooded and stocked with fish for the leisure pleasure of the wealthy.

Luke sat at the table next to Denny and across from an elderly man who had the same sharp intelligence in his eyes as the Flying Spur's matriarch. Assuming he was Denny's brother Big E, Helen took a seat next to Denny where a steaming plate awaited her—beef stew sprinkled with melting cheese and hot biscuits drenched in butter.

"Please tell me there's more cake left, Mason." Corliss placed a glass of milk in front of Luke and a glass of water in front of Helen. Then she plopped into a chair across from Helen, next to a man with dark hair who was wearing a blue T-shirt with the Eagle Springs Fire Department logo. She nodded toward Helen. "You remember Ryder. My husband. And his...*our* daughter. Olivia."

Farther down the table, a little girl with long, wavy brown hair paused her cake-eating to breathe a wispy, "Hello."

Helen gave her a friendly smile. "I've heard a lot about Olivia from Luke." He was fascinated by one of the newest additions to the Blackwell household, perhaps because she was only a few years older than he was.

"And as you've probably guessed, I'm Big E." The old man's smile put Helen at ease.

Mason delivered a slice of chocolate cake to his mother. Corliss wasted no time digging in.

"Olivia rides English," Luke said in between bites of stew. "So weird. Who needs English saddles on a ranch?"

"It's not weird. It's cool. And I like it." Olivia rolled her eyes. "Summer said you can try. You can take lessons with me and Isla. I bet you'll like it, too."

Luke scoffed, shaking his head. "I'll try it if Daddy does."

"Nash? Try something new?" Corliss chuckled, loading her fork with chocolate cake. "That'll be the day."

Ryder nudged her with his elbow.

"I mean..." Corliss covered her mouth, quickly swallowing her cake. "I'm going to give English riding a try, so why wouldn't Nash and Spud?"

"Nice save, Mom." Mason lowered his cell phone, grinning. "If it makes you feel better, little sis, I'll give it a go, too."

"See?" Olivia smirked at Luke, whose mouth had dropped open. "Pretty soon, we'll all be riding English."

"I am a cowboy." Luke slapped a hand over his eyes and repeated, "I am a cowboy."

"You'll always be a cowboy, no matter what riding style you try," Helen reassured him.

"Okay, Olivia. You win." Luke shook a finger at his step-cousin. "But I'm not giving up my cowboy hat."

That elicited a round of laughter.

Helen breathed in the teasing and camaraderie of a large family. Having been an only child, it wasn't what she was used to but she did love the Blackwells so.

Wyatt and Nash entered the mudroom, talking engines and wiring while Nash removed his hat, coat and boots.

"See you in the morning." Wyatt left. He and Harper were living in a trailer out back.

Nash's gaze found Helen's and two things came crashing back upon her—he'd told her he was bringing her home and the fate of his family's ranch now rested on her shoulders.

Helen sat back, muttering, "There must be some way to call off that bet."

"What bet?" Denny may have been old and sick, but her hearing was still excellent.

Helen nodded toward Nash. "Ask him."

The room quieted. Eyes turned toward Nash as he entered the kitchen.

"Everybody just calm down." Nash made a downward motion with his hands.

"Oh, this is bad." Corliss turned her chair to face her brother directly. "He's asking us to calm down before he's explained anything. Bad-bad-bad. This is just like the time he was a teenager and snuck over to Cody to compete in that cutting horse competition, isn't it, Gran?"

"I won that competition," Nash said quickly. Hatless, he ran a hand through his shaggy brown hair.

Corliss laughed. "You were seventeen. And you stole Mom's beauty shop money from the cookie jar for the entry fee."

"Borrowed," Nash corrected.

His sister wasn't letting up. "All without telling anyone, I might add."

"You don't need to add anything," Nash grumbled. "Because I won enough money to pay for gas and return Mom's cash. Sometimes, all it takes is a chance to show your grit."

Grit and chutzpah. He's got both.

Helen rubbed her forehead. Nash's impulsiveness should have made him less appealing, not more so.

Big E rapped the table with his knuckles. "Maybe you should let the boy speak, Corliss. I believe a bet was referenced."

Nash's gaze landed on Helen again. And without regret or remorse, he proceeded to explain the bet he'd made with Phil.

Helen decided finishing her food was priority one. She tried to shut out Corliss's shout of disapproval, Denny's shocked whisper about Nash inheriting Cal's reckless streak and Big

E's continued calls for silence until Nash finished.

"You had no right to make that bet, Nash," Corliss said after sending all children out of the room. She paced the kitchen. "First thing in the morning, Gran and I will drive over to Carson and tell Phil there is no bet."

Helen's spirits lifted. There was hope.

"I shook on it. It's a done deal." Nash's posture stiffened.

"Nash gave his word, Corliss," Denny said softly, staring at her hands. "I won't ask Phil to overlook that."

"But..." Corliss halted and extended her hands. *"Helen."*

Big E caught Helen's eye. "Is there a problem..."

Helen felt her cheeks heat.

"She doesn't ride," Corliss said in a defeated voice that echoed the trepidation inside Helen.

"She *can* ride," Nash said firmly.

Helen trembled inside, disagreeing.

"Had a bad experience, did you?" Big E asked Helen with a compassionate look in his eyes. "Long time ago, I bet."

"I was just a tween, barely Mason's age." Helen began tearing chunks out of her biscuit. "My mom worked the stockyards during the week and competed in the rodeo on the weekends. She was offered extra money to handle some new stock that came in, but she'd been…" Helen's gaze darted to Nash and then back to her biscuit. She tore another crumbly bit off. "…drinking. She saddled the horses and began putting me on the back of one for a ride around the holding pen amidst the other stock." Not realizing the horses were still sorting out their pecking order, nipping and kicking at each other. "Long story short…" She drew a deep breath. "I was bucked off and thrown into a horse that kicked me. I broke my wrist in three places."

"She doesn't ride," Corliss repeated, frowning. "And Phil knows it."

And wasn't that rubbing salt in Helen's wound? Had Phil ever really loved her?

"Fears can be overcome," Big E said slowly. "Ask any former bronc rider or any cowboy who's been kicked."

Helen lowered her hand to her abdomen and her gaze to her plate, thinking of a different, but similar, set of circumstances.

"But it's a slow process," Denny added, putting her arm around Helen. "You only have two weeks."

"Can we enter her in the youth cutting horse category?" Corliss wondered aloud. "She'd have a better chance of placing then."

"That would be cheating, love." Ryder softened his words with a kiss to his wife's temple.

"She'll have to compete as an amateur," Denny said in a faraway voice. "Along with any Tom, Dick, and Harry." In sanctioned cutting competitions, there were three main levels of competitors—open (big money winners and champions), non-pro (decent money winners), and amateurs (everyone else).

"And place," Big E added. "I'm assuming this Phil fella will be competing in the non-pro division and not against Helen."

Nash nodded.

"It would be worse to have to go against him." Was that a silver lining? Helen thought not.

"What a mess." Corliss shook her head. "Nash, how could—"

"I'm placing my trust in you, Corliss." Helen cut off her former sister-in-law. There was no need to beat Nash's decision to death. She gathered her empty plate and utensils. "I'm hoping you'll make this bet disappear by lunchtime tomorrow."

The Blackwells erupted in conversation, each weighing in on the problem. Notably, no one reassured Helen that Phil would let Nash off the hook.

"Helen..." Denny reached for her hand when

she returned from the sink, giving it a squeeze. "Have I ever told you that marriage isn't perfect?"

"Yes." Helen glanced at Nash, who was embroiled in an argument with Corliss.

"I understood why you left Nash before," Denny continued quietly. "But you need to understand that a man like Nash charges through life, acting before thinking things through."

Helen nodded.

"If you want him back, you can bank on him not picking up the drink again." Denny gave Helen's hand a little shake, as if urging her to pay close attention to what was being said. "But you should accept the fact that he's not going to be anything but a bull in a china shop."

"Always leaping before he looks." Helen nodded again, thinking about Nash believing she deserved a prince. "And being unapologetic about it."

Denny sighed, releasing Helen's hand.

"Oh, really," Corliss said to Nash in an especially loud voice. "If I can't get Phil to drop the bet, I wash my hands of you."

Side conversations quieted. Nash looked shell-shocked.

"Can I trouble someone for a ride into town?" Back to Helen's apartment where she could pretend that she wasn't part of a wager that made her a player in the fight for Eagle Springs' future.

As if on cue, all the Blackwells but Nash disappeared.

And Nash… He was staring at Helen in that slow, lingering way of his, as if he had something on his mind but wasn't about to say it out loud.

She gave him a look that she hoped said he better start talking.

"Mama, Great Gran says we can sleep here tonight." Luke scooted into the kitchen, skidding across the linoleum in his socks. "A sleepover at our house. Woo-wee!"

"It's convenient," Nash said quickly, as if anticipating Helen's objections. "And you'll have an excuse to be here in the morning when Corliss comes back from Carson."

In Helen's experience, the most logical excuses were made to cover bad decisions. And suddenly, she realized that staying the night here was a bad decision. Not because hanky-panky would ensue, but because she yearned for Nash to want her home to stay.

She opened her mouth to argue but Nash beat her to the punch.

"It's too late for a working cowboy like me to be out on the road." And as if to prove it, he yawned. "Come on. I'll sleep on the couch. You can have the bedroom."

Silence buzzed in her ears. Silence and her mother's words: *No one's going to gift you what you want, dove. You've got to work for things.*

Like her marriage.

"Okay," Helen relented. "I'll stay, but only if we talk." About bets and kisses, foolish pride and romantic wishes.

"Sure." Nash picked up Luke and led them to the mudroom, and from there once they were shod and bundled up, out the door.

Helen hadn't been in the double-wide mobile home since she'd packed up and left. On first glance, it looked the same, other than the fact that the wall where they'd hung pictures of Nash's cutting horse triumphs was empty.

Nash carried Luke to his bedroom, leaving Helen to look around.

The place felt...unlived in. There was no Christmas tree in the corner. No holiday greeting cards from friends held by magnets on the refrigerator.

The couch they'd bought together in Carson still rested under the big front window with folded blankets in one corner. The kitchen table that had belonged to Nash's parents still sat in the dining room, empty and unused if the coat of dust was any indication. The mismatched horse lamps they'd found in a thrift store galloped in place on the end tables. And there, on a coffee table, was their framed wedding photo. It looked like the only thing in the living room that had been dusted recently.

That photo…

Their wedding day had been filled with such promise. The ceremony had been held in a grove of pine trees behind the Flying Spur's covered arena. There had been joy and laughter. Toasts, hugs and well wishes. She'd believed she'd finally found a place where she'd belonged. No more nomadic life. Being a Blackwell meant she had roots. How wrong she'd been to assume such things.

"Luke's asleep already." Nash closed Luke's bedroom door and went to sit in the corner of the couch, propping his stocking feet on the coffee table next to their wedding picture. He looked beat. "It's a big adjustment for a little guy to take the bus." He'd just started the new schedule since his afterschool babysitter had closed up shop on Thanksgiving. "Why don't you go take a shower? We can talk afterward."

It was too easy to run away.

Helen grabbed her backpack with its clean change of clothes, and headed for the hall bath. It felt too intimate to shower in the master bathroom they'd once shared.

Several minutes later, she emerged, ready to talk, having rehearsed what she'd say. The conditions weren't ideal. Her hair was wrapped in a superhero towel and her skin smelled like grape body wash. But they were going to have an adult conversation and clear the air. She'd decided during her shower that there could be no bet if she wasn't willing to participate. Phil and Nash had ignored her protests. She had to stand firm.

But the conversation wasn't meant to be.

Nash was asleep on the couch, head tilted back, breath slow and even.

After allowing herself a moment of longing-filled gawking, she covered Nash with Luke's brown fuzzy blanket, the one decorated with saddles and cowboy hats. And after another moment's hesitation, she pressed a tender kiss to his temple.

He may be a cowboy in a mess of trouble, but he'd always be her cowboy.

At least, in her dreams.

CHAPTER FIVE

NASH WAS IN the barn long before the sun came up on Saturday.

With the clock ticking on the family loan and his bet with Phil, there was a lot to do. He thought about Helen asleep in their home, her openness to reconciliation, his promise to talk to her and his need to help her overcome her riding anxiety so she could save the ranch and the town. Surprisingly, he felt optimistic about the challenges they faced in the arena.

The four well-bred fillies needed the fresh worked off, which meant exercises on the lunge line. Then it was time for them to be ridden, training with the mechanical cow. The fillies performed well, a good omen for his wager with Phil. If he had to choose a horse for Helen to ride in the competition, it would be Rose. That filly could win riderless.

If only Helen could stay in the saddle.

But first, he'd have to get her *in* the saddle.

Every time Nash put a horse away, he lingered in the barn before saddling another one, expecting to see Helen.

Corliss came to muck stalls and feed stock, giving him the silent treatment. No Helen. The family breakfast hour came and went. No Helen. The sound of the farrier van's engine turning over without catching filled the air. No Helen.

Didn't Helen realize she had work to do?

Patience bone-dry, Nash went to find her.

She was in the kitchen drinking coffee with Gran and Big E, watching his nephew Mason guide Luke in the making of chocolate chip cookies. She wore blue jeans and an orange T-shirt with Luke's small handprint painted on it, and accented to look like a turkey.

Luke stood on a chair at the counter, measuring sugar in a glass measuring cup. The old folks were intently competing in a game of double solitaire. Christmas carols were being played somewhere in the house, perhaps the living room since he heard Olivia ask Ryder when they were getting a Christmas tree.

"Is it two cups sugar?" Luke asked Mason.

"It's one." Mason corrected.

"I'm no good at this." Luke blinked, bottom lip quivering.

"Don't say that, Spud," Mason told him kindly. "It just takes practice. And when you're older, I'll teach you how to play video games so you can join in online with the rest of the family."

"I'm a horseman. I don't have time for video games," Luke said, recovering his spunk. "Or cooking."

"That's my boy." Nash slid into a seat next to Helen. He hadn't had time or energy to play video games in months. "It's mid-morning and you're still inside. Since when do you sit still?"

"Since I had to cancel all my appointments today because of a broken van." Helen passed him her mug of coffee. "Not to mention, Corliss is due back anytime from her visit with Phil."

The reason for Helen staying out of the barn became clear. She hoped the wager would go away.

Nash had faith in her and his horses. So, he was quick to burst her bubble. "You're dreaming if you think Phil will back out. He's like a shark with a whiff of blood in the water." Nash sipped the coffee she'd given him. It was just the way he liked it—hot with just a splash of milk. "We need to begin your training."

Helen glanced away, rubbing her palms over her jean-clad thighs.

Corliss burst in through the mudroom door. The dogs trotted ahead of her, sniffing at people and countertops to see if any treats were around or could be mooched. Corliss took her time hanging up her hat and removing her boots.

She even checked in the dryer, as if laundry was ever her first concern.

"Well, little miss?" Gran looked up from her card game. "Quit your stalling and tell us."

"That was a waste of time and gasoline." Corliss hunted in the refrigerator, taking out a pitcher of iced tea. "He laughed in my face." She reached into a cupboard for a glass. Everything she did was careful and controlled, which meant she was working hard to keep a tight rein on her temper.

"What did you say when he laughed?" Gran asked cautiously, as if testing the waters.

Nash sipped the coffee and watched his sister.

"I told him..." Corliss set the empty glass next to the pitcher and then placed both hands over Luke's ears. "...that Helen was going to ride our best horse, come in first place and never speak to him again!"

"Stop that." Luke contorted himself and swatted at Corliss's hands.

"But no one wins or loses if I don't compete," Helen insisted.

"I wouldn't bank on that." Corliss practically groaned. "I think he shouted something at me while I was driving off about him winning if we forfeit."

"You think?" Gran arched her thin white brows, giving Nash a hard stare.

"I think because..." Corliss paused. "I'm not certain. It's hard to hear well when your truck tires are spinning so fast in the snow."

"We Blackwells are known for not hiding our feelings," Big E said with all the gravitas of a documentary voice-over. "Especially when a man doesn't act like a gentleman."

Nash very carefully stared into his coffee cup.

Beside him, Helen sighed heavily. "If I hadn't broken things off with Phil or broken down, none of this would have happened."

"Never take the blame for something someone else has done." Big E was full of wisdom and significant looks sent Nash's way.

"I'm the one to blame," Nash ground out, man enough to admit it. He'd kissed Helen and she'd gotten herself unengaged, after all.

"I heartily approve of that statement." Corliss poured her tea. "And I hope like anything that Helen can do us proud in that cutting horse competition."

"It'll take work, but she can do it." Nash drew back and gave Helen a smile meant to reassure.

Helen looked pale.

"The Christmas parade is tonight." Oblivious to the tension in the room, Luke changed the subject while spilling sugar on the floor and counter and jolting neat-freak Mason into a frenzy of cleaning action. “I want to get there early to see the Christmas Village and talk to Santa. I want to ask him about a special present.”

A horse, Nash guessed. “I thought you wrote Santa a letter at school.”

“Letters get lost.” Luke gathered loose grains of sugar and sprinkled them in the bowl. And then he stuck his bare hand into the flour tin, adding that to the mix and dusting the counter in the process. “Daddy, this present is important.”

“Spud…” Mason had been trying to wipe up the mess with paper towels. “I think I hear Olivia calling you.”

Nash hadn’t heard a thing.

Regardless, Luke popped down to the floor and scurried off to find her.

“Have you spotted that white horse I told you about, Nash?” Gran tapped the kitchen table.

“No.” Nash lowered his voice, leaning toward Helen. “We have training to do.”

“I…” Helen seemed stuck in her chair.

“You’re going to compete, Helen,” Gran proclaimed with finality. “You’re a Blackwell and we believe in you.”

“But…” Helen was thinking too much about being thrown from that horse all those years ago.

Now who’s the mind reader?

“I got us in a pickle,” Nash said candidly.

"You know that Phil won't agree to you backing out on the bet. Knowing you, you've already texted to ask him about it. And he either didn't respond or told you that competing was the only option."

Helen frowned, not denying it.

Nash felt bad about being right. What he didn't feel bad about was the fact that Phil was ruining his chances of ever getting back together with Helen.

He took Helen's cold hand and stroked it with his thumb. "I keep telling you, if I didn't think you could do it, I wouldn't have taken the bet."

"Well, that's just it. Phil has no faith in me doing this, while you…" She tugged her hand free. "You've misread me completely."

"Come out to the barn and we'll see." Nash gentled his voice. He truly believed in her. "We'll see what you can do."

Everyone was quiet, watching them.

"You owe me a talk," Helen finally said, obviously stalling.

"I do." Nash stood, drawing Helen to her feet. "Come out to the barn and we'll talk all you want."

"I'M A FARRIER. I work with horses every day." Helen stood in the middle of the covered arena, sweating as if it was a ninety-degree, sunny day, not a morning of intermittent clouds and snowflakes. "I've been knocked down, kicked, and stepped on but I keep doing my job. I can ride. Of course, I can ride."

She hunched her shoulders.

I can't ride.

The wind blew beneath the arena's roof, bringing snowflakes and cold. Helen was wrapped in layers. A crash vest hung heavy on her shoulders over her Christmas hoodie. A riding helmet crushed her hair against her head.

Every fiber in her being cried out against her getting on a horse. Every fiber, except her brain, which kept turning to "buts."

But the Blackwells and the town need you to ride.

Not only to ride but to ride well. Oh, boy.

You're a Blackwell. Quit your complaining, dove!

She scoffed, not appreciative of her mother's voice in her head.

Do your best. The rest will fall into place.

Dad's advice was more welcome. Her father would have wanted Helen to give it her best shot. Eagle Springs had been his home town.

And it had become her home.

Her shoulders rolled further forward, bent by the weight of it all.

Because it wasn't just Eagle Springs that had become her home, but the Flying Spur.

She shuffled her feet and glanced around. Seeking help. Seeking counsel.

The arena was empty.

But every direction Helen turned brought proof that the Blackwells cared for this ranch and their horses. They'd invested in their livestock and their future with a big barn, a covered arena, a roofed round pen. The same could be said of their impact in town. The annual rodeo Denny had founded drew competitors from across the western states. The auction yard she'd started had been reborn, expanding from stock sales to other items. All that meant jobs, revenue and a bigger, tighter-knit community. The Blackwells had been building this place, this life, for decades on the capable shoulders of Denny.

Helen's shoulders felt weak by comparison.

Still, she wanted to ride.

Nash led a saddled horse toward her. She would like to take a picture of him, her perfect cowboy, because when she lost the competition in two weeks and let everyone down, she was bound to lose him, too. This time, for good.

He came closer and she realized that the horse he led was Beanie, the gentle brown gelding she'd taken refuge with yesterday. He was one of the board and train horses. "I thought we'd start with this old gentleman."

Beanie greeted Helen with a nose-nudging inspection.

"Sorry, Beanie. No carrots today." She tucked her bare hands in her jeans pockets for warmth. Nash hadn't wanted her to wear gloves, saying she'd get a better feel for the reins skin-to-leather. "Thank you for bringing me the oldest horse in the stable." She hoped he was slow and patient.

"He may be the oldest, but he could teach my fillies a thing or two about cutting." Nash stared at the looped reins in his hands. "Do you remember how Luke was taught to ride?"

She nodded. "Denny and Mason led him around the arena on his pony for hours. Is that what we're going to do?" How many hours were there between this weekend and the competition? Helen didn't know. What she did know was that there weren't enough hours between now and then for her to conquer her fear of riding.

"Do you remember what happened after every session they led Luke around?" Tone far too serious, Nash continued to stare at his hands, hat brim hiding the expression on his face.

An expression she was suddenly desperate to see.

"Denny gave Luke a treat. I think it was a

piece of chocolate candy." Helen paused, struck by a thought. It had been others who'd taught their son to ride, not Nash. He'd been drinking on the daily back then. "You wish you'd taught Luke to ride." It wasn't a question.

"Yes." Her ex-husband raised his gaze, letting her see the regret in his brown eyes. "Giving you the joy of riding might make my past failures sting a little less."

"The joy of riding? That might be a stretch." Helen thought enduring was a more likely goal. "And I probably won't be as motivated by chocolate as Luke was. Don't get me wrong. I love chocolate and I'm happy you aren't going to reward me with carrots. I'm just pointing out that you'll need a better incentive system."

"We'll get to that." Nash's smile emerged, lopsided and endearing. "Do you remember how I like to train my horses?"

"You start quiet," Helen murmured.

The wind swirled though the arena enveloping them in a cloud of snowflakes before whisking them away.

"Yes, *we* start quiet." He stood on one side of Beanie, gesturing to her to stand on the other side. He held the reins loosely beneath the brown gelding's head. "Place your hand here."

When she held the cool reins, he placed his

hand over hers. Both their hands were cold. But at his touch, warmth grew between them.

Please don't let go.

He didn't. "And now, we walk." Nash started forward.

Helen didn't want to move. Not because she dreaded the next two weeks—she did—but because she would have preferred to have him hold her hand while he stared into her eyes and lowered his mouth to hers.

But in this new reality of theirs, kisses were apparently not in her future. Walking was.

They walked on either side of Beanie's head, leading him around the perimeter of the oval-shaped arena. They walked, not speaking. One lap turned into two. Her fingers were warm now beneath his. Perhaps that was all Nash had planned for the day. Walking.

Helen began to relax, to breathe easier, to gather courage to be the karaoke-singing Helen of Old. Which allowed her to venture into teasing territory. "You mentioned treats."

Laughter burst from Nash, as if this was the last thing he'd expected her to say. "We aren't done training."

"I want to specify the terms of my training, including my rewards." Helen smiled to herself, full of ideas.

"That's not how I train or how rewards work,"

Nash said, mirthlessly. Since his accident, he always closed down when she tried to draw him out. And she'd closed herself off as a result, shuttering away a big part of herself, a part that was increasingly pressuring her for release.

"I hate to be obstinate," Helen of Old pressed on. "But my way is how training and rewards will work these next two weeks. I have the advantage, Nash. You can't refuse me anything because you need me." She ruthlessly set aside the fact that the entire town needed her. She didn't want treats from anyone but Nash. Oh, the power. After three years of leaving the relationship ball in his court, this was thrilling. "Here's how this will go. We're going to walk and talk at the same time."

"I don't think so."

She could tell without looking at her ex-husband that he was shoring his guard. As much as he'd been promising they'd talk, he didn't want to follow through.

"I'm not good with silences, Nash. If you're quiet while we train, I'll be thinking about the time a couple of horses tossed me around." Or the most recent time... Her gut clenched. "You don't want that, do you?"

"Helen." Nash sounded very put-upon.

She peeked around Beanie's nose, catching

sight of his frown. "Now, don't you believe talking is my treat. I have a different treat in mind."

He sighed. "Don't say—"

"Kisses." She practically didn't feel the whip of the wind. He was holding her hand and she was holding him over a relationship barrel. If not for the bet, her future might have looked marvelous.

Nash stared straight ahead. "You know that's not wise. Pick a different reward."

"You're in no position to refuse me." When he didn't argue, she continued, "Good. Now that I have you captive, tell me why you kissed me last month."

Silence.

She pressed her lips together, determined to outlast him.

Beanie plodded along. Her boots continued to slog through the inches of soft, loamy soil. The wind gusted past. A snowflake landed on her cheek. Helen noted the speakers mounted in the ceiling and thought it would be nice to hear some Christmas music.

Finally, she couldn't take the silence anymore. "Nash Blackwell. Don't tell me you don't know why you kissed me."

Nash muttered something she didn't catch. And then he said in a louder voice, "I kissed you because I'm the worst kind of man, Helen. I kissed you because I couldn't stand the thought of you with Phil. Or..." He glanced at her over Beanie's long brown nose. "...anybody else."

Her heart soared. Her pace increased. "You want to get back together." It wasn't a question.

"I didn't say that." He frowned.

She wished he'd give her that lopsided grin instead.

She wished he was jealous enough to try and salvage their relationship.

Struck by a thought, she came to an abrupt halt, holding Beanie back. If only she could hold back her words. "Nash Blackwell. That is the most selfish thing you've ever said to me. And that's taking this bet into account."

His fingers over hers tightened and he made a clucking noise, starting to walk forward once more, leaving her no choice but to follow. "You deserve better than a cowboy with a string of mistakes."

"And now you're going to decide what's right for me?" She huffed. "Suddenly, the prince comment makes sense, since I'll never find one in Wyoming. What you're saying is that if you can't have me, no one will. How Phil of you." She huffed again.

Not to be outdone, Beanie nickered.

"See?" Helen flashed a disapproving frown toward Nash. "Even Beanie thinks you're looking at this all wrong. We should be together." Helen of Old was on a roll.

"There is no *we*."

If his goal had been to start quiet, she was upsetting his apple cart because she kept pumping up the volume, fueled by her frustration with him. "I see. So, you're saying you felt nothing in that kiss? No spark. No heat. No—"

"When it comes to you, Helen, holding you in my arms is all I think about."

She recalled the image of him sleeping in the corner of the couch where he could stare at their wedding picture. A jolt of satisfaction lifted her flagging spirits. "You still love me."

"Yes, but I let you down," he said heavily. "And I can't risk doing that again."

She considered his words as they walked toward the far end of the arena, the wind at their backs. "You don't think you'll stay sober."

"Whereas you think I'll never seek refuge in liquor again." There was disappointment in his voice, but it felt more like he was upset with himself than with her. His features were tense. "The temptation to drink is always there, like an old habit. It's there when life throws me impossible challenges. It's there when I look back at my incredible failures. It's there when I can't sleep at night."

That sounded as if temptation was always by his side.

"But then—" she stumbled "—what keeps you sober?"

"Things I'm responsible for. People I don't want to let down, myself included." He settled his cowboy hat more firmly on his head. "You and Luke and my horses. Corliss and Gran. Adele, who needed me after her husband died. This ranch. My heritage. The town." He caught her eye with his sorrow-filled gaze. "Do I need to go on?"

"No." She'd heard enough. "Basically, all the forces around you are keeping you sober. And pride, I *bet*." Emphasis on bet.

He winced. "And they could just as easily make me drink, I suppose." His gaze turned uncertain. "Which is why I can't start up with you again."

"Even though you love me. Even though I'm one of the things keeping you from drinking." She had no qualms using his logic against him.

Nash nodded, bringing them to a stop. He stepped in front of Beanie and cupped Helen's chin in his hand with a loving touch that made her heart ache. "I didn't plan on making that bet with Phil. And I don't plan on picking up a drink ever again. But what I am determined to do is *not* hurt you. And the only way to make sure I do that is to keep my distance." His hand fell away. "Don't fight me on this, please. I'm only thinking of you."

"You're so hard-headed." Her eyes unexpectedly filled with tears. "You annoy me." Which was a shame since she loved him so much.

"I know." He brushed a thumb over her cheek before letting his hand drop away. "You did great walking Beanie. You were able to concentrate on other things."

"And for such a good performance, I deserve a reward." Her gaze fell to his lips. He was so determined to erect defenses against love and passion. And she was equally determined to breach his walls.

"You'll get your treat." Nash reached into his back pocket and produced two baby carrots, giving one to Beanie before extending his hand toward Helen.

"That carrot has horse slobber on it." Helen mucked around horses all day long, but she did not share a plate with her four-legged clients. "Pass."

"I meant for you to feed Beanie." Nash gave her rejected carrot to the gelding. "Now, climb on up in that saddle, and I'll lead you around the arena."

Helen sucked in a sharp breath. "Hang on. Let's walk some more."

"Or we could see just what we're up against." Nash came around to her side,.

"I..." *Can't.* "I..." *Won't.* "I...need a better reward system than carrots." Obviously.

"Like what?" Nash crossed his arms over his chest and stared her down.

Beanie swung his head around and looked at her, too.

"I don't want carrots. I want kisses. I'll ride for kisses." And maybe after more of her kisses, Nash would realize they had something worth risking disappointment over.

"All right." Nash tipped the brim of his hat back and kissed her nose. "There's your reward. Paid in advance."

"That's not fair." But she did as he asked and scrambled into the saddle without any grace.

Mistake.

Her breath stuck in her throat before her right foot slid into the stirrup. The ground felt so far away. She flushed hot. Sweat popped out at the nape of her neck.

Beanie shifted his back legs, making her gasp.

And then her limbs prickled with the ice of fear.

I'm a farrier. I'm a Blackwell. Nash believes in me. I can do this.

And yet, the beginnings of a scream gathered in her throat.

"Easy now." Nash wasn't looking at her. He gathered Beanie's reins. "You're doing great. We'll just take a lap around the arena."

"Don't," Helen wheezed, clinging to the saddle horn. "Don't move him." Or she'd fall. She was sure of it. *"Don't. Move."*

"Helen?" Nash glanced up at her face, and then held out his arms. "It's all right. It's okay."

"It's not." Helen slid out of the saddle like melted butter, falling into his embrace. "I can't do it. Don't make me do it."

Setting her feet on the ground, Nash held her close and stroked her back, making soothing noises in between soft words of reassurance.

He said all the right things to calm her.

Everything, that is, except that she didn't have to compete.

CHAPTER SIX

"I'M NOT CUT out to be a hero." Helen inched forward in the line to see Santa Claus, raising her voice so her best friend could hear her above the rising din.

Santa Claus was about to arrive in Eagle Springs. It was always a guessing game as to who would play him.

The line to see Old St. Nick wound its way around the outer walls of the high school cafeteria. Across the room, Nash and other fathers entertained young children with a game of Duck, Duck, Goose.

Despite Luke's desire to be the first to see the big man and despite cutting the traditional Saturday night Blackwell dinner short, they were still tenth in line.

Santa entered the cafeteria with a jolly *ho-ho-ho* that seemed to make light of his late appearance and ease parental concerns that they'd miss the tree lighting ceremony in forty-five short minutes and the beginning of the Christmas parade after that.

"Not a hero?" Beside Helen, Gwen Calipari tsked as she rocked her sleeping baby girl Daphne. She and her kids had come alone since her husband was out of town. "How right you are, Helen. You're no hero. Heroes help little old ladies cross the street." She nodded toward Denny, who sat at a table with some of the town's old timers. Helen had helped her to her seat. "Heroes don't volunteer to weld broken school equipment for free." Gwen nodded toward the stage at the other end of the cafeteria. Helen had welded the heavy curtain's broken operating mechanism last summer. "And heroes also forgive their true love his faults." She nodded toward Nash, who was slowly running after Gwen's son Caleb around the Duck, Duck, Goose circle. "You're so right. You're no hero, my friend."

"You know what I mean." Helen unwrapped her green plaid scarf and tucked it in her coat pocket as they moved forward in line. "I'm not the type to storm the castle or punch the villain."

"But you can be the type to cling to a saddle horn," Gwen pointed out. Her dark brown curls peeked from beneath a red and green knit cap.

It was Helen's turn to scoff. "Says the woman who doesn't ride either."

"Look..." Gwen took hold of Helen's arm. "You're as tough as they come, Helen. Maybe even tougher than Denny. And that's saying a lot."

Although Nash had said much the same, Helen shook her head.

"What? You don't believe me?" Gwen kept on with her baby rocking. "You forget that I'm the one who picked you up from the hospital after that stallion in Carson kicked you."

Helen recalled the sickening sting of a hoof followed by the rumble of boards on her back as she landed against a barn wall. The damage and internal bleeding a year ago had required surgery. With Nash gone to deliver a cutting horse, Gwen had been her first and only call. Helen and Luke had spent several days with Gwen's family so that she could recuperate. And she'd brought on an apprentice for weeks after until she was cleared for heavy lifting.

"I met you at the doctor's office, too, when you were getting stitches in your arm." Gwen added a side-to-side motion to her jiggle when her daughter tested her lung strength. "All because some horse in the next county bit you."

Helen rubbed her coat sleeve over the scar on her bicep.

"Not to mention, I loaned you my big rubber rainboots when that Clydesdale Bobby Maylar owns pranced around and broke your toe. It swelled up so much you couldn't put your regular boots on." Gwen looked like she was running out of steam both verbally and in her efforts to jiggle. She smiled gratefully when Helen took the baby. "You're lucky I have big feet. So, don't tell me you aren't tough because somehow after all those injuries, you still shoe horses for a living. You got thrown once—"

"And kicked, too," Helen sing-songed to little Daphne, who was trying her hardest to wake up and remind everyone it was feeding time.

"—and you refuse to get back on a horse?"

Helen bit her lip, jiggling the baby.

"My point is that you've had more injuries shoeing horses than riding them." Gwen plunked her hands on her hips. "Why can't you do this?"

Helen's gaze drifted to Nash. "I suppose I haven't thought about the why." She'd been too consumed with fear.

"Maybe you should. Look, in all seriousness—" Gwen moved closer to Helen, fussing with Daphne's blanket "—everybody knows Nash trains the best horses. I've never heard tell of his horses bucking someone off."

"Knowing my luck, I'd be the first."

Grinning, Gwen took Daphne back. "And if you are, I'll bring you a pillow for your tush and a bottle of wine."

"How lucky I am to have a friend like you," Helen quipped.

"Has it occurred to you that this could be your chance to win Nash back?"

"Yes, but that's a long-shot." Helen explained Nash's philosophy about not being the prince she deserved.

"Well, he's right in that respect. You are too good for a cowboy who favors a drink."

"Gwen!" Helen moved forward as a couple with a scared young toddler got out of line. "You know he's not drinking."

"Helen!" Gwen mirrored her tone, startling the baby, who began to squirm. "Let me rephrase. When Nash is sober, you're perfect together. But he's right about one thing. You shouldn't settle when it comes to love. You withdrew when you left Nash and you withered when you were with Phil. I can finally say it now." That was silly because she'd said it before. Many times.

"You know I was playing it safe." Not wanting to rock the boat. "And you'll be happy to hear I'm done with that." She hoped. "The withdrawn wallflower thing, that is."

"Good. Because it was totally unlike you. It was as if you were afraid to say *anything* for fear you might offend someone."

"*Gwen!* It wasn't that bad."

"It was," Gwen crooned to Daphne. "You deserve better...seemed like Phil always thought of you as some kind of accessory."

Helen knew Gwen was right but refused to admit it.

Besides, people were looking at them. And listening, too. The adults in line around them had stopped talking and were staring with unabashed curiosity.

Helen turned her back on the room and more than half their audience. "If I agree, will you change topics?"

"Okay." Gwen tucked the baby blanket tighter around Daphne's arms. "I'm assuming if you have a chance at getting back together with Nash, you're going to tell him you can't have any more children first."

"Gwen!" Helen surveyed their audience to see if they'd heard, but no one looked her way.

Gwen spread a disapproving frown over those who did seem to be eavesdropping. But then her gaze fixed on someone. "Speak of the devil. There's Phil."

Helen turned.

Sure enough, Phil was walking toward them like he owned the room, smiling just as he had when he'd proposed to Helen last month.

"What are you doing here?" Nash moved away from the Duck, Duck, Goose circle and gave his former best friend, turned Xavier Howard flunky, a dirty look.

"I was invited by my nephew." Jake Gallagher pointed to where his sister and her kid, who had Down syndrome, stood in line to see Santa Claus.

"You should have taken your nephew to whatever new town your sister plans to relocate to." With effort, Nash kept his voice down. "How does she feel about you working for the wrong side of this fight?"

"You gave me no choice when you fired me," Jake said with equal fervor and volume. "What was I supposed to do? No one in town was hiring and Jami relies on me and my income to support Patrick." His nephew.

Nash shook his head. "When the blight took all our stock, we didn't need—and couldn't afford to pay—extra hands. I wish I could have kept you on, but..."

"You had a hard decision to make, just like I did." Jake chewed on the inside of his cheek. "Look, you need to know that this Frank Wesson fella doesn't just want to flood the valley and create a playground for the rich. He wants to put you Blackwells at odds with each other and scatter you all to the wind."

"What are you talking about?"

Jake took hold of Nash's arm and moved closer. "Where do you think your family will go if you lose this fight? Chances are you won't pick up and move five families and your grandmother to the same town."

Nash shook him off. “There’s no way your boss can drive a wedge between us. Or make me suffer any more than I already am.”

“Don’t be so sure about that.” Jake nodded toward where Helen stood with Gwen and Phil. “Frank offered Phil a bigger stake in the development if he removed Helen from your corner.”

Nash flushed with angry heat so fast that it felt like there was steam coming out of his ears. He wanted to sprint to Helen’s side and tell Phil to get lost.

But the last time he and Phil had sparred, Phil came out on top.

Nash had to trust Helen could take care of herself.

“GWEN, IT SEEMS like ages since I’ve seen you.” Phil tipped his gray felt hat in her direction.

“What do you think, Daphne?” Gwen spoke to her fussy baby. “Is Phil’s greeting really code for please leave? Little does Phil know that you can’t step out of line to see Santa or you’ll lose your place. I’m not that kind of mama.”

“Gwen,” Helen whispered, not wanting to make a scene.

“Always a pleasure, Gwen.” Phil’s smile never wavered but his gaze shifted toward Helen and it felt icier than a wrench left outside on a snowy day. “I hoped to find you here.”

Standing next to Jake across the room, Nash caught Helen's eye and frowned.

Holding his gaze, Helen shook her head slightly. Then she summoned the gutsy Helen of Old. "We have nothing to say to each other, Phil, unless…"

"Nothing will change my mind about the bet. However, there's another matter…" Phil held out his hand and in his palm a familiar ring glittered garishly under the cafeteria lights.

"You have the nerve to show me that?" Helen was floored.

Gwen's head came up. "Would you take him back?"

"No!"

"Wear my ring, Helen." Phil carried on blithely. "Marry me and I'll make all your problems disappear. I'll even buy you a new blacksmithing van if you insist upon working."

He was building a pretty cage. That attractive smile. The successful shine on his boots. If Helen hadn't witnessed him offering the bet with Nash, she might have believed he was sincere.

Nash, Luke and Caleb had left the game and were in line at the cookie and coffee table. Nash kept glancing their way.

Nash, who thought about kissing her and believed she deserved a prince. Nash, who had owned her heart since she'd impulsively sung him a love song on karaoke night in the Cranky Crow. Nash, who had quietly wooed her with his hard work, humility and protectiveness.

"You should think about the future, Helen." Phil apparently wasn't finished with his sales pitch. "Where will you go if Eagle Springs is no more?"

"And if I agree to marry you, Phil, what happens to the Blackwells?" Helen's gaze swung around to Phil in time to see the barest of cracks in his facade, a hard glint in his eye, quickly concealed. "Will you give up those horses you wanted from Nash? And what about your pride? Could you marry me knowing that a part of my heart will always belong to Nash Blackwell?"

Beside her, Gwen was silent, for once.

After a moment, Phil forced a chuckle that convinced no one he found Helen's speech amusing.

"That's what I thought." Helen shoved her hands in her jacket pockets. Or she tried to. The green plaid scarf blocked her efforts. Phil had bought that scarf for her the weekend he'd proposed. Helen thrust it toward him. "I won't marry you, Phil. I don't pine for you the way Nora Peachtree does. And besides, my son needs good male role models and that isn't you, not by a long shot."

Helen of Old was back. Helen couldn't help it. She grinned.

Phil's cheeks took on a ruddy hue, and his lips were pressed together as if he had more to say but prudence—or an audience—was holding him back. He grabbed the scarf and shoved the engagement ring in his pocket. Then he pivoted on his shiny boot heel and made for the exit, tossing her scarf in the trash.

Gwen hugged Helen, careful not to squish the baby. "Look at you and your newly rediscovered backbone. I'm so proud of my hometown hero."

Helen wasn't. Woulda-coulda-shouldas set in. "I'm a fool. I could have negotiated for a reprieve for the town. I could have been the sacrificial lamb, at least until the Blackwells paid off their debts."

"With that man?" Gwen shook her head. "You'd be negotiating forever. And knowing Phil, he'd find a way to keep you in his clutches."

Nash and the boys approached. Nash didn't spare a moment's glance to Phil's retreating back. And yet, she felt as if Nash had her back.

"Cookie, Mama?" Luke very carefully handed Helen a frosted sugar cookie in a napkin as Caleb did the same for Gwen.

"It isn't Christmas without Christmas cookies," Helen said with forced cheer. One glance at the bright yellow frosting and tiny balls decorating her star-shaped cookie and her mood lifted a little.

"I thought you ladies would enjoy the treat." Nash handed Helen a cup of coffee, that near-lopsided smile of his on full display. "There should only be sweets at the holidays, no sour notes."

"And you wanted to prove to Helen's best friend that you can still be doting husband material," Gwen teased as they moved forward in line. "It's important you impress me, Nash. In case Helen decides to take you back."

Nash blinked blankly before recovering with a laugh. "I've missed your sense of humor, Gwen."

Gwen gave him a mischievous grin that was eons apart from the expression she'd worn for Phil. "Your wife and I are a package deal, honey."

"Ex-wife," Helen muttered, earning a frown from Nash. Movement and raised voices around Denny caught her attention. "Nash, you better go smooth things over. Looks like Denny's causing a ruckus." About the future of Eagle Springs, no doubt.

Nash hurried to his grandmother's side.

The two boys plopped on the floor and ate their cookies, while pointing at, and chattering about, Santa.

"Where do you plan to go if Eagle Springs goes under?" Gwen asked, serious for once.

"I..." Helen's gaze caught on Nash's broad shoulders.

"You'll go wherever that cowboy does," Gwen predicted with a smile. "Which is best for Luke, after all."

But not for me if he won't take me back.

Helen shrugged, feeling deflated. "Can we talk about something else?"

"What do you want for Christmas?" Gwen didn't miss a beat. "I want one of those fancy air fryers. They say the roasted vegetables are so good that even kids eat their greens."

"You wish."

They both laughed.

Idle chit-chat carried them through until it was Gwen's children's turn with Santa. The jolly old elf held Daphne with practiced ease. He was a much better Santa than last year's. Everything was better about this Santa—the shine to his boots, the bright white fur trim on his red velvet costume and the thick, snowy-white beard. There were no tears. He had Caleb mugging for his photo like a professional model.

In no time, Gwen headed off to join her parents for the tree lighting ceremony in the town square, after reminding Helen she had a haircut scheduled at her salon next week.

Finally, it was Luke's turn to sit next to Santa. Helen was floored to see who this year's Santa was—*Big E!*

Laughing, Nash and Helen each took pictures of Luke with their cell phones.

"Have you been a good boy?" Santa, a.k.a. Big E Blackwell, asked Luke.

"I'm always good." Luke nodded solemnly. "Even when Wendy Carsden kicks me at recess."

Helen worked hard not to frown. She wasn't a fan of little Wendy and the politics at school that made excuses for the girl's bad behavior.

Give that little redhead a stocking full of coal!

Santa chuckled, a hearty *ho-ho-ho* that made Helen suspect this wasn't the first time the old man had played a jolly old elf. "And what do you want for Christmas?"

"It's a secret," Luke said, glancing at his parents before whispering to Santa.

"What's that?" Big E tapped his ear. "Say again."

Glancing at Nash and Helen, Luke whispered to Santa once more.

"I'm sorry. I didn't hear you." Big E was grinning from behind his luxurious fake beard.

Luke huffed. "I said, I want my parents to get

hitched again! I whispered 'cuz it's supposed to be a secret."

It wasn't anymore.

Nash's cheeks turned ruddy.

Helen couldn't stop laughing.

"WHERE'S MAMA?"

"Right behind us." Nash carried Luke in his arms, dodging through an unusually large crowd moving from the town square where the Christmas tree had been lit to garner spots along the streets where the Christmas parade would pass. He glanced over his shoulder but didn't immediately spot Helen. He stopped and turned, worry flooding his system. "She was right behind us."

I should have held her hand.

He should have asked her to stay by his side. Especially with Phil hovering around, holding out engagement rings. When Nash had seen his rival's hand extended toward Helen, he'd wanted to run to her and shout that she was spoken for. But a room full of people and the fact that Helen would take any such action as proof that he did want her back had held him in place.

If they were going to get through the next two weeks, Helen needed his support and skill, not his love.

He'd been shaken this morning when she'd been unable to sit in Beanie's saddle. They'd walked Rose together in the afternoon and she'd sat in her saddle for a minute before her face turned green. He wanted to reassure her that he'd keep her safe on horseback but how could he do that when he planned to keep her at arm's length?

Without kissing incentives.

Beyond kisses, he was desperate to give Helen and Luke what they wanted—a reconciliation. And equally desperate not to.

It was bad enough that Helen insisted on returning with Luke to their apartment in town tonight after the parade. After what Jake had told him, seemingly verified by the episode with Phil in the cafeteria, Nash felt like he needed to camp outside her door. Or bring her back to the safety of the ranch.

"There's Mama," Luke cried, waving. "With Great Gran."

Helen and his grandmother had stopped in front of the Christmas Village set up in the empty lot next to Waders & Bait Tackle Shop. Christmas trees and large, inflatable holiday decorations had been erected in the vacant lot, along with a skating rink and a crafting place for kids, manned by volunteers. Nash would have stopped there if his son hadn't been antsy to claim a good spot for the parade.

Standing in the shadow of an inflatable reindeer twice her size, Gran was talking to Dorcas Fenway, who held a sign that read, *"Don't let this be the last Christmas parade."*

A man passed by them, jacket too thin to do much against the freezing temperatures and gently falling snow. He must have said something derogatory about Dorcas's sign, because the trio turned toward him, frowning and talking, although Nash was too far away to hear what was being said.

Jackie Youngblood, owner of the feed store, went to join them, looking like he was adding fuel to the fire.

After Gran's snapping at development supporters in the cafeteria, all they needed was an altercation on the streets of Eagle Springs to cap the night.

He rushed back.

For weeks, tempers had been flaring between those who had sold or wanted to sell to the developer group and those who wanted to keep their homes and Eagle Springs unchanged. Earlier this week, Hayes Lewis had called out his brother Cody as a money-grubber for selling. French fries had been thrown, along with insults. They'd been eating lunch together at

Sweetwater Kitchen and Sheriff Grady McMillan had been called upon to escort them from the premises.

Nash's long strides brought him quickly to his family's side, where a crowd was growing.

"Do you really think a wealthy man in a suit is going to let you re-open your feed store in a luxury community?" Gran was saying to Jackie.

"Yes. Wyoming is horse country." Jackie bit off each word with relish.

"I've seen the development map. There are no riding trails," Gran told him in a superior tone of voice. "The plots of land for homes won't be large enough for a mansion *and* horses. Not to mention, they plan to flood all the existing ranches. Face it, Jackie. You've been bamboozled."

Jackie's face reddened. "Xavier Howard made me a promise. He shook my hand."

"Which will mean nothing in court," Gran said in a softer, more compassionate pitch. "Did money change hands?"

"I received an advance check for signing the sale papers." For the first time, Jackie looked doubtful. "All deals depend upon what happens to the Flying Spur."

Helen shuddered.

Nash put his arm around her shoulders, drawing her close.

"Hi, Mama." Luke reached across Nash to pat Helen's cowboy hat.

Helen gave them both tender smiles, but the expression didn't mask the worry in her eyes.

"Is it true?" Jackie studied Helen. "Are you competing for the Blackwells and the town?"

Helen gave a curt nod, looking like she wished she was anywhere but here, with the future of the town resting in her ability to stay on a horse.

"I'm pulling for you, Helen," Dorcas said, holding up her sign.

Several people nearby seconded her sentiment.

Chances were that none of them knew about Helen's fear of riding.

But a few others—ones Nash knew had already cut a deal, like Kevin Parker over at Two Springs Ranch—sized up Helen and smirked. Had Phil shared Helen's fears with the development group? It felt like it.

Nash's fingers curled into Helen's shoulder. He should have asked Jake about that when they'd been talking earlier.

"Guys, only the kids in the front row get candy." Luke twisted in Nash's arms, pointing the way they'd come. "Last year, I got weeds."

"Not weeds. Mistletoe," Helen corrected,

staring up at Nash, expression transitioning from apprehension to humor.

"Whatever," Luke said impatiently. "I want candy."

And for your parents to reconcile.

It was two against one—Luke and Helen versus Nash. And the mischievous way Helen was looking at him made it hard to remember why Nash and Helen couldn't be together. He realized he'd been giving Helen a goofy smile. He stopped. Now wasn't the time to moon at his ex-wife. "Come along, family." Nash handed Luke to Helen and then took Gran's arm.

Gran set a slow pace. "Some people are going to be hurt when Frank's plan is said and done."

"You can't protect everyone, Gran."

"Tell that to my conscience." She was scanning the crowd. "Have you seen that meddlesome brother of mine?"

"Big E?"

Helen poked Nash in the back and shushed him.

"Nope." Nash took the hint. "Sorry, Gran."

She harrumphed and resumed moving forward.

"I don't think I've ever seen a crowd this large," Helen marveled when they finally found the spot on the sidewalk where Adele had staked out space for the Blackwell clan.

Adele had chosen a location in front of Barn Owl Bookstore and Café.

Helen set Luke down while Nash escorted Gran to a folding chair Corliss had brought. His sister laid a thick, red checked blanket over her lap.

"The size of the crowd has to be a positive sign, despite people like Jackie," Helen said when Nash returned to her side on the curb.

"It's not a positive. It's a mark in time." Nash put his hands in his shearling coat pockets instead of reaching for Helen's hand. "It's a farewell of sorts."

Luke had joined his cousins. He was glommed on to by Adele's twins Quinn and Ivy, who were wearing matching pink polka dot snowsuits and holding small candy canes.

"Lukey! Lukey!" the twins cried, wrapping their arms around him.

Luke stood still but glanced back to Nash and Helen, a suffering expression on his face.

"Aw, that's cute," Helen said.

Luke's shoulders fell. "Mama."

"Come on, girls." Mason came to Luke's rescue. He lifted both Quinn and Ivy, resting one twin on each hip. "You missed Santa at school earlier, girlies. You don't want to miss him because you were hugging on Luke, do you?"

The twins shook their heads, sending their

delicate blond curls fluttering beneath their knit caps in the evening breeze.

"I refuse to allow my kids to suffer by making them visit Santa." Adele stood nearby, holding her fiancé's hand. She glanced at Sheriff Grady with love in her eyes. "I screamed every year they took a picture of me beside Santa."

"We have the photographic evidence," Nash teased. "In case Grady wants proof."

"Don't you dare ask to see it," Adele warned her fiancé.

"One year, Adele got herself so worked up that she upchucked on Santa's boots." Gran chuckled. "There's always one in the family who dislikes tradition, whether it's the Easter Bunny or Santa."

"You really think this is the end for Eagle Springs, Nash?" Helen stared at him, looking like she needed reassurance. "I keep hoping for a Christmas miracle."

"Me, too." Nash dug deep but had no reassurance to give her. In fact, it was the opposite. Having her by his side gave him a sense of optimism that had been lacking these past few months. "But the rest of the town? They've given up hope. To them, this is the last Christmas parade. The last lighting of the town Christmas tree. And no one wants to miss the last anything in Eagle Springs."

Helen sighed. "Unless something changes, it

will be the end. Next year, we'll all be somewhere else."

He hoped her somewhere else would also be his.

"Head high." Nash touched Helen's chin, giving it a tender lift. "You aren't a quitter." He certainly didn't hold ending their marriage against her. "Remember the time you told that crotchety old cowboy, who tried to stiff you for smithing, that you'd camp out on his doorstep until he paid you?"

Helen rolled her eyes. "I'm the first to admit that I can be stubborn. But this is different."

"It's only different if you give up before the challenge really starts," he said softly, perhaps too softly for her to hear since she didn't answer.

Or maybe she did hear, since a small smile blossomed on her beautiful face. He took her hand in his.

If he had to guess, she was thinking about kisses because he was thinking about kisses, too.

Reluctantly, Nash pulled his hand back, searching for something to fill the awkward void between them. He found what he was looking for, spotting his brother Levi and his fiancée approaching on the sidewalk. Levi's ten-year-old daughter Isla joined the crowd of Blackwell kids, squirming her way to Olivia's side.

"Hey, Levi. Summer." Nash waved them closer. "Summer, I was hoping you could help me with something."

"If I can." Summer glided up to them in new jeans tucked in stylish black boots, a blue wool pea coat, and a bouncy reddish-brown pony tail. She walked as gracefully as she rode in the English style. "What do you need?"

"Hope and a prayer?" Levi gave Nash a dark look.

"No." Nash gestured toward Helen. "She has a fear of riding and—"

"It's a fear of falling off," Helen corrected him, arms moving to cross her chest.

"—she needs some positive reinforcement." Nash nodded at Helen. "I thought since you were a national riding competitor, Summer, that you'd have some ideas we could use about regaining confidence in the saddle."

"And you didn't want to ask your bull-riding brother?" Levi was acting just as ornery as those bulls he used to ride.

Nash tipped his hat back. "What's your problem?"

"Nothing, which is what you've told me about your wager," Levi said brusquely. "I had to ask around to find out why the rate of ticket sales to the Holiday Showcase doubled today." He lowered his voice. "When were you going to tell me? Or submit Helen's entry application? I paid her fee, you fool. You never should have taken that bet."

"You're complaining about increased ticket sales?" Nash murmured, letting his brother's hostility roll off his back.

"Hon, didn't you listen to your grandmother's lecture earlier about supporting Nash?" Summer rubbed Levi's back until his frown eased. And then she faced Helen. "How willing are you to ride?"

"If I say I'm one hundred percent unwilling, half the population of Eagle Springs will come for me," Helen said mulishly. "But the truth is I'm determined to ride. It's just that..." She trailed off.

"She's got the yips," Levi said carefully, keeping his disapproving gaze on Nash. "Anxiety. Worry. It's like the nerves you get going up the first big hill of a rollercoaster. Am I right?" He spared Helen a glance, expression softening.

She nodded.

"She likes rollercoasters," Nash said, earning frowns all around.

"If you've built up a fear, you have to break it back down, starting with how you frame things," Summer said kindly. "Negative reinforcement doesn't help."

"I was thinking about chocolate as a reward,"

Nash murmured, sneaking Helen a teasing glance and dodging her elbow.

"What I mean is..." Summer touched Helen's shoulder. "You have to think and speak positively about your goal. Stop the negative thoughts and outcomes before they get completed in your head. So, if you catch yourself thinking, *'I'll get thrown,'* complete the sentence a more positive way."

"I'll get thrown if I don't hang on," Helen said dutifully.

"That's it." Summer's smile was encouraging. It was easy to see why she was a popular instructor to young riders in the area. "Your homework is to practice positive framing."

The couple moved on to talk with Gran.

Helen's eyes sparkled for the first time since before Nash's wager. Or at least, it felt that way. And she didn't stop with the eye sparkle. She put her hand on top of her cowboy hat, sliding it back on her head. And then she brought her lips close to Nash's ear to whisper, "If Nash kisses me, he'll realize he can't live without me."

"Helen." Nash tried to sound stern.

"What?" She drew back, but only a little, feigning innocence, but not successfully. "I'm just practicing."

The flirt.

This was the woman he'd fallen for. Not

the woman whose spirit he'd crushed with his drinking. "That's not what Summer meant."

Helen's smile grew. "If Nash has the relationship yips, he needs to move slowly, starting with hand-holding."

"What's gotten into you?" *Please reach for my hand.*

She rocked down on her boot heels, smile dimming. "I'm on that rollercoaster, I guess."

Nash didn't know what to say.

A barbershop quartet rounded the corner, singing about partridges in pear trees. There were street vendors everywhere, weaving through the crowd, selling everything from candy canes to school Christmas pageant tickets to sprigs of mistletoe.

Helen tracked the path of the mistletoe vendor as they passed. "You'd have more excuses to kiss me if there was mistletoe in the barn."

"That's what you say every Christmas," he said absently, realizing that she hadn't said it to him in years. He didn't chase the vendor down, but he wanted to. How he wanted to.

In the distance, drums began a rolling cadence. The high school band was undoubtedly getting ready to kick off the parade a few blocks over. Kids up and down the street bounced and fidgeted, shouting about the parade starting and Santa coming.

Luke was one of them, gyrating so much that his gray felt hat fell to the slushy street, muddying the crown. Nash grinned. He couldn't wait for the hat to earn throwaway status.

Several people gave Nash and Helen more than passing notice.

Helen lowered the brim of her cowboy hat and moved a few steps from Nash. "Either folks are wondering if we're back together or news of this bet is spreading. Maybe I should have accepted Phil's second engagement offer. The least it would have done was buy you Blackwells time instead of betting everything on me."

"You don't want to marry Phil," Nash said gruffly, needing to raise his voice above the din to be heard. "Why the continued angst? You sat on Rose after lunch, and we'll work on getting you walking tomorrow. Think positive thoughts. Yips be gone."

"I can do it." Helen brought her fists up to her shoulders in the universal sign for a willingness to work hard. "I'm ready, coach. Put me in. But let's be clear. I'm not doing this to be able to reclaim the joy of riding or become a cutting horse junkie. I'm doing this because I…" Her gaze skittered away.

Because I love you, he silently finished for her.

"Why are you doing this, Helen?" He wanted

her to say the words out loud, the way she used to. It was selfish and he knew it.

Helen drew a deep breath and started over. "I'm doing this for Luke, to show him he can face a challenge head-on. And then there's my loyalty to Eagle Springs and your family. I don't keep in touch with my mother or her kin. There's no one left on my father's side of the family that I know of. A person has to fight for the ones they care about."

With each word, she was distancing herself from him. Not by moving physically away, but by setting an emotional boundary and lumping him in with all the other folk she cared about.

He didn't like it. He didn't like it one bit.

But what was he going to do? If he put his arms around her, she'd get ideas. He'd told her where he stood. It was just… In his heart, he wanted them to stand together. Hand in hand. But in his head, he knew he'd had his chance. He had to let her go. Especially if she did this for his family and Eagle Springs.

She frowned. "A year from now, this will all be under water. No more Cranky Crow or Sweetwater Kitchen. No more walking down Main Street and greeting people you went to school with. No more guessing as to who in town will play Santa this year. And do you know what people will remember? They'll remember that I was the one who let them all down."

Helen, who had found a family here in town. She could have settled anywhere. She could have married anyone. But she'd chosen Eagle Springs and she'd chosen Nash Blackwell.

His hand sought hers. His fingers closed around hers, resolutions be damned. "They'll lay blame where it belongs, at the feet of folks like Frank Wesson, Xavier Howard and Phil Mitchell. They'll think back on nights like tonight and regret that they didn't do enough to stop the takeover. They'll be sad that they put a price on happiness or regret they didn't have more time with close friends and loved ones here." He brushed his thumb over her cheek. "But they won't blame their situation on anything you've done or tried to do."

She didn't believe him. He could see it in her eyes.

The marching band went by, playing a tune he barely recognized other than its general association with Christmas.

"Of all the..." Gran nodded toward the other side of the street after the band had passed. "Those vultures couldn't stay away."

Across the street, a group of men walked through the crowd. Most of them stood out to Nash because of their new jackets, new cowboy hats and new boots. Xavier Howard led the group, confident smile firmly in place. Brock Bedford, from the bank, scurried after Xavier. Phil paused when he was directly opposite Helen and stared at her the way Luke stared at toys on display in the general store's window. Jake sauntered along, bringing up the rear. He tapped Phil's shoulder, nodding toward the others in their group disappearing through the crowd. He and Phil moved on.

Nash was reminded of what Jake had told him—that the development guys wanted to drive wedges between the Blackwells, including himself and Helen.

I won't let that happen.

Nash tucked Helen's hand in his jacket pocket. "I think you should move out to the ranch."

Helen turned to look at him, eyes wide.

"For the next two weeks," Nash quickly clarified. "We can take advantage of the extra training time until Wyatt gets your van fixed."

"How practical." The words were colder than her fingers.

"It's sentimental, too." Nash squeezed her hand. "We can give Luke a perfect Christmas on the ranch."

Helen's gaze softened.

"We'll stop by your place on the way home

so you can pack." He wasn't taking any chances on Phil running interference.

She faced him as Olly Hampton drove his antique tractor as part of the parade. It was draped in gold garland and white twinkle lights. Olly wore a fuzzy green Grinch costume.

Helen tugged her hand clear of his pocket. "If I move back in with you, Nash, I'm going to be me. I'm going to speak my mind even if I know you'd prefer I didn't. I'm going to frame things positively, from me riding a horse to us giving things another try. Those are my terms. Do you accept?"

No. He shouldn't. And yet, his mouth had gone so dry he couldn't get that one little word out.

"I take your silence as a yes." Helen grabbed hold of his hat brim on both sides and tilted it to a jaunty angle. "Everything about the next two weeks is going to be a challenge. But you've always liked challenges."

Maybe when he was courting her. Maybe when he was training horses without deadlines. But not challenges like this.

He should argue. He should set boundaries. He should—

"There's Santa!" Luke bounced around like a bunny rabbit. "Look, Daddy! Look! The elves are passing out candy canes for Santa!"

"Look, Daddy, look," Helen murmured, wearing a triumphant smile, green eyes sparkling just the way he liked.

"Is that..." Gran leaned forward in her chair and then began to laugh. She pointed at Santa riding atop the town fire truck with Ryder, the fire chief, at the wheel. "Why didn't anyone tell me what my brother was doing? That rapscallion makes me laugh even when I've lost all hope."

Nash wished he could laugh.

But he was in a serious predicament, coming and going.

CHAPTER SEVEN

"HELEN, WAKE UP, HONEY."

Helen snuggled deeper under the covers. "Just five more minutes." Sleep was precious for single, working moms.

The smell of coffee wafted through the darkness.

"Time to get up." A hand touched her shoulder and gave it a gentle shake.

Still lost in a dream about sitting on Santa's lap and Santa being Nash, Helen mumbled, "Go away. Mommy is about to kiss Santa Claus."

Masculine laughter filled the air. "I shouldn't laugh."

Her eyes flew open. "Nash?" She sat up, squinting even though light was coming from the hall. Outside the window, it was dark. "What's wrong? Is Luke okay?"

"Luke is fine." Nash handed her a hot mug of what smelled like coffee. "We need to train today, remember?"

Reality came crashing back, more effective than caffeine at prying her eyes wide open.

"We're training before the sun comes up? Won't it be freezing?"

"It's in the forties. Come on. I have a feeling you'll do great today..." Nash cleared his throat, looking away. His hair was still in need of a cut. His whiskers in need of a shave. And his eyes conveyed that he was in need of some tender loving care. "Power of positive thinking, remember?"

Helen dutifully said, "I'm the greatest rider in the world. Go, me." The words were without feeling because inside she was feeling too much, yearning too much. And it had nothing to do with riding.

"You can do it, Helen." Nash turned on the bedroom light, revealing circles under his eyes.

She wanted to hug him. If not for her sake, then for his.

"Picture yourself sitting on Rose, the way you did yesterday." He gazed upon her tenderly. "Picture yourself riding tall in the saddle."

She drank the coffee he'd brought, trying to hide the fact that the visual of her in the saddle bothered her, so much so that his tender glance lost its meaning. "I can do hard things."

"That's the spirit." Nash sat on the bed next to her. "Imagine the look on Phil's face when you win."

She couldn't argue with that. She rather liked that image.

Helen grinned.

"I'll do you one better." She leaned forward. "I'll imagine the big kiss I'll earn from you when I don't eat dirt in the competition." She wasn't foolish enough to think she could be in the top three, but she could manage that.

Trust all my positive thoughts.

Nash sat back. "Wow, you said you were reclaiming your spunk, but—"

"And while I'm at it," she said in a louder, stronger voice, "I'll imagine us growing old together, sitting in front of a festive tree and enjoying its beautiful lights while our grandchildren enjoy their Christmas stockings."

Nash opened his mouth, probably to argue.

But Helen wasn't done. "And I'll imagine the huskiness of your voice as you tell me you love me every night." She sighed dreamily. It was a really good image. "And do you know why I can visualize all those things? Because they are all more likely to happen than me winning a ribbon in the Holiday Showcase."

"Hold up. No negative thoughts, remember?"

"When I think of riding, I think of my mother. And those memories don't make me happy." Or optimistic.

"Not all your riding memories are bad. You and I have ridden double."

She nodded. Those were pleasant, kiss-filled memories.

His gaze drifted over her face. He smoothed a lock of her hair away from her forehead. "Helen, have you ever wondered why you didn't get back in the saddle as a child? I think it's because a part of you doesn't want to please your mother. She forced you to take on all kinds of challenges a little girl shouldn't."

"My dad didn't have horses." Helen sipped her coffee, forcing herself to remember days she'd rather forget. "Mom would tell me I had to be tough to survive in this world. She'd challenge me to be brave." Except it wasn't that simple. She'd couch her requests with endearments, like *I was roping stray bulls when I was your age, dove*, or *I never complain about work that gets me paid, dove.* And then when she was drunk her words would turn harsher. *Life crushes the weak ones like you, dove.*

Helen shook her head, trying to shake off the feeling that she'd never be good enough for her mother or Nash. "She was quick to point out my flaws." Which, in turn, made Helen feel vulnerable.

He took her free hand, holding it gently. "You picked up that gauntlet she threw down, but you resented her for it. And maybe you resented the things she had you do, too. Like riding."

"I was a disappointment to her. She and Denny were cut from the same cloth. They just weren't both watered at the same trough." Her mother ran on hostility and resentment, while Denny ran on love and responsibility. "And my refusal to get back in the saddle was a mark in Mom's book that I couldn't erase. She went on the road and never looked back." Later, after two weekends and no calls from her mother, Helen had panicked.

Dad, can you come get me?

She'd been so frightened to place that call to her father because Mom had told her that Dad wanted nothing to do with her. That had been a lie. "I should have known Dad loved me. I should have seen through her lies." If only things had been different for the three of them or at least for her mother. Perhaps then Helen would have family other than the Blackwells.

"You're not doing this for her," Nash said with certainty, and she loved him for it. "Of all the people you mentioned last night, you didn't mention her."

Helen gripped Nash's hand, trying to banish all thoughts of her mother. "I can see what Summer was saying about the power of positive thinking. And I can understand the motivation behind rewards for lessons where I try really hard."

"But..."

"You should kiss me." She smiled her most sultry of smiles.

"Why?" Nash's eyes widened.

"I want a comparison." Her smile transitioned into a pout.

"To Phil?" Nash scooted back, scowling.

"No. Your kiss a few weeks back was an impulsive drive-by. It's been years since you kissed me sober." Oh, she was pushing, and she knew it. "I need an incentive for the hard day ahead, Nash."

Instead of rising to the challenge, he left, high-tailing it all the way to the front door and exiting the premises.

"I scared him off." Helen set her coffee on the bedside table and sank down under the covers, pulling them up over her head. "I should have bought mistletoe last night."

To sprinkle around the ranch, giving her the opportunity to dole out quick kisses.

But Nash was right. She'd never been one to shy away from the hard things. It was just this one thing—riding—that was her Achilles' heel. It was wrapped up tight with her memories of her mother and the insecurities she brought out in her.

"This dove can do hard things, Mom."

Like conquer her fears and win back the man of her dreams.

"LET'S DO SOMETHING DIFFERENT." Nash had been standing at Rose's head for over ten minutes while Helen sat in the saddle gritting her teeth and gasping every time Rose shifted her weight. He didn't think they were making progress.

"Hallelujah. Break time." Helen flung herself out of the saddle and stumbled in the dirt. She would have fallen if Nash hadn't steadied her. "Thanks. Darn crash vest and helmet throw me off balance."

"Standing still seems to be throwing you into a panic." It was daunting. Helen wouldn't allow Nash to take one step forward. He led Rose across the arena and toward the barn. "A change might do you good. I need an extra set of eyes on a project." And he needed to occupy Helen's mind with something else, the way he had yesterday when they'd walked Beanie around the arena.

"My eyes are good." Helen walked next to him, regaining some of her confidence with each step. She wore scuffed brown cowboy boots, blue jeans, and her stained green work jacket. She appeared the part of a working ranch hand. "What are we looking at?"

"Not at. *For.* Why don't you go check on Luke?" The sun had been up for an hour and their son was under strict instructions to get himself dressed when he woke up and start over to the main house. Hopefully, Luke was watching television with Olivia or helping Mason bake, but Nash wanted to be sure. "Meet me back here in twenty minutes. And if they're baking, don't eat too many cookies."

Gran had decided last night that a plate of cookies might help her cause with Eagle Springs' residents who had yet to sell. She'd enlisted Mason and Corliss to canvass this morning.

"Okay." Helen didn't hesitate to escape.

It wasn't until she'd gone that Nash realized he was disappointed she hadn't bussed his cheek before leaving. He squashed the sentiment.

No kisses. That was his mantra for the next two weeks.

But he smiled thinking about how Helen had tried to wheedle one from him this morning.

"No one ever said saving the ranch was easy, Rose," he told the filly as he led her toward her stall.

Twenty minutes later, he had Beanie saddled and was leading the older gelding out to the ranch yard.

"Are we introducing a change of scenery into my training?" Helen marched up to greet them. She'd ditched her padded vest but still had on her riding helmet.

"Kind of." Nash swung into the saddle and then extended a hand toward her. "Come ride with me."

Helen froze.

"Come on." He curled his fingers in invitation. "The very first time I brought you out here, you rode with me." And they'd taken other rides like this on Jet in thc early years of their marriage.

"Yeah, well." Helen fidgeted, coming back to life, which he took for a good sign. "Back then, I didn't want you to think I was a wimp."

"I've never thought you were a wimp." He guided Beanie closer to her. "Do you remember what happened during those rides?" Kisses. Lots of them.

Careful, Blackwell.

"So, this is my carrot." Helen's eyes bounced around Beanie—his head, his legs, his twitching tail. "We're riding to the springs, and then you'll kiss me."

He shouldn't, but if he did, it would be one kiss. One brief kiss. One fabulously brief kiss.

He nodded.

"Sweet!" Helen grinned.

Nash settled his hat more firmly on his head, reminding himself to stay the course and in his predetermined lane. "Just one kiss. You named the reward system, not me." Nash tried to hide the longing he suspected was spilling from his heart into his eyes. "If you're really intent upon returning to your spunky old self, now's your chance to prove it."

"Were you this bossy when we were married?" She extended her left hand.

"Nope." He slipped his left foot out of the stirrup and took her wrist.

She slid her boot into the stirrup. In one smooth move, she was up and sitting behind him.

Her arms came around his waist and she rested her chin on his shoulder, keeping her helmeted head below his hat brim. "I should have asked for kisses *and* chocolate."

With her arms wrapped around him, she could have asked for the moon, and he'd have given it to her. His heart beat faster, and he began to question his commitment to his goals.

Helen shifted behind him. "Who owns Beanie? He's such a good horse." Her words brought him out of his reverie. "His plaque says Sylvie."

"A couple in Carson bought him for their teenage daughter Sylvie as a surprise Christmas gift. While he's here, I'm just making sure he doesn't have any bad habits. But if he has any, I've yet to find one." He guided the gelding toward the south pasture. "They'll be picking him up on Christmas Eve. Now, if anyone asks, we went to look for the white horse Gran *claims* she saw in the woods."

"Is that doubt I hear in your voice?" Helen's breath was warm on his neck. "Those wildlings do come down from the mountains during winter, along with elk and deer. I've seen them occasionally when I drive to my more remote clients. As I recall, Denny has the sharpest eyes of all you Blackwells."

"That was before she got sick." Nash guided Beanie to the south pasture gate, taking his time opening, moving through and closing it to see how the horse would react before picking up the conversation where they left off. "Gran called me Cal the other night. I didn't make a big deal out of it but there were tears in her eyes when she realized what she'd done."

"Poor Denny." Helen sounded teary herself. "The stress of being sick and trying to save Eagle Springs must be taxing."

They rode into the trees at Beanie's leisurely pace. With the sun out and little wind, it was warm for winter by high country standards. Beanie's hooves sank in a few inches of soft snow.

"You okay back there?" Nash asked after a bit.

"I'm fine." Helen's arms tightened around his waist. She added in a whisper, "I'm fine because I'm with you."

He laid his right arm over hers, wishing things between them could be different. Knowing that couldn't be. He wasn't the steady, predictable man Helen needed, the bet with Phil proved it. He forced himself to remove his arm over hers.

Helen sighed, her warm breath caressing his neck. "We need to take Luke to chop down a Christmas tree."

"To set up at the ranch, right?" Not her duplex?

Man, he was pathetic, obsessing over being with her.

"Yes, at the ranch. Happy memories of a person or a place can carry you far." There was doom and gloom in her tone.

"Okay, but Helen…"

Before he could chastise her to think positively, a twig snapped deeper in the woods ahead. He brought Beanie to a halt.

And there, staring at them without any sign

of fear, was a white horse that looked to be about two years old.

"Gran wasn't seeing things," Nash whispered.

"What a beauty," Helen said just as quietly. "A filly?"

"Yes." Nash searched the tree line for any other horses, but there were none.

"What are you going to do?" Helen shifted behind him. "We don't have any rope."

"Nothing." Nash urged Beanie forward, focusing on the trail and their mount, not wanting Beanie to get spooked and make Helen anxious again. "I'm curious to see what that horse does. Knowing her behavior might help us catch her later."

They drew even with the filly and then proceeded deeper into the woods.

"She's watching us." Helen twisted, half turning to look back.

And if that wasn't progress for Helen on horseback, Nash didn't know what was. Not that he planned on pointing it out to her.

"She's following us," Helen added.

"Ignore her."

Helen faced forward. "We should have brought a rope."

"I'm not chasing any animal through the snowy woods on horseback. It's dangerous enough when you can see the ground. And besides, Beanie isn't my horse to gamble with."

"Ah, that's sweet."

"And we can tell a lot about a horse by what they do around people."

"If she follows us..."

"She might not be a true wild horse. Gran says people used to dump horses in the wild when they couldn't afford to keep them or if they had behavior problems so bad they couldn't find a buyer."

"That's sad. That filly looks so young."

"Horses are like anything else, Helen. Their lives can get ruined, young or old, sometimes even by people with the best intentions."

She fell quiet. Was she thinking about their situation? Or her childhood with a negligent mother?

Beanie's ears swiveled actively, an indication that the filly was still in the vicinity.

They continued through the trees on the trail made by countless Blackwell rides to the springs. It was one of many natural springs in the area that had given the town its name, fed by the underground aquifer that provided the ranch with water.

When they reached the springs, Nash helped Helen down first and then dismounted, spotting the filly about fifty feet back. He grinned, pleased. “I’m curious about her and she’s curious about us.”

“She can join the Nash and Helen Blackwell Curiosity Club,” Helen quipped, brushing snow from a huge rock that was the perfect height for sitting and enjoying the view of the springs. The water bubbled gently in a small pond and trickled into a creek that would meet with several other trickling waterways, eventually becoming part of the popular fishing spot Blue Mist Run.

Nash fastened Beanie’s reins to a branch and joined Helen, bumping her gently over with his hip. “Make room.”

“So bossy.” She turned to face him, green eyes sparkling.

“Why do I think you’ve got kissing on your mind?” Perhaps because he did, too.

“I rode all this way without panicking. What do you think I’d have on my mind?” She arched her brows. “Wild horses?”

Responsibility warred with longing. Was it too late to walk away? “Helen…”

“You owe me a kiss, cowboy.” She reached for him, hands coming around his neck.

And much as Nash wanted to renege on that deal, his arms circled her waist. He drew her closer, and he gave her exactly what she wanted—a kiss that said she'd done well, that she was his woman and he was her man.

If only while they kissed.

HELEN'S TOES WERE cold in her boots.

But her heart was warm.

Because Nash was holding her. Because Nash was kissing her. Because Nash had suggested they come to the springs where they'd shared their first kiss. Because he'd agreed they take Luke out to find a Christmas tree, one they'd set up at their house.

Their house.

Helen sighed, leaning into Nash.

He still loves me.

He wouldn't kiss her so fervently if he didn't.

Helen drew back and stared into his rich brown eyes.

"I thought you'd kiss me a bit longer." Nash smoothed her hair to one side.

"I like you, Nash," Helen said, recalling the words she'd said to him six years ago when he'd kissed her here. "But I'm an independent woman and I'm not easy to be with."

He laughed. His laughter filled the clearing around the springs and startled the filly.

Except for the sound of retreating hooves, it was déjà vu.

Or it would have been if Helen had the same

things to offer him that she'd had all those years ago. Her hand drifted to her abdomen. "Do you want to have more kids?"

Please say no.

He drew back, frowning slightly. "Helen…"

She'd forgotten about his opinion that she deserved a perfect prince of a man rather than him. "Assuming a twist of fate of some sort happened, and you got married again to me or…or someone else." Her voice felt hard as rock, the words grinding out of her. "Would you want to have another child?"

"It's a moot point." All trace of humor was gone from his demeanor. "I'm unreliable. I'm not marrying you or anyone else."

"Will you forget marriage and hypotheticals and your opinion of yourself and…and just answer the question," she said sharply, losing her composure over the need to know his answer. "In a perfect world, would you want to have more kids?"

Nash's eyes widened. "Yes. Okay. *Yes*. I have four siblings. I like big families. I always assumed I'd have one of my own."

Helen's heart sank.

Nash shoved his hands in his jacket pockets.

And it was good. It was good that he didn't reach for her intent upon another kiss. It was good that he didn't draw lines in the sand about kissing incentives. It was good because she had an answer, one she'd been afraid to hear.

Nash wants more kids.

And despite his noble words about not intending to get married again, to her or anyone else, she knew the truth. Someday, the right woman would come along and make him believe in himself and love again. That woman just wouldn't be Helen. The stallion who'd kicked her a year ago had made sure of that.

"Good to know, cowboy." Helen stood, putting space between them. "We should head back."

Nash didn't move. "You asked me once how I was so sure we were meant to be together." He studied her expression, obviously clued in that something was wrong. "You were right to have doubts."

She scoffed. "I was right to leave you. But I've been wrong about everything since." Including thinking they could salvage what they'd had and live happily-ever-after.

CHAPTER EIGHT

"USE THAT CHARM of yours when the Harmons answer the door, Luke." Denny held on to her smile, along with a plate of cookies and holiday confections.

"Why do we have to smile?" Luke tipped his gray felt cowboy hat back so far it fell off his head onto the front porch. His fancy hat was getting dingier by the day.

Denny bent to one knee to retrieve it since her great-grandson didn't appear to want to do so, being too busy smiling at the closed door like he'd been told. "You know how at Halloween you say trick or treat?" She plunked his hat back on his head.

"Yeah." His smile broadened, but it was a posed expression, unnatural, like the one they'd captured in his school picture last fall.

"That's October, Luke. In December, we bring plates of treats and say Merry Christmas with a big smile." Denny tried to get to her feet but couldn't. "Can you hold this for me?" She handed him the plate of cookies.

Luke did as he was asked, turning to face

the door behind which the Harmon family either hadn't heard her knock or weren't going to answer.

Denny tried to get to her feet again, but her legs lacked the strength.

She glanced toward the empty sidewalk. She and Luke were working their way down Belmont Street with a wagon filled with holiday goodies. Elias had told her he'd meet them at the end of the block. He was nowhere in sight.

The door swung open.

"Trick or treat!" Luke cried, holding out the plate.

Denny forced a smile on her face, staring up at Ken Harmon. "Merry Christmas, too."

Ken rubbed the graying stubble on his chin. "Never thought I'd see Denny Blackwell down on her knees."

"I'm not..." Denny fought to control her frustration. "This isn't..." She swallowed back a thick lump of pride in her throat. "I'm trying to teach my great-grandson about community spirit, Ken. It's something we've always had an abundance of in Eagle Springs."

Ken harrumphed but he opened the door wider to accept the plate of sweets from Luke.

Still on her knees, Denny tried really hard to keep that smile on her face. "The thing I've always loved about this town is that folks share the holiday spirit and lend a hand when one is needed."

"That may be true, Denny." Ken flipped back the clear plastic wrap on the plate and selected a piece of fudge drizzled with caramel. "But with the money I'm being offered by Xavier Howard, I can afford a new start in a town that cares about community just as much as this one did. No plate of cookies is going to change my mind. Merry Christmas, Denny. And Happy Halloween, young Mr. Blackwell." He closed the door and locked it.

"Huh." Luke turned to face Denny, who was just about his height standing as she was on her knees. "I didn't get any treats."

"Maybe because you didn't dress up," Denny muttered, feeling out of sorts. "Other than that fancy hat of yours."

"Huh," Luke said again. He walked toward the porch stairs.

"Wait." Denny grabbed on to his shoulder. "I need help getting up."

But her small great-grandson wasn't strong enough to pull her to her feet. She sent him off to find Elias.

And then Denny sat on the porch and scooted over to the top step. At least from there, when Elias came, she wouldn't look so pitiful.

The front door opened behind her, and Ken

came outside, sighing heavily as he sat down next to her. "Thank you for the grocery store gift card, Denny," he said thickly, acknowledging the monetary gift she'd tucked beneath the white wedding cookies. "How did you know Jackie laid me off from the feed store?"

"People talk, as you well know." She clasped her knees and wished for strength of spirit and body. "It's not always destructive gossip they pass along."

He made a sound that she took for agreement. "You helped me once before, years ago. We had three kids in diapers. It was pretty much a choice between buying those diapers or food. And then you showed up, stocking our refrigerator and filling us with hope."

"I've always thought no one in Eagle Springs is a stranger."

He made that sound again, rising to his feet. "Let me help you up." He extended his hands, and she took hold. "We haven't signed anything yet," he told her, guiding her down the steps.

"If you could just hang on a few weeks more," she pleaded, having swallowed her pride, most likely permanently.

"There are financial penalties for holding out," Ken admitted. "They're making it hard not to sign right away."

"I understand." And she wished things were

different. “But just so you know, we Blackwells are going to fight ’til the end.” Impulsively, she hugged him. “Merry Christmas, Ken.”

“Merry Christmas, Denny. I wish… I wish things were different for us all.”

CHAPTER NINE

"HOW'S YOUR PROGRESS, HELEN?" After lunch on Sunday, Corliss climbed up the arena pipe fencing to sit on the top rung next to Helen. Corliss shivered, tugging her jacket tighter to her. "I always forget how cold the rails are in winter."

"They warm up pretty quick. As for me… I'll be fine if I can ride behind Nash and hang on to him." Helen gestured toward the roan filly being put through her paces by a big man under Nash's watchful eye. "Dan told me he's been riding since he was a kid. He looks good on Queenie. He'll be competing against me in the Holiday Showcase."

"Pfft. That's no big deal. Didn't you ride as a kid, too?" Corliss snuck a glance at Helen's face. "Your mother was involved in the rodeo. You must have had horses growing up."

Helen blinked. "We did have a horse. I haven't thought about Bunny in a long time." When she recalled the years with Mom, it was always the bad bits. "I used to ride Bunny in our backyard. We didn't have a traditional backyard, of course. It was a pasture."

"Every cowgirl has a Bunny." Corliss's features turned nostalgic. "Mine was Katie. She was a small, black and white appaloosa mare. I don't know where we picked her up. But she was such a good horse. Patient and kind. Finding the right mount is kind of like finding the right spouse."

And here we go...

"I appreciate you having Nash's back in this." Corliss gave Helen a stern look. "But what are your intentions toward my brother? I worry about him."

"Not drinking, you mean?" At her nod, Helen breathed a sigh of relief, grateful that she wouldn't be adding stress on the personal front. "He's determined to stay sober and single." And she had to honor that.

"Gran and I were hoping that you two could work things out." Corliss had always been caring but unabashedly prying, more like Denny than the other Blackwells. "No matter how the competition shakes out, I think you two need each other."

Helen made a non-committal sound.

Dan brought Queenie to an abrupt halt.

"That's what I was talking about," Nash said in a firm tone. He wore a thick jacket but it was open, as if the winter's cold didn't reach him the way it did her. "You have to give her some direction with your legs. Queenie wants to please you but she's still young and trying to figure out the sport we call cutting."

Dan frowned. He was middle-aged with thin, salt and pepper hair beneath his straw cowboy hat. "When Adele mentioned there was a Nash Blackwell filly for sale, I thought she'd be further along. I've already signed up for the Holiday Showcase."

"Now Dan..." Nash began in his trainer-knows-best voice.

"If Nash talks him out of this sale..." Corliss hopped down into the arena and marched purposefully toward the two men.

"I'm sure you know why we're selling stock earlier than we like," Nash said, without losing any of his conviction. "And I'm sure my sister told you that I'm willing to work with the pair of you for the next few months, no charge. Queenie will come along. But I wouldn't expect her to win the Showcase this time around."

Dan looked uncertain. "It's a lot of money for a horse. I could buy a good truck for the price you're charging." He gave a wry chuckle. "As my wife is quick to tell me."

Corliss reached Nash's side. "Queenie won't last long once we get the word out about her no matter what her level of training. It's a fair price and a priceless bonus of training with my brother. The track record of his horses speaks for itself." She may or may not have stepped on Nash's boot. It was hard to tell from this distance.

Nash gave his sister a dark look but when he spoke, it was in a lighter tone. "Just because I said I don't expect Queenie to win the Showcase this year, I didn't say she couldn't win next year. Or any other competition you enter come spring. That is, if her training continues." Nash tipped his hat. "I'll let you put her through her paces again, if you like." He handed Corliss the mechanical cow remote and then walked over to Helen and leaned against the fence, jaw working.

"I'm sorry you have to sell Queenie before she's ready," Helen said.

Nash glanced up at her briefly, eyes tinted with frustration. "I'm sorry you have to compete before you're ready."

"Unlike Queenie, I might never be competition ready." When he frowned and began to say something positive, she cut him off. "I had a good time riding with you. And Corliss reminded me that I had good experiences as a kid with our family horse. I can see myself getting through this without dying. Trust me, this is me being positive."

"I could sweeten the pot with more kisses?"

He glanced at her again, quirking a brow, gaze dropping to her lips.

Her pulse kicked up. "I… I don't think that's wise." Helen wanted to reach for him. She clung to the cold fence rail instead.

"Am I misreading something?" He faced her. "When we were at the springs, you kissed me back."

Tell him. Tell him about the accident.

Helen opened her mouth, but nothing came out.

Nash's brows lowered. "Have you decided to take Phil up on his offer of marriage as a way to shut down competing?"

"No." She shook her head.

"Mama!" Luke ran up to the railing from behind her. "Great Gran said you saw a horse in the south pasture. Can I have it?"

Helen and Nash exchanged glances. Nash's was flat. She imagined he was thinking he didn't have time to tame the filly enough to trust her around their little boy. Helen was sure her eyes reflected that same worry. It was nice to feel like they were on the same page.

"That wild horse isn't a good choice for you, son." Nash knelt down to Luke's level, reaching through the rails for Luke's hand. "Even if we catch her, it might take months for that filly to be gentle enough for you to share a stall with, much less ride."

Helen nearly fell off the arena rail. "If she's caught, you aren't going to keep her here?"

"If she's caught—and that's a big if—" Nash said slowly, "Adele will need to see if she has an owner already or if she's part of the herd that roams up in the hills."

"She'll be mine," Luke said firmly. "I can tame any horse, just like my dad and my great-grandpa."

"Maybe when you're older," Helen said, with her mommy hat firmly on.

Luke thrust his chin out the way Nash did when he was challenged. "Great Gran said she started letting Daddy train horses when he was five."

"I'm not Great Gran." Helen climbed down from the rail.

"But, Mama—"

"Listen to your mother." Nash got to his feet. "She seems to know what's best."

Helen glanced sharply at her ex. "You did not just say that." With an abundance of nose-bent-out-of-shape sarcasm.

"We'll talk about this later," Nash said to Helen without defining exactly what "this" was.

"Nash." Corliss called him over, smiling as

if she'd closed the sale and ending all other discussions and arguments.

"IT'S THE CANDY cane song, Mama." Luke sat in the back seat of Nash's truck as Helen drove into town Sunday night. He danced as best he could in his car seat. "Turn it up."

Helen obliged, filling the air with the breezy pop tune. They were going to pick up their Christmas decorations. There was no sense searching the ranch for a good tree if they weren't ready to put one up and dress it properly.

They approached a truck parked on the shoulder of the narrow two-lane highway just as the song ended. It was gray and a newer model, but the hazards were on, and an older cowboy was flagging her down, looking small next to the silhouette of a small grove of pine trees lining this section of road.

Given Helen's recent breakdown, she was sympathetic to his plight. She slowed, pulling up next to him. She turned off the radio and lowered the passenger window.

"Thanks for stopping." The older cowboy had once been good-looking, with classic features. His clothes weren't new, but they weren't thread-bare either. Oddly enough, there was something about him that said he was trustworthy. "It's in the forties but my engine overheated. And I can't seem to find a tow truck service out here."

"I can relate to that. Broke down myself the other day."

"Boom," Luke said.

The old cowboy spotted Luke in the back seat. "That's a fine cowboy hat you're holding, son."

Luke's hat was in his lap since it wasn't compatible with car seat usage. He held it up proudly. "Thanks, mister. It used to be new. Daddy says now it's just dirty."

The cowboy chuckled.

There was something about the man's demeanor that Helen instinctively liked. It was a fleeting feeling she couldn't explain.

"Do you need a lift into Eagle Springs? I know the tow truck driver, but he clocks out at five now." And it was long past.

"A ride would be much appreciated. I'm meeting a friend at Sweetwater Kitchen. We'll figure a way to get my truck towed and fixed after we eat."

"Sweetwater Kitchen is on our way. Get in." Helen waited for him to climb inside and buckle up before heading on down the road.

"What's this?" The cowboy picked up a leather glove in the cupholder that was monogrammed with the Flying Spur brand. "I recognize this. If I'm not mistaken, it's the Blackwell brand."

"Yes, the Flying Spur. I got those for my ex-husband one Christmas, not realizing that he doesn't wear gloves when he trains horses." In fact, he rarely wore gloves. What had she been thinking? Perhaps she didn't know Nash as well as she thought. Perhaps another woman could give him gifts he cherished and children he wanted.

"So, your ex-husband regifted the gloves to you?" The cowboy returned the glove to the cupholder, shoving it in so the brand didn't display.

"No. This is his truck. Mine is being repaired."

"The glove must mean something to him then, if he's keeping them where he can see them often."

"Yes, I suppose." Helen's gut clenched with uncertainty.

Luke waved his hat around. "Are you gonna be here for the craft fair, mister?"

"Hadn't planned on it." The old man turned in his seat to look at her son. "Should I? What's that?"

"It's fun and part of Christmas." Luke kicked his feet against the back of the man's seat. "I'm gonna dance there. On a stage and everything."

"It's more than just a craft fair," Helen said, grateful for a change in topic. "The school kids perform. And all the clubs in town set up booths in the school cafeteria. Each one offers a different holiday craft for you to make. You pay a small donation at the booths to craft gifts and such."

"Mama, I was telling it," Luke huffed.

Helen smiled. "Sorry. Go ahead."

They passed the auction yard. Adele's truck was parked out front next to Grady's police cruiser.

"Last year, I painted a rainbow for Gran, and I made Mama a necklace." Luke's young voice rang with pride.

"How nice." The cowboy looked at Helen. "What club are you in?"

"Oh, well." She had a long list. It was kind of embarrassing. "The parent-teachers, of course, mostly because my best friend roped me in." Gwen. "And the Future Farmers, because my former sister-in-law is involved with them." Corliss. "I also support the Vocational Club because I feel like kids should have paths to choose other than college." In honor of her father, the welder. "And the school choir because they let me join even though I couldn't carry a tune." She flashed him a smile. "I did a lot of clapping and swaying." Ecstatic to be included.

The old cowboy sat back as if in awe. "You really are active in town."

"Most people are." They passed the indoor rodeo arena where the Holiday Showcase was to be held. Helen looked in the opposite direction. "The way I heard tell, it wasn't always like that. When Denny Blackwell came to town, she tried to get everyone involved."

"Denny Blackwell." The cowboy muttered her name, not as if committing it to memory but as if it left a bad taste on his tongue.

Was he someone who'd accepted money from Xavier Howard?

Helen quickly jumped to Denny's defense. "She really is the heart and soul of this town and the Blackwell family."

The lights from Eagle Springs came into view as they passed the fairgrounds.

"If you get a chance, check out the town square," Helen continued. "It's beautiful with the big Christmas tree decorated. Years ago, Denny raised money to put benches around the square. Each one is dedicated to a cowpoke who lost his or her life on the job, someone who was special to a town resident."

"Is her former fiancé one of them?" the cowboy asked in a husky voice.

"Yes. Look." Helen turned early to drive

around the town square. "It's pretty in wintertime. Cal's is the bench on the north side."

"I look like Great Grandpa Cal," Luke piped up from the back. "I'm gonna be as good a horse trainer as he was. Maybe better."

The man turned to look at Luke again.

"Yep." Helen agreed. "Even though Cal isn't with us today, Denny made sure your daddy learned Cal's cutting-horse training methods. He'll teach you, Luke. And someday you'll maybe teach your children those same techniques."

"I could start Great Grandpa's stuff now." Luke kicked his feet again. "Daddy and Uncle Wyatt are gonna catch a wild horse for me."

"Cal's techniques, not Denny's?" Ignoring Luke's remark, her passenger glanced at Helen curiously.

"Denny credits Cal for everything." Helen slowed the truck as they approached the town square. With the snow and the colorful lights on the large tree, it was Christmas card pretty.

"You can let me out here." The old cowboy rapped on the window glass.

"Oh. But Sweetwater Kitchen is another two blocks down."

"I see it." He put his hand on the door latch. "I'd like to check out the memorials. And the walk will do me good."

"In the snow?" Helen came to a careful stop. "Are you sure?"

"This isn't my first snowfall, young lady." He got out, taking a good look at her and Luke both, as if committing them to memory. "Merry Christmas. Much obliged for the ride." He closed the door.

Helen made sure he was okay before driving on.

"Who was that, Mama?"

Helen realized she didn't know.

AFTER SUNDAY DINNER, Nash sat in the kitchen of the main house and in what felt like a bad mood.

There'd been a change in Helen since they'd kissed at the springs this morning. And he couldn't put his finger on what was wrong.

"We sold a horse." Corliss nudged him with an elbow. "Why are you looking so glum?"

"I want to know what happens if we don't pay off the loan in time," he blurted, which wasn't what he'd been upset about at all.

"We won't accept defeat, boy," Gran said decisively.

"But maybe we should have a contingency plan." Nash tried to sound diplomatic. "Just in case. I know everyone here's thought about it."

And with Helen gone, it seemed the right time to discuss it.

"I haven't," said Corliss, glancing at her husband Ryder. She set down her fork. "But obviously, you have."

"No." Ryder shook his head vigorously. Guiltily. "I mean, Xavier Howard came to see me last week and—"

"Last week?" Corliss coughed. "And you're just now telling me?"

"—he offered me the fire chief position in Mountain Ridge."

"But you turned him down." Corliss was wound up tighter than a fresh spool of fishing line.

"I turned him down," Ryder reassured her.

"If he made you the offer, he also made one to Grady to stay on as sheriff," Big E quickly surmised. "I'll speak to him in the morning."

"Frank Wesson wants to make us a house divided." Nash shared what Jake had told him about the developers wanting to cause chaos within the Blackwell family. "Has anyone talked to Levi and Summer? Or Wyatt and Harper?"

"Wyatt and Harper are spending the evening at an ice festival in Carson," Gran said slowly, as if she had something else on her mind. "I imagine they're having dinner before heading back. There's not much of an opportunity to cause a rift there."

"Not so fast. Harper's step-father is the bank president," Big E pointed out. "Just because they approached Harper before for her social media savvy and she turned them down doesn't mean they won't approach her again."

"I'll text Wyatt." Corliss reached for her cell phone.

"You'll wait until they return," Gran said firmly. "Let the newlyweds enjoy their time alone."

"Fine. I'll text Levi about Summer then." Corliss stood, took her cell phone and headed into the dining room.

"Well, at least you and Helen are patching things up," Mason said to Nash with his big teenage grin. "No worries there."

Nash said nothing.

"Or not," Mason muttered, turning to bend over an open cookbook on the counter.

Corliss came back into the kitchen. "They just offered Summer a more lucrative sponsorship for her competitive riding, much like the deal they extended to Harper. Summer refused. They also extended an offer to Levi to buy the rodeo grounds. You can guess what Levi said."

And how colorful his word choice might have been. Nash smiled.

Gran slumped in her chair. "For a man who claims to ache with loss over Cal's death, Frank sure is dead set on destroying Cal's family down to its roots."

"I guess he needs to be taught that Blackwells stick together." Big E patted Gran's shoulder.

"I think he'd prefer it if *Wessons* stuck together," Ryder muttered.

"Hey, we're not Wessons." Corliss nudged him.

Ryder raised his brows. "You want me to change my name to Blackwell?"

"No. We don't, Ryder. But you bring up a good point about families and legacies. I may have committed to Cal, but we never got the chance to marry," Gran admitted. "And now, it feels as if Frank's holding that against me. And us."

Big E nodded. "Adding insult to injury, I suppose."

"What's done is done," Corliss said, sounding on edge. "Nash, how can we help you with Helen?"

"I was just thinking about that." Nash made some calculations regarding the pace of Helen's training in his head. "I need fresh cows. At least, by early next week."

"You know that's not possible." Corliss shook

her head. "We have about twenty yearlings in the pasture. Make do."

"No." Nash frowned. "I've used all those cows repeatedly over the past few months. They're getting too smart to train with and some of them are bigger than five hundred pounds. You know as well as I do that large, cunning cows are a cutting horse trainer's worst enemy. They can outsmart and undercut a horse's confidence." Which was why cutting horse competitions always provided new cows for their events.

"We might have enough money in the cookie jar to buy you one." Corliss opened up the ceramic cookie jar on the counter that was shaped like a cowboy hat. It was the one they kept money in, not sweets. She reached in and then got a panicked look on her face, drawing the jar closer. Her knuckles banged around the crockery. "It's gone. Our emergency fund. There's nothing in here." She glanced at Nash, slack-jawed. "Who..."

"It was me." Gran held up a hand, raising her nose in the air. "I bought grocery gift cards to include in our Christmas cookie platters." She lowered her hand but not her nose.

"But Gran..." Corliss seemed speechless, which was rare.

"People are being laid off, little miss. Without jobs, how are they supposed to put food on the table?"

"How are they..." Corliss ran a hand through her hair. "How are we supposed to put food on the table?"

"We'll manage," Gran said crisply.

"Gran... How could you?" Corliss ran out, teary-eyed, which wasn't at all like her.

"Mom?" Mason trotted out after her.

Nash bet Corliss wasn't just upset about not having enough money to buy him one fresh cow. "Is there something going on I don't know about?"

"No." The way Gran said it wasn't convincing.

"Yes, there is," Big E said gruffly. "Tell the boy your good news, Ryder."

"We're pregnant," Ryder said evenly. "And Corliss is a bit...emotional about saving the ranch and Skyfire." The cutting horse they'd promised Big E as collateral for the loan he'd given them to buy four cutting horse fillies. The horse Corliss loved like no other. The horse she'd lose if Helen failed.

Nash bit back an oath. "Congratulations," he said instead.

"Now's as good a time as any to remind you folk that I can spot you the money for the bank loan," Big E told everyone. "We can end this tomorrow."

"You think paying off our mortgage will stop Frank from coming at us?" Gran pushed herself to her feet, voice shaking. "I've been thinking on that a lot these past few days. If we pay off the mortgage, he'll go after Levi next. He took out a big loan to buy the rodeo arena and chances are they'd call it in if he won't sell. No matter what happens to us, Frank will buy those two empty seats on the town council and rezone the land where Adele's auction yard sits. He'll dig and twist and lie and cheat until we're all wiped out and done for. He might even go after Barlow next." Gran's other son, who'd made a name for himself in oil.

Everyone in the kitchen was quiet, most likely because everyone agreed with Gran.

"This is where we make our last stand." Gran slapped the flat of her hand on the table. "This is where we draw the line."

No one argued with her.

CHAPTER TEN

"GIVE CORLISS SOME space today," Nash's youngest brother Wyatt warned Helen on Monday morning. He spared her a glance from where he'd contorted himself underneath her van's steering column.

"It's barely nine o'clock." Helen had gotten Luke on the school bus and saddled two horses for Nash to allow him time to focus on training. "What happened to Corliss?"

"I don't know. And I don't ask." Wyatt reached into the van's innards. "She has a thunderous expression on her face and everything she touches goes bang."

As if on cue, something in the barn went *bang*.

"I can talk to her. Maybe it would help."

"No, Helen." Wyatt twisted a wire free. "If we keep our heads down, we'll be fine."

"Yes, but she won't feel better if she keeps it all bottled inside." The way Nash did. It seemed as if the Blackwell route was to shoulder burdens alone. "What time do you expect the part for the van to be delivered?" The circuit that Wyatt believed had gone bad.

"They said by ten o'clock." Wyatt scooted out of the van. "It'll be a miracle if it arrives by then since I ordered it on Saturday, and we live in the boondocks."

"I'm due a miracle," Helen muttered, hoping to get back to work later today. "A Christmas miracle."

Harper joined them, Western chic on full display. Her jacket today was white with a red and black southwestern pattern. "What's with Corliss?"

"Don't ask," Wyatt and Helen said at the same time.

"We're all giving her space," Helen explained.

"Okay..." Harper smiled at Helen. "I have time this morning. How about you show me some of your farrier equipment?"

"Sure." Helen moved to the back of the van, opening the double doors. The interior had built-in storage for nails, tools, and different styles and sizes of horseshoes. "These are my chaps." She freed them from a hook on the side and held them up to her waist. "They protect me from stray sparks and sharp hooves. Mostly. I tuck all the most common tools I use in their pockets."

"They're like cowboy chaps with storage."

Harper snapped some photographs with her phone.

"Yes. Part overalls, part regular chaps." Helen rehung them on a hook. She pointed out some other equipment highlights. "That's my forge. And that's my anvil. They both pull out on an axle, like a drawer." She extended the anvil arm, dropping the metal brace beneath it. "They're both so heavy that they need a support leg while in use. And that's about the extent of my tour."

Harper kept taking pictures. "You have an entire blacksmith shop in a van. That is very cool. I want to capture you at work. Are you going to shoe any horses here?"

"No." Helen stowed the anvil. "Not for another few weeks. As soon as the van works, you can come with me though."

"I'd love to. Do you ever make stuff out of old horse shoes?" Harper reviewed the pictures on her phone. "You know, like wall hooks or hearts?"

"I've dabbled, but I can make more money actually shoeing a horse than crafting with their shoes. I either donate used shoes to friends who craft or sell them to a woman in Cody who I went to farrier school with. She crafts full time. Has an online store and everything."

"This is so interesting." Harper tucked her phone in a pocket. "You must have super strength."

"Watch out, sweetheart." Wyatt came around to the back of the van, joining them. "I've seen Helen arm wrestle dudes at the Cranky Crow. And win."

Helen felt heat creep up her cheeks. "That was in my wild youth." And she'd only taken on competitors she thought she could beat.

Nash appeared at the corner of the van behind Wyatt. "Helen is always the life of the party." He turned, gesturing for her to follow him, presumably back to the barn.

"*Was*, handsome." Helen frowned. "I *was* the life of the party. Do you think that's what I do on the weekends when you have Luke?"

He kept walking. "People tell me if they see you at the Cranky Crow."

"Well then... People should also tell you when they see me arm wrestling or drinking or hopping on stage to sing love songs to random cowboys." She stomped angrily along behind him. "And do you know why they don't tell you that? Because I'm not doing any of those things anymore. If they see me at the Cranky Crow, it's with Gwen and we're sharing a plate of nachos. We don't close the place down either. Sheesh."

Nash opened the barn door for her. "What's gotten into you?"

"It's Helen of Old," she muttered, marching past him.

"Helen who?" He followed her inside.

"Exactly."

"KEEP YOUR HEAD DOWN, NOSEY." Nash rode the flashy chestnut filly across the arena.

It didn't matter that he told her to keep her head down. He'd had to put a headsetter on her beneath her bridle, a rope-made halter attached to the girth strap that kept her from lifting her head unusually high.

She kept fighting it, which was part of her problem training as a cutting horse. She didn't keep her head down when the cow, real or the mechanical one, made a stop, which meant she led her movement with her shoulder. Shoulder-led movements slowed a horse down. And bad habits deterred buyers from paying full price.

"She's proud, just like the Blackwells," Helen said from her position near the gate where he'd asked her to watch him work, hoping she'd talk about whatever was bothering her.

He hadn't understood why she was angry when he'd come to get her. And since he stank at intimate or loaded conversations, he wanted her to take the lead.

So far, no luck.

"Nosey can be taught to keep her pride and her head in check." Just like him. Was that what Helen had gotten stuck on? His pride? Nash eased Nosey into a fast trot and then brought her to a quick stop, turning her head slightly as he pulled back on the reins. "Do you see what I'm doing?"

He couldn't be sure, but he thought Helen sighed. "Yes. That's all I'm doing is watching."

"You're learning."

"Sure I am."

Nash wasn't giving up. "I'm teaching her to stop and anticipate the cow cutting in a different direction." He guided Nosey forward and to the right with rein and heel. "Then I'm stopping her and prepping her to head the other direction."

Nosey stopped, bobbing her head as she tested the length of rope on the headsetter, but it was a smaller movement than before.

Nash used the remote to move the mechanical cow at its slower speed. He put Nosey through her paces. She was still turning too slow, using her whole body instead of pivoting and leaping forward with explosive power. Chances were that she'd be a good horse for ranch cattle, rather than a serious competitor. But horses had surprised him in the past, mostly when paired with a passionate and skilled rider. Nosey was the type of horse who needed a knowing rider to cue her along her development.

Corliss entered the arena leading Java, the blue-blooded bay.

"Hang on," he told his sister. "I'm not through with Nosey."

"I didn't bring her for you," Corliss snapped, mounting up, back rigid. "I'm going to put her through her paces. You know it helps sales if horses are acclimated to a variety of riders."

On the one hand, Nash knew she was right. On the other hand, pride reared its ugly head and said, *"That's my job."* He knew all too well that he didn't have time to listen to pride. "Good idea," he told her.

"You agree with me?" Corliss huffed, as if she'd been looking for a fight and was disappointed.

Nash laughed. He led Nosey through her next steps.

Wyatt appeared next to Helen. "I got your van started, but—"

"Great!" Helen ran for the gate.

"—nothing in the dashboard comes on." Wyatt turned to follow her, raising his voice. "I wouldn't risk driving it in case there's a system failure."

Nash brought Nosey to a stop, watching Helen and his youngest brother.

"Wyatt." Helen slowed and faced Mr. Fix It. "I was so excited."

"I know. I'm sorry." Wyatt playfully wobbled the cowboy hat atop her head, a tease that created a stab of envy in Nash's chest. "I'm researching what part we might need next."

Helen pouted. "Can I at least try to start her up myself?"

"Sure," Wyatt reassured her. "I left the keys on the front seat."

"Hey, we need to train." Nash brought Nosey trotting toward the gate, wanting Helen to stay.

"I'll be back to watch you in a few minutes." She disappeared into the barn without so much as a backward glance.

"But—"

"Let her go, Nash," Corliss said in that cool voice she used when she was upset.

Let her go.

Everything inside Nash rebelled against the notion, but everything inside him also rebelled against the loss of the ranch.

"Hey, give me the mechanical cow remote." Wyatt held out his hand. "I can operate it for you guys."

Nash tossed it to him. "Don't you have stuff to do?"

"Other than provide my brother with emotional support? No." Wyatt went to stand in the middle of the arena and began moving the mechanical cow back and forth at varying intervals and speeds. "Shouldn't you be happy that I'm helping you carry this heavy load?"

"He'd rather have Helen," Corliss pointed out, still sour.

"I'm happy for you and Ryder," Nash said to his sister through gritted teeth. And he was. He'd even been thinking how it would be nice to have another baby—his and Helen's baby—if things worked out for the ranch and with Helen. "Any time you need to take a rest, you just let me know, Corliss."

"Don't push me, Nash." Corliss was working well with Java. The filly responded beautifully, with grace and the promise of power when she got older.

"You see that?" Nash patted Nosey's neck. "That's how it's done. Tight turns and small bursts of speed."

"I hope that horse you're riding isn't one of my fillies." Phil leaned his arms over the top railing, wearing a fancy wool coat and that dreaded gray felt hat. "A headsetter means problems. I expect perfection from a Nash Blackwell horse."

Nash turned Nosey to face Phil, stunned.

Corliss brought Java to Nash's side. "Who let the fox in the hen house?"

Had Helen seen Phil? It wasn't likely since Phil looked as if he'd come around to the arena from the side facing the main house, rather than through the barn. She'd either been in the barn proper when he pulled up or sitting in her van.

Good.

"This is private property, Mitchell." Hands on his hips, Wyatt walked over to stand next to Nash and Corliss.

"Someone call Sheriff Grady." *Trespassing.* Nash was going to enjoy seeing Phil arrested and charged.

Phil's smile never wavered. "Given our bet, I have every right to be here."

"You have no right!" Corliss called, making the horses' ears swivel back.

Nash held out a hand toward his sister and said quietly, "We've got this."

Corliss scowled.

"I heard you sold a horse," Phil continued, unperturbed. "It occurred to me that I should pick out which horses I want of the three diamonds remaining."

"Not a chance," Nash practically growled.

"Why bother, Phil?" Helen came to stand one section of fence away from her ex-fiancé, head held high. "You aren't going to win that bet."

Atta girl.

"Confidence looks good on you, Helen," Phil

said in a silky voice that raised the hair on the back of Nash's neck.

"Easy," Wyatt cautioned in a near-whisper.

"You like my confidence, do you?" Helen pointed toward the arena, so brash and annoyed that Nash wanted to kiss her. "If hell freezes over and you win the bet, those are your horses if you still have the cash to buy them at the agreed-upon rate."

Phil shook his head. "Not the chestnut."

Nosey, he meant.

A growl collected in Nash's throat.

Helen mimicked Phil's head shake. "Nothing in the bet stated which two horses you'll receive for your money. I was there, remember? You wanted Nash Blackwell horses. If I don't place, you'll get what you get, and you'll be grateful for it."

"Ooh," Corliss breathed softly. "You go, Helen."

Phil frowned.

"Now get out or I'll call Sheriff Grady and have you arrested." Helen pointed toward the path, presumably back the way Phil had come.

"I'll show you out." Wyatt moved purposefully toward their nemesis.

The pair disappeared around the corner of the barn.

Nash rode over to the railing where Helen stood, then dismounted, climbed the fence, and reached over to help her up on the rails across from him. "That was spectacular!"

And then he kissed her. He kissed her as if he had every right. He kissed her as if everything was going to be all right.

And when he was done, he looked deep into her green eyes and smiled, intending to kiss her again, assuming she'd be agreeable.

Instead, Helen dropped to the ground. "I'm going to make some client phone calls. I've got to rearrange my schedule for tomorrow and Wednesday." She walked off without so much as a teasing comment about rewards and futures together.

"What was that?" Nash wondered.

Nosey nudged the back of his shoulder, and then rubbed her muzzle near his cheek, begging for attention.

"She's something." Corliss rode up behind him.

"Yeah." Nash turned, gathering Nosey's reins. "This filly wants to please. She just needs a chance."

"Not the horse." Corliss rolled her eyes. "I'm talking about Helen."

"Yeah, but she…" Nash glanced toward the barn. She'd walked away. Something was wrong. Very, very wrong.

"I meant, *what* Helen said." Corliss arched a brow in front of Nash.

"It's what she didn't say." Nash swung into the saddle.

"What she didn't say?" Corliss was like her little terrier Arrow, worrying on a big bone. "We aren't talking about the same things."

In that case, Nash chose to ignore the question. "Let's get to training. Time's a-wasting."

And when it came to Helen, he had to make every moment count.

CHAPTER ELEVEN

"WHAT'S THE RUSH in cutting down a Christmas tree?" Nash pulled a sled with a Christmas carol–singing Luke sitting on it. There was about an hour before sunset on Monday afternoon. He slogged through the snowy meadow north of the arena. "I have training to do." And it was easier for him to talk to Helen when Luke was elsewhere.

"If you need to train more, you can do it tomorrow." Helen walked a few feet ahead, blazing a trail through about half a foot of snow.

"We don't have many tomorrows, Helen."

She said nothing.

A pit formed in Nash's gut, large enough for his heart to fall through and tumble toward his toes. "We'll train after dinner."

"We can't. We're going to put up our tree tonight." Helen sounded adamant. "Happy memory-making time. That's more important than training."

Nash's jaw clenched. "You told Phil earlier that you were going to win the bet. That means we should train." And train harder. And talk through whatever was bothering her.

"I'm not up to speed in the saddle." She picked up her pace. "And watching you train… I've watched you compete and train enough over the years to know what you're doing. I'm not going to learn how to ride by osmosis."

"Ouch. Maybe we should talk about what's really bothering you." Young audience or not.

Rather than elaborate, she joined Luke in song. *"Fa-la-la-la-la. La-la-la-la."* Regardless of the tension between them, what Helen lacked in harmony, she made up for with enthusiasm.

He gave her props for that, even as he recognized the avoidance tactic. He'd used it enough himself, although never by bursting into song.

Now Nash knew firsthand how Helen must have felt when he wouldn't talk in more detail about the accident. Frustrated. Shut out. Alone. The more he dwelled on it, the more the negative feelings filled his inner well and the stronger the siren's call for something to assuage the bad.

He focused on the smooth blankets of snow on the landscape, the crisp, cold air in his lungs, Helen's and Luke's voices lifting toward the sky.

He joined them in song. Surprisingly, singing with them made him feel better.

This part of the property had once been grazing land for the small herd they'd kept for beef and training purposes. The herd they had now was smaller still and currently roamed the pastures on the other side of the main house.

There was a grove of pine trees ahead on the slope. A scattering of trees of various sizes dotted the landscape between here and there. Saplings that were knee or shoulder height. Nothing as grand as the trees he and Helen used to cut down each holiday.

"Mama, 'Jingle Bells,'" Luke cried when they'd finished "Deck the Halls." He led his parents in the first verse.

Helen sang loudly and unapologetically off-key.

Two songs later, they reached a larger group of trees on the edge of the grove—four to six footers.

"Tell me if you see my horse, Daddy," Luke said as they came to a stop.

"I'm pretty sure she'll stay in the south pasture." Nash knelt to Luke's level. "There's no cattle that way. She's got all that land to herself."

"Aw. Bummer." Luke scooted along the sled until he was lying on his back, smashing that gray felt hat behind him.

At this rate, the hat would be ruined before Christmas.

Helen ventured farther up the hill. Nash ran a little to catch up, to Luke's delight.

"How about this tree?" Nash stopped at the first six-foot-tall tree he found, one Helen had passed by.

The tall pines acted as a block against the mountain wind.

She returned to give it a thorough inspection. In the fading light, Nash could almost overlook the tension around her eyes.

"I don't like it," Luke said.

Helen nodded. "It's not for me either. It's got a twisted trunk and broken branches on the one side, like it was used as a backscratcher for a passing bear or something."

When she said, *"Bear,"* Luke's eyes popped wide open.

Nash continued on beside Helen, pulling the sled while walking backward, no small feat. "Tell me if you see your perfect tree."

"It's too early."

"What does that mean?"

"Have you forgotten? We planted some saplings that first spring we were dating. I just can't remember where we planted them."

Nash did. And it was down by the springs. He kept moving forward, feeling the burden of the training, the ticking clock, his lost marriage, his missed second chance with Helen. Suddenly, choosing a tree together in order to make a nice memory for Luke seemed like relationship-ending closure. He didn't want that. Not at all.

"Stop. This one's good." Helen circled a tree that was only about four feet tall. "What do you think?"

"Too small." Nash surveyed other, grander options nearby.

"It's just my size." Luke scrambled out of the sled and bounded over to it. "I love it."

"It's too small," Nash grumbled, preferring larger trees, although any tree that wasn't one of the ones they'd planted together was a winner.

"But I think this year, this is the tree for us." Helen touched a branch. "It's a delicate tree that says it needs love."

Nash felt the need to argue. "If we leave it here another year or two, it'll be bigger and stronger."

Helen gave him a look that said what everyone in Eagle Springs feared—that there would be no next year. Not for the town, for this tree or for their love.

AN HOUR LATER, the Christmas tree had been cut, dragged home on the sled and placed in a stand in the corner of their living room.

After stringing the tree with lights, Nash felt twitchy and on edge. He should have been merry. Helen had Christmas music blaring from the clock radio in the kitchen. She and Luke happily sang along as they dug through Christmas boxes for their favorite decorations.

"I'm going to put these on." Luke stood guard over a pile of ornaments he'd chosen. "And the star."

"That's fair." Helen was barely talking to Nash. The distance was growing between them and he hated it. "Daddy has strung the lights. I'm hanging the beaded garlands. And you can do the ornaments as soon as I finish." Helen circled the tree, draping her golden garland beads and humming along to "Frosty the Snowman" on the radio.

Nash sat within touching distance on the couch. Did she bump into his leg or touch his knee as she passed? No.

He gritted his teeth.

"Mama, are you done?"

"No." She fiddled with the drape of the garland. She was wearing jeans and a red hoodie with the make-believe Santa University logo.

The radio announcer read a dedication, a Christmas love song to a couple who'd been married fifteen years. That couple was probably laughing together in the kitchen as they made dinner. Nash had put frozen pot pies in the oven. Geez, he was messing everything up lately.

"I like it when people smile at Christmas," Luke said out of the blue. "It's better than trick or treat."

"We're smiling." Nash bared his teeth.

"We smile all the time," Helen echoed, although without much enthusiasm. With her back to Nash, he couldn't see if she was smiling.

"Not everybody smiles." Unable to wait any longer, Luke snuck a shiny red ball onto the tree. "Gran and me delivered cookies and fudge to people in town. I smiled. Gran smiled. And not everybody smiled back."

Nash hated that folk in Eagle Springs had treated his family that way.

"I'm sorry, Luke." Helen hugged their little boy. "Everybody should smile at Christmas."

"Even those who have worries on their plate," Nash said dutifully.

"I'm smiling." Luke grinned, putting another ball on the tree. "And that's because I know Santa is going to bring me my wishes. Daddy found my horse. And Mama and me are back home."

Helen's hands dropped to her sides, and her smile fell as well, probably on the carpet near her stocking feet.

Nash came to her smile's rescue, teasing Luke. "I thought you wanted a bike for Christmas."

Luke nearly dropped the bauble he was holding. "No, Daddy, a horse."

Helen turned away, moving into the kitchen. She opened the oven, presumably to check on the pot pies.

Nash continued to tease. "And what would you call this horse if I catch her?"

"It's white. So…ice cream?" Luke practically threw his ornament on the tree. It came to rest on top of a branch.

"Ice cream?" Nash scoffed. "Try again."

The love song ended. The radio announcer began reading his messages from sponsors.

"Milk?" Luke grinned, coming to lean on Nash's legs.

"Naw." His spirits were lifting, raised by one clever little boy.

"Cotton?"

"That's better. But…"

"Hmm." Luke tapped his chin. "Snowflake?"

"Sneaker?" Helen called from the kitchen where she leaned against the counter, watching them with a guarded expression on her face. "I'm only suggesting it because your great-grandmother's sneakers are white. I saw them in the mudroom."

"Sneaker is sneaky." Luke giggled, racing around the living room. "Sneaker is my horse!" He stopped suddenly, dropping to the carpet. "Oh, my gosh. What if Santa brings me a horse on Christmas? I'll have two."

"Don't count on it, Luke," Helen said gently. She was really good at the parenting thing. "There's probably another boy or girl wanting a horse."

"Yeah," Nash seconded. "Don't be greedy. Santa gives out coal to the greedy kids." And adults who couldn't communicate with their loved ones. Nash drew a labored breath. Something had to change and he was afraid it was him.

The radio announcer finished his long list of endorsements. The next holiday song began.

"Mama, the candy cane song!" Luke leaped to his feet and flailed around as "Candy Cane Lane" camc on the radio. His arms swung out as he shimmied closer to her. "Look at me! I'm a happy elf. Come on, Mama. Be a happy, dancing elf."

Helen's gaze flew to Nash. "Uh..."

"Don't mind me." He waved them off. Dancing wasn't his thing. It was hers.

"Ma-ma!" Luke kept bopping around, moving back toward Nash. "You're missing it."

Helen blew out a breath and then joined him,

boogying her way into the living room and to Luke's side.

Nash was spellbound. They both danced as if they had no worries in the world, as if they didn't care if anyone watched them or not.

"Come. On. Daddy!" Luke gyrated toward Nash. "Everybody dances to 'Candy Cane Lane'!"

Helen was smiling, cheeks pink. But she wasn't smiling at him.

Nash continued refusing the offer to dance. "You all know I don't do that."

"Daddy," Luke chastised.

"Scrooge," Helen was more direct.

She and Luke laughed. Nash laughed with them.

Them. His family.

But he still refused to dance.

"WHY DON'T YOU ever dance?" Helen stood in front of the Christmas tree after Luke had gone to bed, adjusting ornaments. She knew she should be in bed, too. But she wanted a few moments alone with Nash, wanted to record these precious times in her memory because she suspected they'd be their last like this. "You never dance, except for the slow songs."

"I have two left feet." Nash finished putting dishes away and came to stand next to her, hands in his jean pockets.

"Two left feet? You could say that about my riding skill and yet, I'm trying." She flung her hair over her shoulder. And since it wasn't that long, it didn't go far. "Dancing isn't about accuracy or judgment. It's about happiness—enjoying a good song, celebrating good friendships, rejoicing in love." Helen moved a little away from him and temptation. He'd kissed her this afternoon—a doozy of a kiss, one that made her determination to keep her distance hard to maintain.

Still, she couldn't resist giving him a verbal nudge to open up, even if it was only about a simple topic like dancing. Who knows? Maybe it would help him in his next relationship.

Her heart panged, protesting the thought.

She moved a shiny gold ornament higher up on the Christmas tree.

"I'm not demonstrative like you," Nash said in a subdued voice. "I can't dance or sing in front of people."

"Or talk through things that burden you." Helen faced him, unable to resist re-opening old wounds. "Someday, you're going to realize what you're missing out on."

He caught her hand, eyes so full of longing that she wanted to cry. "I know what I'm missing out on. Is this sudden cold shoulder of yours because you've finally agreed with me that I'm not good enough for you? If it's something else..." Nash seemed to gather himself. "I'm ready to talk about that night if you're ready to listen."

That night? The night of his crash?

Helen went numb, which kept her from crying out, *"Of course, I want to listen!"*

She somehow managed to nod instead.

Nash swallowed, gaze shifting to the bare wall where his cutting horse career had been documented in photographs and ribbons. "To celebrate my win, I had a couple of beers with friends before I left Torrington. Two hours. Two beers. I thought I was good to drive home. That's within the legal limit."

Helen's overall numbness morphed into the tight-skinned prickle of dread. He'd been drinking before the crash. He'd never admitted that before.

"And everything was fine until an hour later when I came over the pass. You know, the one with that big curve that winds its way around the mountain peak." He spoke slowly and his eyes were glazed, as if seeing something other than a blank wall. "The tractor trailer came from the opposite direction in the lane next to the mountain, swinging wide into my cliff-side lane as if he'd taken the corner too fast."

Helen nodded. This part, she knew.

"The driver clipped the front fender of my truck." Nash stared at his hands. "Maybe if I'd driven home in daylight... Maybe if I hadn't had that second beer... Maybe I'd have been able to keep control of my truck."

"The police report said the other driver was at fault," she reminded him softly.

Nash's features tensed, as if refusing to believe it. "The horse trailer fish-tailed. It felt like I was a kite being buffeted by the wind—toward the mountain, toward the guard rail and back toward the mountain." His voice was taut and raspy. "I knew the guard rail couldn't save us. I knew it. I knew it with gut-wrenching certainty but there was nothing I could do. We hit it and rolled down the cliff. And I thought that was it, it was over."

She laid a hand on his shoulder, knowing the sequence of events but never having heard how he felt or how it affected him.

"We rolled and all I could think of was Jet and how frightened he must be." Nash worked his throat, finally managing to swallow.

"Because you were frightened, too?" And alone.

He nodded, staring toward Helen even though she knew he was seeing something else.

"You thought about the soul that was in your care and in danger," she gently pointed out. "Jet."

He didn't seem to hear. "When I came to… When I got the airbag out of the way and forced the crumpled door open, there was blood in my eyes and…"

Other places.

In addition to his head wound, his right arm had been broken and his right ankle banged up from the pedals.

"It's all right," she told him, moving her hand back and forth across his shoulders.

"It was quiet…" His gaze shifted back to the empty wall. "So quiet."

"The noise from the crash probably scared every creature for miles around."

He blinked. "But I… I didn't hear *him*. Jet." Nash swallowed thickly, gaze traveling to the dining room cabinet where he used to keep his whiskey. And then it came back around to rest on Helen. And this time, he was present. There were a myriad of emotions in his gaze—pain, regret, guilt, helplessness.

Helen smoothed the unkempt hair from his eyes.

Nash stopped her, taking her hand in his and holding on tight. "Jet was always such a strong, stubborn horse."

And Nash had loved him.

"The horse trailer was mangled. Nothing should have survived that. But he… When I got the trailer door open… He nickered… Almost as if he knew I needed to know that he recognized me." A tear rolled down his cheek.

There were far more tears tracking down Helen's face.

"I'd never seen a horse…" He swallowed again, visibly struggling to continue. "It was bad. So bad… Sometimes it comes back to me at night and I…" He blinked and it was as if he was seeing Helen for the first time in several minutes. "And when that happens, I reach for you."

But she wasn't there. And hadn't been for years.

Helen was there for him now, wrapping her arms around him and drying her cheeks on his T-shirt.

He rested his cheek against her hair. "But the hardest thing was making my way back to the truck to find the gun, leaving him alone and suffering, and knowing that I'd have to end his pain."

Helen clung tighter. She clung tighter and loved him more than ever. "You did the right thing."

"For the wrong reasons," he said heavily. "And later, when you came to the hospital with Corliss and Gran, I knew that a better man would have headed home after the competition to celebrate with his family. I should have been responsible. I should have wanted to return to my wife and son. Instead, I celebrated a victory with people I barely keep in touch with. A victory that turned out to be hollow."

And his last. He hadn't competed since.

"I know the decisions I made that day and during the two years afterward hurt you," Nash was saying. "I know it's hard for you to put your heart in my hands once more, but I thought over the weekend that there was hope for us. It surprised me. It… It flew in the face of everything I believe. But that moment at the springs… We were… It was…" He paused, perhaps expecting Helen to pick up where he left off.

But she couldn't say the words that would sever what was left between them.

His expression turned regretful. "And then I guess you had second thoughts. None of which I blame you for. I can't give you what you want—a loving husband who puts you first, one you can trust to stay sober."

Cold washed over Helen. Not because Nash hadn't rushed home after a competition to be with her—he deserved to celebrate his hard work—but because he continued to believe he didn't deserve a second chance with her. And if she remained silent, he'd believe she agreed that he'd made too many mistakes to be forgiven, to be loved, to be entrusted with her heart again.

She drew away from him, moving backward until she bumped into the branches of the Christmas tree. "I'm afraid it's the other way around."

"Don't say that." He reached for her. "Never say that. I don't care about Phil."

"That's not it. Nash, I..." Helen edged to the other side of the Christmas tree. Now she was the one who couldn't find the words. Instead, she pulled up her sweatshirt and lowered the waistband of her jeans, revealing her scar.

"What's this?" His hands fell to his sides.

"It's the reason I put distance between us since you kissed me at the springs." She covered herself once more, unable to look at him. She felt so hollow. So...so lacking. "A horse caught me when my guard was down."

"That scar isn't new." There was tension in his voice, tension, and an accusation.

"It's new since you saw that much of me." This was hard. So hard. Helen felt as vulnerable as she had when her mother would chastise her for being weak. She forced herself to look at Nash.

He was still handsomely disheveled, but his mouth was taut. At least, it was until he peppered her with questions. "When? How? Were you in pain? Why didn't you tell me?"

Whether it was pride or love or a combination of both that had him upset, she waved it all aside. “I didn’t have to tell you. We weren’t married anymore.”

“I know that.”

“But you always seem to forget to put the *ex* in front of *wife*,” she said, trying to be as gentle as she could in getting the message across that her body was no longer any of his business.

“And this is the reason for your distance?” He shook his head. “You think I won’t find you as beautiful with a scar? You think I won’t love you because your body is no longer perfect?”

“No. I…” *Just tell him.* “I can’t have any more babies,” she blurted, wiping at the sudden tears.

Nash took a step back, legs bumping into the couch. It seemed to be a good thing, because he sank onto the cushions as if his legs could no longer be trusted to support him.

She forced herself to explain. “So, you see, it doesn’t matter what you think about yourself, Nash. I can’t give you what you want.”

He was silent for a long time, staring at his hands. His scarred, scraped and bruised hands. And then his gaze came up to meet hers. “You’re doing it again. You’re leaving me before I leave you, rejecting me before I reject you—which I’ve never done, by the way, not even when I was self-medicating with alcohol.” There was a sharpness to his voice she’d never heard before.

Helen tried to discount his conclusion. Her mouth opened to speak, but nothing came out. Because it was true.

He sat up, leaning forward. "You pushed me for an answer about wanting more kids. You didn't give me all the details to weigh. If you had, I would have told you that I'd rather have *you*, just as you are, than any other woman who can have children or not." His tone was sharp, his words raggedly delivered, as if she'd sucker punched him.

And maybe she had, but he'd been so earnest about wanting kids at the springs and he came from a family of five siblings, not to mention his uncle Barlow had five children of his own.

Helen drew in a long breath, then let it go. "What we just shared needs some time to digest." Because she didn't know what to think or believe anymore. She passed by the Christmas tree.

"Helen."

She went to the bedroom, not answering when he called her name again.

CHAPTER TWELVE

"WHERE ARE YOU, SNEAKER?" Denny sat in a chair in front of her bedroom window on Tuesday morning, on the lookout for the wild white horse that her grandsons were trying to entice closer to the ranch.

Wyatt had laid portable fencing on the ground. Once raised, it would close off the southern pasture into a triangular-shaped enclosure. Nash had put out hay and a breadcrumb trail of buckets with oats. It was Denny's job to spot the horse and then the boys were going to pull the fence up in place. The hope was that the horse wouldn't hurt itself trying to escape.

Movement in the ranch yard caught her eye.

Elias walked from his motorhome toward the barn, cell phone glued to his ear. If that man wasn't talking to someone in person, he was on the phone.

Denny experienced a moment of guilt. He'd been by her side for the better part of four months. He had a wife back in Montana, a son he'd reconnected with recently, ten grandkids and a passel of great-grands. Christmas was less than three weeks away. She needed to tell him to tend to his own life and business. Nothing he did now was going to make a huge difference in how long she lived or in the outcome of what went on in Eagle Springs.

"I'll tell him tonight."

Her gaze drifted to the snowy south pasture. And there, at the far end, a small white horse emerged from the trees and picked its way carefully up the slope toward a small mound of hay.

"Oh, Cal. She's got good lines." No knock-knees. A long, graceful neck. Intelligence in the alert way she walked, ears perked forward.

Cal would have taken one look at her and said she was a filly fit for a queen. He'd have trained her for a trail riding horse. But the Flying Spur was known for their cutters. Still, Denny could almost hear Cal's voice, the way she had back when they were kids and the Blackwells had gone to the Wessons' for Sunday social.

"That's no working horse," Cal would say. "She's not got the barrel for high range riding or the look in her eye like she wants to stare down a bull and show him who's boss."

His mother would have laughed, as she'd been meant to. His father's chest would have swelled with satisfaction. And Frank would have tossed his arm across Cal's shoulders and given him a playful noogie with his grandparents looking on. The Wessons had been a close-knit family.

If what Elias had uncovered was true, Frank was alone now. He'd never married, which might explain why he'd become obsessed with Denny and her family.

"That man could use a little love in his life." If she knew where he was staying, she could bring him a Christmas plate. "Without the grocery gift card." Frank wasn't in need of Denny's money.

The filly finished eating the first bit of hay. She lifted her head, ears swiveling, nostrils flaring.

"Be brave, honey," Denny urged, watching and waiting.

The filly picked her way uphill toward a bucket with oats.

Denny picked up her phone and called Wyatt.

CHAPTER THIRTEEN

"FORGET THE FACT that Gran was right about the horse," Wyatt told Nash on that sunny Tuesday afternoon. "This will never work."

They stood outside the barn, staring across the ranch yard toward the south pasture. The white filly walked along the edge of the webbing and plastic fence posts Wyatt had laid on the ground, and they'd covered in snow, which was now melting because of the unusually warm day.

The filly was a welcome distraction for Nash, who'd been worrying that Helen hadn't returned from the few errands she'd claimed she had to take care of. In the back of his mind, Nash wondered if she was returning at all.

"She's treating the uneven ground like a cattle guard," Nash noted. "She might work up the courage to jump across."

"I should have run the ropes from the pulley system over here." Wyatt rubbed the stubble on his jaw. "If I move closer to raise the fencing, she'll spook."

"Maybe." Nash rather thought he'd spooked

Helen when he'd told her she was more important to him than increasing the number of children he had. Nash had tossed and turned on the couch all night, wondering how to convince Helen he was sincere.

"Our plan always relied on that filly not being spooked by humans." Wyatt scratched the back of his neck. "Why was that again?"

"Because she followed Helen and me on our ride." Nash walked toward the south pasture. "The only way to test a theory is to test a theory. I'll head to the right. You head to the left. Don't look at her. We'll see if she runs."

"This isn't my first experience with an unbroken horse," Wyatt grumbled, veering to the left along the driveway.

The filly backed slowly away from the fence line, ears swiveling, tail twitching, clearly nervous.

"Almost there," Nash murmured half to himself. His end of the fence was just ten feet away.

The filly swiveled her head, looking toward the driveway. And then she spun and bolted toward the trees, a beauty in motion.

Corliss's truck rumbled along the driveway, the cause of the filly losing her nerve, Nash thought.

The truck pulled up next to Wyatt. Two windows rolled down. Nash ambled over to join Wyatt.

Mason sat behind the wheel. Corliss sat in the passenger seat, bent over her phone. She allowed her son to drive around the ranch even though he was only thirteen. Nash didn't mind him driving because Mason was thirteen going on thirty, more helpful and sensitive than anyone in the family except Adele.

"Did Sneaker get away?" Luke unbuckled his seat belt and practically fell out of the rear window.

"Yes, she did. And it's all on you, Spud," Wyatt teased. "The truck spooked her."

"That's not true," Corliss said testily.

"Aww." Luke sat back on the seat, looking adorable with his expression of disappointment and the mangled gray felt hat. He tipped the brim up. "I guess I'll be helping Daddy train the other horses until you catch her, Uncle Wyatt."

Nash grinned.

It would have been great to have more kids like him.

But a life without Helen…

Nash didn't need more than Helen and Luke.

"Well, Spud, while you're training horses, I'll be making culinary history in the kitchen with Olivia." Mason reached around and high fived his step-sister.

Luke grinned, clearly enjoying the teasing.

"I guess you have to like riding English to be good in the kitchen."

Mason and Olivia started razzing on Luke, who took it like a pro, repeating his go-to defense. "I'm a cowboy, not a cook or an Englishman."

Nash chuckled, wishing that Helen was here to see how well the younger Blackwell generation got along. Maybe then she'd realize he'd meant what he'd said last night. She and Luke were enough family for him. He glanced down the driveway, wondering when she'd be coming back.

If she came back.

His entire being tensed at the thought of Helen giving up on him.

"Which horse are we training, Daddy?" Luke poked his head out the window.

"You can help me with the board and trains after you get a snack and do your homework," Nash told him, striding toward the barn across the slushy yard, reminded of all the responsibilities resting on his shoulders. His parents had always told him that if you took care of your duties the rest of your life would fall into place.

He hoped so.

"I don't have homework," Luke called after Nash. "I'm in kindergarten."

Nash turned as he neared Helen's blacksmithing van. He kept walking, moving backward. "Eat first. Train later."

His heel caught on something, and he went down.

Painfully.

You're leaving me before I leave you.

Nash's words stayed with Helen while she led Beanie around the arena during her morning training, a session from which Nash had been absent.

They echoed forebodingly in her mind when she borrowed Nash's truck to go into town to do some Christmas shopping Tuesday morning. They played on repeat in her head when she went to Cody to pick up an order of horseshoes around lunchtime. They lingered with her now when she stopped by the beauty shop where Gwen worked in the afternoon.

"Shouldn't you be practicing riding at the Flying Spur?" Gwen snapped the plastic drape around Helen's neck.

Christmas music filled the salon, which had four small Christmas trees and sparkly silver garland draped around every station's mirror.

"I committed to two hours a day." Helen stared at her reflection. Her eyes seemed haunted. Her cheeks gaunt. "One hour in the morning. One hour at night."

"And when will your van be fixed?" Gwen played with Helen's hair, fluffing and gently pulling the ends to test the length.

"Wyatt says tomorrow. But it'll be tomorrow afternoon." The day would be shot. Helen didn't like to total the number of days she'd had no income. That she no longer had to pay an afterschool babysitter and that her grocery bill was reduced while she stayed with the Blackwells was little consolation.

"No offense, Helen, but you look like someone stole all your Christmas presents." Gwen caught her eye in the mirror. "You're finally back where you want to be. Is Nash still claiming he's not your prince?"

"No." She explained about Nash saying he wanted more kids and then him saying he only wanted her and Luke. "I want to believe him but..." She lowered her voice. "What if he wakes up one morning five years from now and looks at me with regret?"

"And what if you don't believe him and you wake up five years from now without him?" Gwen grabbed a spray bottle, aiming it at Helen's head. "No shampoo today, right?"

"Right."

Gwen wet Helen's hair all around and combed

the moisture through. "Do you remember how I said in high school that I wanted to marry a wealthy quarterback?"

"Because of all those muscles and the big paydays? Yes."

Gwen set to work trimming Helen's ends. "I have no regrets about marrying a computer geek and traveling ATM machine repairman."

"This is different."

"It's not. I had a picture in my head of my future, just like Nash had for a big family. But dreams change. Even circumstances change. I'm sure Nash didn't dream of losing two years of his life to whiskey." Snip-snip-snip.

"Gwen—"

"If Nash wanted kids that badly, Helen, he would have had some since the divorce." Snip-snip-snip.

"But Gwen—"

"He's still in love with you, Helen." Gwen tugged the ends of Helen's hair beneath her ears, checking to see if the length was even. "Trust what he's saying. Trust what your heart wants." She fluffed Helen's hair.

"I want him." A drop of water trickled down the back of Helen's neck, making her shiver. "It's just… You didn't see his face when he talked about wanting more kids and a bigger family. It's important to him."

"*You're* important to him." Gwen set her hands on Helen's shoulders. "The fact that he finally talked to you about the accident and said he wants to try again… I know you've been disappointed by Nash and your mother, but this seems real. Or as real as the solid relationship you had with your dad."

And she'd left him, too, traveling the world looking for something, absent when her dad died. "I—"

"A man who stares at his wedding photo and admits he's thought of kissing you isn't going to get hung up on you not being able to have more babies." Gwen rummaged around her station for her blow dryer and a round brush. "You're going to be together another week and a half. Make the most out of it. Don't run away."

"I…" Helen waited to see if Gwen was going to interrupt her again.

Gwen looked at her. "What? What's wrong? Why aren't you arguing?"

"Is it my turn to talk?" Helen grinned when Gwen smirked. "I will put on my big girl panties and trust. Ride out this chance with Nash."

"That's the Helen I know and love."

AT THE FIRST sound of his truck returning, Nash made a limping beeline toward the ranch yard.

He opened the truck door for Helen after she'd turned off the engine. "Where have you been?"

"Running errands. Why are you limping?" She hopped out of his truck and went to the back, lowering the tailgate and grabbing a box of horseshoes. She wasn't wearing her cowboy hat. Her hair had been cut, curled and fluffed. It bounced when she walked and caught the fading rays of sunshine. "Were you worried? You look worried? Or in pain." She stopped talking and moving and took a good look at him.

"I tripped over Wyatt's tool box and twisted my ankle. It's not bad." What was bad was his pleasure in her concern for his well-being. "You were gone all day. I was getting worried." Nash took the heavy box from her and carried it toward her van.

"Give me that." She practically ripped the box from his hands. "That limp is too pronounced for you to be walking around. And that look in your eye makes me think you were worried about me bailing on your bet."

"Guilty." What was the use arguing with her? He opened the back door of the blacksmithing van and helped her shove the box across the floor.

"Dinner!" Corliss called from the main house.

"Sheesh, my sister has been keeping tabs on

me since I fell." He began hobbling toward the house. "She and Wyatt took over training. They weren't happy that I kept correcting them."

"I suppose that's something I have in common with Corliss and Wyatt." Helen slid next to him and put his arm over her shoulder. "Lean on me."

Always.

"At least, they offered to help you," she continued. "That's supportive."

"Helen." He lowered his voice as they approached the porch steps. "They're worried about my ability to keep up the quality of training." And about Helen's ability to compete.

"But you're the best, injured or not. And… Before we go in, I have something to say." Helen came to a stop, glancing at the house and then at Nash. "I thought a lot about what you said last night in response to the fallout of my injury. I believed you when you said you still care for me. I believed you when you said I deserve a prince. Therefore, if you're okay with no more kids, I want us… to be us, again."

He breathed a sigh of relief.

And then she threw herself into his arms and kissed him, practically knocking him to the ground because of his injury.

"I got you," he murmured against her lips, ignoring the shooting pain in his bad ankle.

"I hope so," she murmured back, soft and warm in his arms.

"Nash! Helen! Dinner is ready." That was Corliss, out to ruin a romantic moment. She slammed the door behind her.

Helen drew back, smiling, stomach rumbling. She laughed, the joyful sound lifting his annoyance with his sister. She grabbed his hand and led him toward the porch steps.

He slowed and stopped.

She stared down at his boots. "If it's hurting and swollen, your siblings are right. You do need to take it easy."

"We'll see."

And they did, because when he removed his boots in the mudroom, he had a tennis ball–sized swelling around his ankle.

"I'll ice it," he quickly assured Helen. "It'll be fine in a couple of days."

"You'll ice it and you'll rest," she told him in a tone that dared him to refuse her.

He didn't take that dare.

They entered the kitchen in the midst of a dispute between Gran and Big E.

"I'm not leaving." Big E sat rigidly in his chair. "What kind of brother would I be if I left the battle now? I don't care how much we argue. I'm not going anywhere." Contradicting his words, the big man stood and stomped toward the mudroom. Not that he was finished with his tirade. "You may not know this, Delaney, but family doesn't cut out when times get tough. They may disagree, but you don't send them packing when they do."

Gran closed her eyes, breathing raggedly.

The mudroom door slammed.

His grandmother opened her eyes, gaze landing on Nash and Helen's linked hands. "Eat," she commanded, looking away.

"I left your plates in the oven to keep warm," Mason told them. "Helen's has cheese on her broccoli."

Helen ushered Nash to a chair flanked by two vacant seats. She helped him prop up his ankle on one chair, then went to make him a bag of ice.

Luke stood on his seat across the table, trying to get a good look. "That's some bruise, Daddy."

He'd had worse, not that he wanted to admit that in front of Helen.

"I'll grab the first aid kit." Corliss popped up, not nearly as tense as she'd been a few minutes ago. "We'll wrap it."

It took a few minutes to submit to Corliss and Helen's ministrations and then eat. Meanwhile, Ryder and Olivia were doing the dishes. And Mason was wiping down the tables and chairs.

"Are you ready to head back?" Helen put a gentle hand on Nash's arm.

He wanted to return the kindness, but Gran was rapping her fingers on the table.

"Nash, can I talk to you a minute? Alone?" She waved the rest of the family out, including Helen and Luke.

But not before Helen placed a kiss on top of Nash's head.

After the kitchen emptied, Gran stared into her tea mug.

"Are you trying to read the tea leaves?" Nash shifted the ice bag on his ankle. "Or have you forgotten what you wanted to talk to me about?"

"Of course, I remember." Gran shook her bony finger at Nash. "I was just waiting for Elias to join us. He and I wanted to discuss things."

"He was pretty mad. I don't think he's coming back."

She tsked. "He never stays mad at me for long." She glanced toward the mudroom.

"Why don't we have this conversation tomorrow?" He started to ease his ankle from the chair to the floor.

"That darn brother of mine..." Gran held out a hand. "Stay put and hear me out. I wanted to talk to you about the pressure you might be feeling."

Nash set his foot on the floor. "I'm fine, thanks."

"But Nash..." She hesitated again, the way she did when the conversation was prickly and scattered with pitfalls. "Our way of life... Our lives... *Your* life...is being pulled apart at the seams."

He had a sudden, gut-clenching clarity about the direction this conversation was going. "I'm fine."

"When Cal was alive, he'd reach for the drink when the pressure built."

"I'm not Cal." Nash got to his feet. "I know you think you're helping me but—"

"Cal was a risk-taker, too. But when things got tough, he'd take the easy way out, reaching for a drink if the easy way failed."

"You think I made this bet because it was easy?" Nash didn't move. He wanted to but the shock of his grandmother's lack of faith in him kept him rooted in place. "You think I agreed to train four fillies in a handful of months because it was easy? You think convincing Helen to face her fears is easy?" He wanted to howl. But he kept his voice down because if he didn't, Corliss would come running. And the last thing he and Gran needed was for Corliss to choose sides between them.

The last thing I need is to lose the faith Corliss placed in me.

Although he might have lost it when he'd made that bet.

But he was pretty darn sure she didn't lose sleep at night wondering if he was going to douse the mounting stress with alcohol.

"All I'm saying is that everything could go south at the Holiday Showcase. If things fall apart there or with Helen, what will you do?"

"I won't drink." He hobbled to the kitchen sink, dumping the ice bag in it. And then he turned and faced the grandmother he used to idolize. "I need your support, not dire predictions. Don't compare me to your precious Cal ever again. We're not the same. He failed you. I won't."

Nash made it to the mudroom, but he couldn't immediately escape because it was tricky to put his boot back on over his swollen ankle. While he struggled, he heard his grandmother leave the kitchen.

Big E entered, clearly apprised of the topic of conversation and wanting to add his two cents because he opened with, "It's not that we don't trust your resolve but—"

"I'm not interested in anything you have to

say on the matter." Nash cut him off, shoving his boot on and trying to push past the old man, but Big E caught his arm and held him firm with surprising power.

"Your grandmother is scared."

"She's not scared." Nash tugged his arm free. "She thinks I'm Cal reincarnated. Doomed to destroy everything good around me. Fated to go to an early grave."

"She wants you to be aware of the danger is all. Put yourself in her boots and take a breath." Big E slid his hands in his expensive jacket pockets. "Delaney wants the best for you, but she wants you to be careful. There's a lot riding on you and Helen. We're here to help you see it through."

"I'm aware of the pressure. I've been calling my sponsor every morning since those fillies were delivered." Instead of every week. "I think what you two fail to recognize is that I went to seek help to quit drinking. I adopted the rules of the program. And I stick to them."

"And Cal didn't." Big E nodded, stroking the white stubble on his chin. "You're right about that."

Nash nodded briskly, some of the tension leaving him. "If I have the urge to reach for a drink, I know what to do. Separate myself from the situation."

"I respect you, Nash. And I'll be here if you'd rather talk to someone than run."

"Thanks." Nash turned to go. Now that he was calming down, his ankle was on fire. But... *Run.* Nash wasn't the runner around here. He faced Big E again. "Could you do me a favor?"

"Anything."

"Helen's mother abandoned her after she had that riding accident. Could you find her?" Assuming she was still alive. "Her name is Linda Oliver."

Big E tilted his head as he studied Nash. "Shouldn't Helen be asking me that?"

"You can ask her if you like. It's that Helen runs from things when times get tough. And maybe if she had a chance to talk to her mother, she wouldn't always look for a door." Nash wished he'd thought of the idea sooner.

CHAPTER FOURTEEN

"You crossed a line, Delaney." Elias entered the living room looking as upset as he had when he'd stormed out at dinner. "You handled the conversation with Nash all wrong."

He was right. Not that she planned to admit it.

Denny sat stiffly on the couch across from the yet to be decorated Christmas tree. There were boxes of ornaments stacked beside it waiting to be opened. Those who would have done the decorating and enjoyed it were upstairs, avoiding Denny. Yes, she'd made a fine mess of things. "He'll forgive me in the morning."

"Will he?" Elias waited a beat and came to sit next to her. "Forgiveness usually follows an apology."

"Stay out of this, Elias," Denny said tightly.

"Nash isn't Cal," Elias said quietly. "And everyone deals with their demons differently."

Denny rubbed her hands over her face, sickened by the things she'd said to Nash but convinced that her concerns needed to be aired. "We can't turn a blind eye. That's what everyone did with Cal." And look how that turned out. "If we lose this fight, I don't want the family to fall apart."

"It won't."

"It already has." She fought to keep panic from her voice. "Both my sons left. Hudson moved to Arizona when he retired from practicing medicine. Barlow was always too big for Eagle Springs. He's in Cheyenne, raising his children in the ways of oil, not horses. I'm afraid Hudson's children will scatter to the winds after this and lose touch with each other the way we did."

"There's a difference. These grandkids of yours won't be running away from something."

"They won't have regrets, you mean?" Denny laid a hand over his. "They'll carry bad memories if we lose to Frank. It won't be the ache of loss over not being with their parents when they pass on." That was her burden. "But they'll wonder what their life would have been like if only..." She shook her head. "If only. If only. Pride kept me from answering that call. I am my own worst enemy. And I'd do anything to keep what happened to me and Cal from happening to Nash and Helen."

Even hold hard conversations that might make Nash never want to speak to her again.

CHAPTER FIFTEEN

After closing down the barn for the night, Nash moved slowly and with some pain from the ranch proper toward the driveway, knowing his ankle needed rest but craving air.

Gran's faith in him was shaken. After further consideration, given how Corliss and Wyatt had been hovering around him lately, he thought they had their doubts, too. Maybe not about his horse training product but about his ability to keep it together when things came down to the wire.

Keep it together… That was code for something else.

Say it, Nash.

To stay sober, come what may.

He'd thought he'd proven his victory over whiskey. Their lack of confidence stung.

Something moved near the fence.

Nash stopped, peering into the shadows outside the ranch lights.

Light glimmered off the back of a large animal on the other side of the south pasture gate.

"Sneaker." Nash started quickly forward before the stab of ankle pain made him catch himself. He adjusted his steps to a smoother hobble, not wanting to startle the filly. He shuffled fifty feet down the driveway to the place where Wyatt had rigged the pulleys for the portable fence.

He heard the filly move slowly around, saw her out of the corner of his eye. She was still near the bucket of oats and water trough. He wrapped his fingers around the slim rope in the pulley.

Now.

Nash hesitated to draw the fence into place. If the filly startled and ran upon hearing something behind her, she might not see the webbing in the dark. She could run into it and be injured.

Or need to be put down.

Nash's stomach soured.

There was a time and place for everything. A time to close ranks and be strong. Or, if no one believed in him, to walk alone.

He turned back around, heading for the mobile home and the last bastion of safety.

Helen.

"WHAT DID DENNY WANT?" Helen smiled at Nash when he returned to the mobile home.

Luke was playing in the bathtub, while she prepped the coffeemaker for the morning.

Nash didn't say a word. He wrapped his arms around Helen and buried his face in her hair.

"Hey. What's this?" Helen slid her hands under his jacket, running her palms over his back. "Is your ankle worse?"

He shook his head, continuing to hold on in silence.

Luke sang "Jingle Bells," splashing too enthusiastically. Helen didn't dare leave to chastise him. She was too committed to console Nash through whatever crisis he was dealing with, convinced he'd share when he was ready.

Besides, she'd missed being held in his arms. She'd missed being the one he leaned on when things got tough.

And so, Helen didn't say anything either. She thought about the times they'd held each other in the past. The night he'd proposed. The morning they'd discovered they were pregnant. The moment she'd arrived at the hospital after his car crash and had climbed into the bed with him. There was love and strength to be found in each other's arms. Right now, he needed both.

Slowly, Nash's breathing became less ragged, his shoulders less tense. And finally, he raised his head and looked at her. "You're the only person who believes in me."

"That can't be true."

He nodded, shuffling to the sink to get a glass of water. "Your lack of experience. My injury.

My so-called resemblance to Cal. The specter of my past. The family thinks I'm going to crack."

"It's been a long haul since the bank called in the ranch's loan. Their nerves are fraying." She went to him, placing her hands on those broad shoulders, willing her love to bolster his flagging spirits.

Luke sang louder, splashed harder. The floor had to be sopping wet by now.

"They've decided on a predetermined outcome," Nash said in a faraway voice. "You'll lose at the Holiday Showcase, and then you'll leave me. And I..." He took a sip of water.

"Nash." She wanted to promise him none of those things would happen. But they were in uncharted territory. "Let's just take this one day at a time."

"Are you worried?" He turned to face her, expression strained. "About what happens after the Showcase?"

With them, she thought he meant.

Helen laid a hand on his cheek. It was rough with stubble and cool from him being outside. "I'm not worried about you following through on your end with the training. I'm worried about me doing you proud."

"You'll be fine..." He turned his face, kissing her palm. "And the drinking?"

"I believe you when you say you don't want

that life again." It wasn't exactly a vote of confidence. And if she was being honest with herself, she'd wondered the same as Denny had—for no more than a second. "I will do everything in my power to support your sobriety."

He considered her words. Then he nodded. "I can't tell you how grateful I am that you're by my side in this."

Helen slid an arm around his shoulders. "Let's get that ankle taken care of." She helped him over to the couch.

"Is nobody coming?" Luke splashed more water in the bathroom.

"Three minutes, young man," Helen told him, helping to remove Nash's coat and boots. She propped his ankle on a pillow and put an ice pack on it. "Let me save our little cowboy from shriveling into a prune."

Nash captured her hand. "Thank you. I dragged you into this mess. I wouldn't blame you if you washed your hands of me."

"We're in this together." She kissed him briefly, wishing for better days ahead but knowing the hardest tests for both of them were just around the corner.

"ARE YOU A FROG?" Helen wrapped Luke in a towel and dried him off as the bathtub drained. "The floor is covered in water."

"Ribbit." Luke grinned, bending his knees and giving a little hop.

Something on his leg caught her eye. "Where did you get that?" Helen inspected a small purplish bruise on his shin. "Did you fall in the barn?"

"I told you before. It's Wendy Carsden at recess, Mama." Luke sighed.

"I talked to your teacher about that just last week." And she'd been assured that Wendy's hurtful behavior would stop. "I'll call her tomorrow."

Luke shrugged. "Freddie from my class said I should kick Wendy back."

"You'll do no such thing. I'll make sure Wendy gets time out or detention or something."

"Aunt Corliss says Wendy likes me and won't give up kickin' until I kiss her." Luke pulled a face. "Yuck."

She set aside the towel and reached for his jammies. "You're too young to be kissing girls."

"'Xactly." Luke picked up a yellow car from the bottom of the bathtub. "Great Gran said when people push you around, you've got to push back."

She tugged a dinosaur-themed sleep shirt over his head. "There will be no pushing."

"Big E said I should hire me a lawyer." He stepped into his matching pajama bottoms.

"He said I should call the lawyer that got Aunt Adele sprung out of jail. Mama, what's a lawyer?"

"That was all a misunderstanding." Could things get any more chaotic in Eagle Springs? She held Luke still. "Just to recap—no kisses, no kicking, no pushing or putting people in prison."

"You're funny, Mama." Luke kissed her cheek and ran out of the bathroom, as if leaving all his cares behind him.

An enviable skill.

CHAPTER SIXTEEN

THURSDAY MORNING, HELEN drove her van to her first appointment in days. Snow sprinkled sparsely. It didn't stick on the road or on her windshield. Christmas carols rang out from the radio.

Helen was determined that today be a good day.

After two days of rest and icing, Nash's ankle was almost its normal size. And the gloom of his family's concerns for him seemed to have lightened, such that he wasn't such a grouch when Wyatt and Corliss took on much of the physical demands of cutting horse training.

Helen had made progress, too. Just this morning, she and Beanie had been trotting around the arena's perimeter. Nash had been pleased.

Nash…

Helen's train of thought derailed. Ten minutes from the Flying Spur and she missed Nash already.

They were going to make it this time—she and Nash. Forever, just like he'd promised her all those years ago. The doubts were fading, just like Luke's bruise.

Of course, their relationship would be easier once the Holiday Showcase was behind them. There'd be less uncertainty and more of a feeling of permanence and normalcy, like they'd had before.

Just this morning, Nash had walked her to her van and said, "Be careful out there today. Let me know if you get injured." There was worry in his eyes before he'd kissed her goodbye.

It was nice to have someone care about her well-being, to feel cherished.

She sighed dreamily and turned into the driveway of a small ranch. Her first client was an old beauty, a palomino brood mare. She was scheduled to drop at any time, which must have made her stressed, because she was a fidgety girl with shifting weight and a twitching tail instead of her usual well-behaved self.

"She'll have that foal tonight," Helen predicted as she processed Darryl Merriweather's payment on her phone when she was through.

"Wanna bet?" Darryl cackled as if this was the funniest comeback ever. A man in his sixties, he'd lost most of his hair and from the sound of things, his sense of humor as well. "Get it? Bet? Like you and Phil?"

"Hardy-har." Helen handed Darryl his bank card. "And the bet is with Nash and Phil. Not me."

Her next stop was a miniature horse ranch run by one of Denny's good friends, Tia Edwards. Three horses needed shoes. The minis were so small, Helen couldn't use her shoe jack to rest their hooves on while she worked. Their hooves would have rested at an awkward, uncomfortable angle. Helen had to get low—bend, bend lower and bend lower still until her thighs burned.

"I should never have given up my gym membership." Regular squats and lunges would have made her legs stronger.

"Like you need a gym." Tia chuckled, tucking a strand of gray hair in her knit cap. "You are a wonder, Helen."

"And you are too kind." Helen set down Piper's small black hoof and straightened, stretching her lower back and shaking out her quads.

"It's a deserved compliment." Tia finger combed Piper's forelock. "You wouldn't catch me riding in a race car at my age. But look at you, hopping on one of Nash's quicksilver beasts."

"They're actually very sweet horses," Helen said evenly, because that was preferable to thinking about how nimble his horses were.

"Sweet horses who spin on a dime." Tia

laughed louder. "I got my ticket to see this. Wouldn't miss it."

"I hope I don't disappoint you." You and everyone else in town. Helen bent to check her work on Piper's hoof.

"Now, Helen. I know things look grim. But the only way you'd let me down is if you didn't show up. I believe in you."

"That's so nice." Helen's phone rang before she could ask Tia if she had any Christmas plans.

It was Adele. "I have a problem at the auction yard and was hoping you could squeeze me into your appointments this afternoon. *Plee-ease.*"

"Anything for my former sister-in-law." Who might be her sister-in-law again if Helen could stay in the saddle.

"WE GOT HER." Wyatt poked his head over the stall door where Nash was putting a headsetter halter on Nosey.

"Who?" Nash buckled the halter in place and led the filly out of the stall. As a result of Helen's tender loving care, he was hardly limping at all today. "I hope we don't have visitors. I've got cows in the arena."

"I know." Wyatt pulled a face, closing Nosey's stall door. "I helped Corliss round them up before lunch."

"Right. Sorry. I'm a little scattered today."

"Understandable," Wyatt said. "But I'm talking about Sneaker. Harper and I were taking a walk and saw her amble up to the oat bucket at the gate. We were near the pulley system, so I just cranked it up." He grinned. "And what do you know?"

"You caught her?" Nash tied Nosey to a hook in the breezeway and followed Wyatt to the ranch yard door. "She didn't bolt or test the fence?"

"No. It's like she's used to being close to the ranch now."

"Or she's been handled in the past." Nash shook his head. "Although it's nice that we got her, it's the worst time to take on another horse. I've got to tell Luke to keep his distance."

"Like that will work." Wyatt didn't sound convinced.

And truth be told, neither did Nash. "It will. I'll be firm."

"When's the last time you worked the fillies with live cattle?" Wyatt opened the barn door.

"Last week. Their performance gave me direction to fine tune this week." Nash emerged into the fresh air. From where he stood, he could see Sneaker in the south pasture. No matter how many times he looked at her, he was surprised to see perfect conformation in the wild filly. "She doesn't look anxious by her confinement. Did you see a brand on her?"

"None. That doesn't mean she's wild."

Nash nodded. "It might take a while to verify that." There was a slight chance she'd been microchipped or had a lip tattoo. Both would require her to submit to close inspection.

"In the meantime, Helen's coming along well." Wyatt held out a hand to Harper. She'd been waiting for him outside.

"She is." Nash nodded a greeting to Wyatt's wife.

"We have a buyer for Java!" Corliss charged out of the main house, hands in the air as if she'd just scored a touchdown, startling the white filly.

She galloped around the enclosure.

Corliss didn't care. She kept running and shouting. "A man down in Texas has been looking for a horse of her temperament for his daughter."

"You sold Java? Not Rose?" The star of the stables.

Corliss came to a stop in front of Nash, brimming with happiness. "Rose is the better horse but we're asking more money for her. Duh." She greeted Wyatt and Harper. "Anyway, our buyer wants a real cuddler. You know, a horse that loves to be cuddled like a teddy bear. Apparently, his daughter is trying to get a college scholarship as a member of a rodeo team. She loves-loves-loves horses and needs a better competition ride."

Wyatt whistled. "This guy is willing to pay nearly forty thousand dollars for a horse because he wants his daughter to land a scholarship? I think he should just pay for the scholarship."

"That does seem odd," Harper seconded.

"Don't question why. It's a sale." Corliss nudged Wyatt's shoulder. "Two fillies sold. We're halfway there." Halfway to paying Big E back and making enough for our share of what we owe the bank.

"That's great news." Nash decided not to worry about their inability to place Rose. "Java will thrive with a loving rider." He'd have been crushed if Phil ended up with her.

They spent a few minutes marveling over their sales and Sneaker's origins.

Corliss faced Nash. "I need you to call all your cutting horse buddies and try to sell them on Rose and Nosey."

Nash shook his head. "I don't have time to make all those calls. My friends will want to catch up. It'll take all day." Maybe two.

"Don't argue. We need a sale." His sister was having none of his excuses. "Wyatt and I can pick up the slack, training-wise, just like we did yesterday."

Nash frowned, leaning against the side of the barn and easing the weight off his bad ankle. "This is an important training step today. I want to be in the saddle. I *need* to be in the saddle so I know what to work on over the next few days. And..." He cut Corliss off. "I don't think we can sell the last two horses until after the Holiday Showcase." It pained Nash to say it. "If Helen... You know. We may have to sell Rose and Nosey to Phil."

"Don't say that." Corliss held up a hand, walking away. "If it makes you happy, work the fillies with the cows today. We'll help tomorrow while you do those calls. And leave the contingency planning of the fallout from Phil's bet to me."

"What are you talking about?" Nash demanded.

But Corliss was already on the move and marching to the beat of her own drummer.

"THANKS FOR CALLING ME, ADELE." Helen stood inside the auction yard's office later that afternoon.

"Not at all. I'm grateful you could work me in." Adele came around the front counter and led Helen toward a side entrance. She was the gentlest of the Blackwell siblings. Soft blond hair and a heart of gold. On a table behind her was a collection of objects that Helen couldn't believe were up for sale—a bag of Christmas-colored yarn, a set of stone garden gnomes and a fancy sewing machine. "We had a mare come in today with the worst shoeing job I've seen in a long time. I need to take pictures of her to post online for the auction coming up."

"And you can't take pictures without her hooves in good condition." Helen followed Adele down a hallway and into a wing with individual stalls. "Has anyone handled her?" Because sometimes a bad shoeing job was a product of a misbehaving horse more than the farrier's skill.

"I led her in." Adele picked up a lead rope on the ground. She hung it on a wall hook before continuing down the aisle. "Whirligig was skittish, but she didn't misbehave."

They reached the last stall. The mare was a trim buckskin. Her main coat was a toasty tan. Her mane, tail and socks black. She shifted in her stall, half turning away from them. Being shown a horse's backside was never a good sign.

"Hey, sweetie," Helen crooned, trying to win the mare over. "We mean you no harm."

The mare shifted again, facing them but

keeping her distance. Her hooves were too long, and one had a worrisome, vertical crack.

"I don't think Whirligig likes us," Adele frowned.

Helen pondered the mare's name. Difficult horses often earned powerful names. "Do you remember Becky Trimble from high school?"

"Yes. But this isn't her horse." Adele looked confused.

"Becky was a bully." No two ways about it.

"And she had a way of wearing people down," Adele said thoughtfully. "Like she couldn't be one of the pack. She had to be alpha, lording it over the rest of us girls."

"Exactly. This mare is Becky, and no one's ever tried to make her behave. She thinks she's alpha." Helen was certain of it.

"But she has such kind, intelligent eyes." Adele pivoted to look at Helen squarely. "If this mare has a behavioral problem, I need to tell people. She has an excellent pedigree but maybe her attitude is why she's being sold so cheaply."

"It could be nothing but an aversion to getting shod." But Helen didn't think so. "Some horses just have to learn it's not that bad. She could be a dream to ride." Not that Helen was volunteering to find out.

"Whew. That's a relief. If you bring your

van around here, you can work on the other side of the double doors." Adele pointed to the nearby doors. "I have a lot to do, including preliminary research on Sneaker. Grady's going to help me. Sneaker might have been stolen or reported missing."

"Nash told me they caught her." Helen wondered if she should be worried for Luke's safety with a wild horse on the property. That boy had no fear.

"See you in a bit." Adele was already on the move.

"Okay. Harper should be here soon. She wanted to take pictures while I work." Too bad Helen was feeling Whirligig wasn't going to be the easiest cover model for Wyatt's wife.

Twenty minutes later, Helen had shed her cowboy hat and jacket. She'd put her working chaps on, set up her anvil and fired up the forge outside the barn door.

"I'm here." Harper burst into the breezeway from the office, carrying two portable lights on tripods. "I won't take long to set up. I promise."

"Okay." Helen led Whirligig out of her stall.

The mare pranced sideways.

"No." Helen gave her halter a little correction, directing her to walk straight. And when she complied, she praised her with several pats and kind words. "Come on, now. You need to prove to me that you're no Becky."

Whirligig eyed Harper, who was fiddling with a tripod light ten feet away. Harper wore her fringed blue leather jacket, blue jeans and knee-high, high-heeled black city boots.

"Pay no attention to the photographer, sweetie." Helen used cross ties to secure the mare to both sides of the barn's breezeway.

The cross ties kept her head in place. But the mare was a fidgeter. Whirligig shifted her rear quarters to one side and then the other, testing the boundaries of movement.

"Do all horses move around like that?" Harper looked nervous.

"No. Whirligig is like a kid testing her limits in the hairdresser's chair." Helen tried to settle the mare with a soft tone and reassuring touches.

"I need to put the other light behind her."

"Maybe we shouldn't." No way was Helen risking Harper's safety with a strange horse. "You can get all you need from the front, right?"

"If need be." Harper sounded relieved.

"Let's see if we can't make your hooves pretty again, sweetie." Helen ran a hand across the mare's smooth neck, around her powerful chest, and then down her leg.

The mare dutifully shifted her weight and allowed Helen to pick up her front hoof.

Her hooves were clean, but Helen fussed with them anyway, wanting to comfort the mare that being handled was no big deal.

Harper snapped some pictures and for a while, Helen believed she'd misjudged the mare.

That is, until Whirligig nibbled the back of her hoodie.

"Hey." Helen flinched, keeping a hold of the mare's hoof.

"Did that hurt?"

"No. But it surprised me." Helen set Whirligig's hoof down.

The mare had her head turned away from Helen, as if shielding herself from an anticipated swat for misbehaving.

Helen's heart immediately went out to her. She spent a few minutes loving on her head and neck until she sensed the mare relax. "That's much better, isn't it? I should have given you that introduction first. Apologies."

She bent and lifted Whirligig's front hoof.

And was nipped, again. This time, her teeth caught Helen's short braid and gave it a painful tug.

"That wasn't nice," Helen said gently. She resumed her tender touches, glancing at Harper. "I'm going to need an assist in here. Can you stand by her head and give her some loving?"

"Oh, but..." Harper looked down at what she was wearing and then flashed her fingernails at Helen, which were acrylic and painted a cheerful sky blue. "I'm not exactly dressed or groomed for this." Nor did she seem to have the courage, something Helen wasn't going to fault her for.

"I suppose I can call Adele." Helen tried to remember where she had put her phone. "It's just that she's really busy."

Harper frowned. "No. Don't do that. If you can overcome your fears and ride a horse, I can help you calm a horse?" She said it like a question, and she eyed Whirligig nervously. "If we could just pause for a couple of photo opportunities..."

"No worries." That was code for, *That's an inconvenience but I'll make do.*

"Wyatt is going to be impressed that you helped me," Helen said instead.

"I'm trying to fit in. Ranch life can be outside of my comfort zone." Harper held up one arm, causing the blue leather fringe to sway near Whirligig's nose.

Thankfully, the mare didn't spook. In fact,

she heaved a sigh of relief as Harper scratched beneath her dark forelock.

Helen didn't waste time getting back to work.

As if catching a wild horse and recovering from a sprained ankle wasn't enough to slow him down, Nash's day was further interrupted by a school emergency.

Apparently, when neither he nor Helen had answered their phones, the school had called Corliss because his five-year-old had been in a fight and was being sent home. His sister had run to the barn to tell him.

Nash entered the school office with a chip on his shoulder. There was no way Luke had started a fight. His kid got along with everybody. Whoever was picking on Luke wasn't going to see a Blackwell smile today. Or a limp. He modulated his stride, slowing down and gritting his teeth to show no weakness.

The office was empty except for Luke and the staff, a pair of young ladies he'd never met and hadn't heard of.

"Daddy!" A teary-eyed Luke hopped off a visitor's chair and ran into his arms.

"It's okay." He hugged Luke with every ounce of strength he had. "Daddy's here and everything's okay."

One of the school secretaries ushered them into the principal's office. It might have been Nash's imagination, but the secretary seemed apologetic.

Mrs. Carsden, the principal, was relatively new. He may not have remembered her name, but Nash knew that much. She was about his age and looked tougher than a prison warden.

"There was an altercation during afternoon recess." The principal got right down to business. "Luke pushed another student."

Luke's little lip was trembling.

Something wasn't right here. "You're saying my kid started a fight?" Because that was hard to believe.

"She kicked me!" Luke blurted, earning a disapproving stare from Mrs. Carsden.

"Who kicked you?" Nash brought Luke from the other guest chair to his lap, trying to console him. "Not the principal." Even though it felt like there was no love lost between them.

"It was Wendy." Luke thrust his chin out. "She kicked me again, so I pushed her away."

"She kicked you again? Has she done this before?" Nash sent the principal a dark look. "What kind of place are you running here?"

"Yes, Daddy. I got a bruise the last time."

"Still, violence is never the answer," the principal said crisply.

Nash couldn't believe it. She was practically defending little Wendy. "My son is being bullied and finally stands up for himself and that's all you have to say?"

Mrs. Carsden sniffed dismissively. "The procedure is to report events to a teacher. He should have told Ms. Lamb."

Nash leaned in to look Luke in the eye.

"I did tell her, Daddy. But Wendy didn't listen." Oh, Luke was hot. Angry, even, talking fast and loud. "And everybody's been telling me I shouldn't take it no more."

"Everybody?" Nash asked carefully, mostly because this was the first time he'd heard of the misbehaving Miss Wendy. "Who is everybody?"

"My friends. Aunt Corliss. Uncle Wyatt. Great Gran. Big E. Like I said. Everybody."

Everyone but Nash. What kind of father was he that he hadn't even known his kid was being bullied?

Only the kind of father who was working his fingers to the bone trying to save the family ranch. Not that his work was any excuse for being out of touch with his son.

Nash's stomach did a slow, sickening barrel roll. He drew an equally slow, deep breath.

"Mr. Blackwell," the principal began. "You should think about the example you set for your son."

Nash nodded.

"You don't want to raise a child who can't handle hard situations calmly."

Nash nodded, still busy silently berating himself as a dad.

"If we aren't able to negotiate a truce with someone we have a dislike for, the strife of the relationship might get put on others unfairly."

Nash blinked. "I'm sorry. I don't follow. We're talking about kindergartners?" Weren't they? It didn't sound like it. It sounded like she was talking about him.

"You know what I mean." Mrs. Carsden gave Nash a disapproving smile, as if he'd come into her office smelling of hard work and horses and she considered that inappropriate. "You had an argument with another rancher in town and chose your wife to fight your battles."

Nash's jaw dropped open. "Uh… *Ex-wife*. And she agreed to do it. Not that it's any of your business, Mrs…." Her name escaped his fired-up brain even though her placard sat on the desk in front of him.

"Mrs. Wendy's Mom," Luke said miserably.

"What?" Nash suddenly realized there was a framed picture behind the principal of an innocent looking little redhead of about Luke's age. "You're Shin-Kicking Wendy's mother?"

The principal got to her feet. "Luke Blackwell is being suspended for a day for fighting."

"Hold up." Nash stood, slinging Luke to his hip and ignoring the shooting pain in his ankle. "What happened to Shin-Kicking Wendy? Is she suspended too?"

"No—no." The principal laughed. Triumph wasn't a good look on her. "Wendy has apologized and is returning to school tomorrow."

"With her cowboy boots," Luke muttered. He swung his feet on either side of Nash's waist. One foot swung precariously close to Mrs. Carsden's nameplate.

"I get it now," Nash said in a voice that came from a dark place where protective instincts were triggered and didn't always result in friendly outcomes. "You don't want a blemish on your little girl's school record. But see, that's where you've gone wrong because we'll be speaking to the sheriff!"

Luke gasped, although Nash was fairly certain his son had no idea what he was talking about.

The principal looked uncomfortable.

Carsden. The name was suddenly ringing a bell.

"I suppose we should have expected this, seeing as how you've already sold out to Xavier Howard." Nash headed for the door. "Let this be a lesson to you, son. Blackwells don't back down from bullies."

CHAPTER SEVENTEEN

If Nash had been expecting sympathy from Helen for the bumps in his day, those thoughts were vanquished by the sight of her when she arrived home long past the dinner hour.

Helen walked into the barn at the Flying Spur doing her best Gran impression, moving as if each step was painful.

"Rough day at the office?" He limped to her side, hooking an arm around her waist. "Same here."

"I'm beat. Is there a full moon or something that makes every horse fidgety or cranky?" Helen sank down on a bench. "Can we skip training tonight?"

Nash sat next to her, curbing his impulse to argue or to launch into the whole Shin-Kicking Wendy ordeal. "Can you give me just a couple of times around the arena?" He felt guilty for asking. "There are limited opportunities to practice."

Instead of answering, she rested her head on his shoulder, which knocked her straw cowboy hat to the ground. Neither one of them moved to retrieve it.

"Did you hear Corliss bought a horse from Adele?" Helen extended one leg, groaning as if it were stiff. "She came by the auction yard when Harper and I were there."

"Yeah. I asked her where she got the money and she told me she had investors." Like they needed any more debt. "Corliss wants me to train her. I suppose we have room since Queenie's gone and Java is shipping out tomorrow for Texas."

Helen extended her other leg. "And you? Will you have time to train Whirligig? She's a bit high maintenance. But I think with time and love, she'll stop nipping."

"I have no choice." Nash stood, extending a hand to Helen, filing Whirligig's bad habit away for later. "She went along with my bet. I owe her."

"Right." Helen put her hand in his. "Pull me up?"

He hauled her to her feet. "You don't have to do any heavy lifting. Just ride."

"Can I close my eyes?"

"No."

"Can I shower and eat first?"

"No. You look like you'll go straight from the shower to the bed." Nash wondered how she'd managed being a working mom the past two years. It must have been a struggle. And he hadn't been much help, hiding out on the Flying Spur and taking part in Luke's life when called upon to do so.

Groaning, Helen walked forward. "Please tell me I'm riding Beanie."

"It's Rose." He pointed to where she stood waiting by the arena barn doors.

"Can I ride with you, Mama?" Luke burst into the barn from the arena end, skipping past Rose. "Great Gran says I need to be a good rider if I'm to train Sneaker. I need all the practice I can get."

At Luke's appearance, Helen put a facade in place, standing tall and smiling to greet their son, another strong example of good parenting that put Nash to shame. "Do you want to steer or ride shotgun?"

"I'm in front." He scampered into the tack room, presumably for a helmet.

"Should we be building his hopes up like that?" Helen asked. "He's only five."

"He can do it." Gran stood in the doorway Luke had just dashed through, her nose in the air. They still hadn't mended fences. "I was working with horses when I was his age."

"Back in the olden days before electricity and safety guidelines." Nash was only half joking.

"You should say the Golden Days." Gran moved to greet Rose, stroking the black filly's long, elegant neck. "Don't be a hypocrite, Nash. You were working horses when you were Luke's age."

"Also the olden days," Nash said firmly, easing Helen closer to her ride. "The sun's gone down and you've eaten dinner, Gran. Shouldn't you be inside knitting or getting ready for bed?"

"I still run this ranch," Gran ground out. "And you'd best remember it."

"You ran out of *or elses* a long time ago." Nash handed Helen her riding helmet, which he'd left on a bench near Rose. Together, they led Rose out the barn doors and into the arena.

Several other Blackwells were waiting for them at the arena fence—Wyatt, Corliss, Big E, Levi. Even the ranch dogs had assembled.

"Did you sell tickets or something?" Nash frowned at his family.

"Don't mind us." Corliss grinned. "We're just here to check on our investment and provide moral support. Specifically, we're here to cheer on Helen's successes."

"Small as they may be." Helen climbed into the saddle, paling as was her habit.

"Aw. I thought I was driving." Luke ran up to Nash, mashing his helmet on his head and clicking the strap buckle in place. "Why do I have to sit in back? I can ride Rose by myself. She lets me get on in her stall."

Rose shifted around, lowering her head to sniff Luke, who giggled and said, "I can't wait to ride Sneaker."

"Can we not talk about that now?" Helen clung to the saddle horn. "You'll have to wait a long time to ride Sneaker."

"Nah," Luke said as Nash set him behind Helen.

"Wild horses aren't as hard to tame as you think." Gran settled in a folding chair next to the rail. "Isn't that right, Nash?"

Nash refused to lend support to his grandmother's whims. If she had her way, he'd start working with Sneaker tomorrow. And they didn't even know if they could keep her.

"You can halter break a wild horse in an hour," Gran went on.

"With the right horse," Nash clarified, unable to resist. He glanced up at Helen, whose color was returning to her face. "Do you want me to hold the reins? Or can you walk her alone?"

Helen's gaze darted toward their audience. "I can handle it but...can you walk beside us?"

"Always." He gestured for her to begin her circuit.

"Sneaker is smart," Luke weighed in, as one-track minded as his great-grandmother. "I'm five and I'll be riding her by Christmas."

Helen made a strangled noise.

"I'm a little busy with the other horses, Luke," Nash told him quietly, hoping his grandmother couldn't hear. "I can't make any promises."

The more they walked, the fainter Gran's ramble became. It was time to tell Helen about Luke's school drama.

"Just so you know…" Nash quickly recounted the events of the afternoon. "Were you aware Wendy was getting a free pass to bully kids?"

"Just me," Luke said morosely as they reached the far end of the arena.

Helen reached behind her to pat Luke's leg. "It's been a sticky situation the past month or so."

"It won't be sticky anymore," Nash said with more than a little pride. "We filed a report with Grady."

"He took pictures of my leg and everything," Luke confirmed, sounded thrilled by it all. "I earned a gold sheriff's badge." A sticker, but he'd been thrilled all the same.

"There's an experience I never aspired to give my child." Helen shook her head.

"It was all well-handled," Nash assured her. "Grady was very sensitive about the whole thing."

"Cool," Helen said unenthusiastically.

Rose tossed her head as they reached the opposite straight side.

Helen gasped and clutched the saddle horn with both hands, dropping her reins. She drew a shuddering breath and picked them back up before Nash could. "I'm good. Nobody panic."

"You're so brave, Mama." Luke hugged her. "I love you."

"I love you more." She patted his arm and spared Nash a small smile.

They walked nearer to where the rest of the family was gathered. Corliss was giving Gran a look of startled disbelief.

"Nash has been doing a fine job helping Helen get comfortable with riding again," Gran said as if she'd been holding court the entire time they'd been gone. "Look at her progress and just try to argue with me. Luke can be riding Sneaker by the Showcase."

"Sweet!" Luke cried, raising his arms in the air.

"That's not happening," Helen murmured but not loud enough for Gran to hear.

"Okay, I'll say what everyone is thinking." Wyatt tipped his hat back and knelt near Gran. "No one has time for what you're talking about. That horse will have to wait her turn."

"And no one wants to invest time in a horse

that we don't know we can keep," Corliss added. "Give Grady and Adele a chance to investigate."

"Pshaw. She's ours," Gran said. "I'm not too old to show Luke how to train Sneaker and my days are blessedly free."

And the crowd, as they say, went a little wild, resulting in Gran getting bent out of shape and shaking her finger at everyone, accusing them of thinking she was ready to be put out to pasture.

"CAN'T WE RIDE TOGETHER?" Sitting on Beanie, Helen looked nervously over the Blackwell yearlings in the arena and then back to Nash. "I'm a little nervous."

Who was she kidding? She was terrified.

It was Sunday morning and Nash wanted Helen to ride Beanie alone through the midst of those brown cows. Sure, they were kind-looking cows when they were out in a pasture. But up close?

They had the look of zombie cows of the apocalypse. She shivered.

"You're doing great." Nash reached for her hand, giving it a squeeze. "You can't ride double when you cut cows from a herd. Beanie will be making quick turns. Too much weight and he could injure himself."

"Forget it then. I'm a big girl." She patted

Beanie's neck, thinking that the Clydesdale who broke her toe would be a good double-riding cutting horse. But he'd probably also be too slow for Nash.

"I'll ride with Mama." Luke scrambled between the pipe rails and joined them. He'd been hanging out with the Blackwells, who'd not only brought chairs, but bowls of popcorn. "I'm good at cutting, Mama. I ride with Daddy sometimes 'cuz I'm so small."

"TMI," Helen murmured, not wanting to think about her baby riding like that.

"What do you think?" Nash studied Helen's facc.

"It won't be too much for Beanie?"

"Luke is no burden," Nash reassured her.

"Then Luke can be my security blanket."

Nash sent Luke to get a riding helmet from the tack room. "Do you need me to make your fan club disappear?" He nodded toward his family.

Helen shrugged. "You can't make the audience at the Showcase disappear, so I better get used to it."

In no time, Luke was back and ready to go. Nash lifted him to sit in her lap.

Helen clutched her baby tight.

"Too much, Mama," Luke said in a strained voice.

"Okay. Okay." She loosened her grip enough that Luke didn't complain.

Nash mounted Whirligig, the fidgety, mare Corliss had purchased. The dun heeded his every command.

Traitor. She didn't nip him once.

Nash walked his mount to the other side of the small herd to keep them from scattering. "Walk Beanie through the cows, honey."

Helen guided Beanie forward. When the gelding realized they were going in, it was as if he was a completely different horse. He cocked his ears and snorted, head high, gathering himself like a sprinter before he took his mark at the starting line. And then he strutted forward, like he was used to being large and in charge, unafraid of zombie apocalypse bovines.

Nash clucked, urging Whirligig forward. "As soon as a cow makes eye contact with you, Helen, go for it."

As if on cue, a cow lifted its brown face and looked at Helen. Or Beanie. She couldn't tell.

"That one, Mama," Luke said.

She used the reins to point Beanie in that direction, guiding him into the cluster of cows.

The cow ducked its head, shying away from eye contact and the now approaching Beanie. Helen let Beanie track him down and separate him from the herd, lowering the reins and letting the gelding do all the work.

The cow made a run for the open arena.

Beanie leaped forward and in a few long strides, cut him off. The cow gave the horse a sideways glance. Yes, the horse. Helen was not the threat here.

"Are you screaming, Mama?" Luke half turned to look at her.

"Yes. Turn around. And hang on." Because Beanie was gathering beneath her, preparing to explode after the cow when it moved.

Beanie and the cow danced. Back and forth. Helen hung on. Luke whooped. The dance continued. Right and left. So many times that Helen's teeth were on edge. But she held onto her precious little boy.

And by luck or skill, they both managed to stay in the saddle when Beanie came to a stop and blew out a breath.

From his seat in her lap, Luke took a little bow. The Blackwells hooted and applauded.

Nash rode over, grinning as if she'd won a gold medal. "You were awesome. How did it feel?"

"Like I was in Dorothy's house being spun in the twister." Helen didn't care if Nash got her *Wizard of Oz* reference or not.

"It was so fun, Daddy." Luke reached both

hands to the sky. "Let's do that again!" He kicked his feet as if urging Beanie to take off.

Oh, no. Helen held on tight to the reins.

"But first, let Mama catch her breath." Nash brought his horse closer, peering at Helen. "You did great. This time, when you pick out a cow, hang on to those reins until you push the cow out of the herd. Don't let Beanie take over too soon. Okay?"

Helen nodded. "I was flung around like a rag doll." How could she not admit it?

"She was." Luke giggled.

"Yeah, but it was your first time. You'll get it." Nash's gaze dropped to her lips.

Helen licked her lips and sat up taller. "Are you promising me a reward right now?"

He grinned. "You betcha."

Be still my heart.

"Go get 'em, Helen," Corliss called.

"You're my hero," Harper shouted.

The Blackwells began cheering. And maybe their support helped. Helen didn't give up.

No, she hung on. For five more cows. A few times, Beanie dropped low, crouching like a dog getting ready to chase after a much-loved toy. Helen bet gymnasts couldn't do the acrobatics she was doing to stay on that horse. But no way was she going to fall off and take her little boy with her.

They couldn't catch the last cow. It was crafty.

"Stop." Nash called it. He was frowning.

"Sorry." Helen croaked. She was ready to take the blame.

"It's not your fault." Nash gestured toward the herd before dismounting. "They learn. Hence the need for cows who've never been in a cutting competition before."

Of which she was certain she'd heard him complain on more than one occasion that they had none.

"That was so much fun," Luke swung his leg over the saddle horn and dropped into Nash's arms. "Wasn't it, Mama?"

"Don't I get points deducted for not looking confident?"

"Yeah. But we'll get there. We still have a week." Nash grabbed hold of Beanie's reins.

"A week." She scoffed. Helen dropped out of the saddle and hung on to Beanie's saddle horn. Her legs were wobbly, and she felt nauseous.

"Are you all right?" Nash placed a hand on her back.

"I'm seasick." Meanwhile, her son was skipping around the arena, having the best of times.

Nash leaned in, speaking softly, "I know the cows are getting craftier, but it might be a good idea to take a break and come back for another round."

She shook her head. Vehemently.

"Helen…"

"No. Tomorrow. I'll do it again tomorrow." She buried her face in Beanie's neck and willed herself to follow through.

CHAPTER EIGHTEEN

"TWO STEPS FORWARD..." Nash rinsed his empty coffee cup at seven o'clock on Monday morning.

It was a new week and he had new training plans for his horses and Helen. He went to put his boots on.

"Where are you going so early?" Helen emerged from the bedroom, looking rested and kissably rumpled and making Nash feel every kink in his back from sleeping on the couch.

Because they were taking things day by day, they weren't fully committed to a reconciliation. It was killing him.

Helen yawned again. "And why aren't you encouraging me to get out of bed to train?"

"We need fresh cows." Because the ones they were using were only getting smarter. And since they had no money to buy cows, he was going to have to get creative.

"Come here." Helen crooked her finger. "Let me give you a proper kiss. For luck."

"Gladly." He took her into his arms and kissed her thoroughly. And when he was finished, he told her, "You were a rock star yesterday on horseback."

"Yeah." She rolled her eyes. "A regular champion."

"Hey." He cradled her face in his hands. "Look at the totality of your work. You've gone from being a pedestrian to being an equestrian."

She rolled her eyes a second time. "So cheesy."

"But you love me." He headed for the door, a man on a mission.

He called Adele as he drove toward the main road and explained the situation.

"What? You think I have cows available to let you *borrow*?" Adele sounded a bit frantic. "Quinn, we don't eat the dog's kibble."

Nash grimaced. He'd called at a bad time. "Uh, I was hoping you had a direct line to a rancher with heifers, yes. And yes, I was hoping they'd be willing to help the fight to save Eagle Springs. Or perhaps accept my voucher for future horse training as payment?"

"No dice." Adele huffed. "Ivy, did you just use that planter as a..." She practically growled in frustration. "Nash, it's Monday morning. Do I really need to explain this to you?"

"Yes. Please."

"Okay. Here we go." Dishes clashed together

as if being dropped into the kitchen sink. "The stock I receive arrives a day or so before auction, sometimes even the day of. And if they arrive early—which none have—it would cost me to transport them to the Flying Spur and then transport them back. And what if they were injured? I'd have to pay the veterinarian bill or cover a loss in reserve price, if the stock value went down because of that injury."

"Right. It was a long shot. Have a good day." Nash felt like crud just for asking. He drove to Levi's house next. Levi lived with Summer and Isla in a large, renovated barn. He wasn't surprised to find him up and moving, and had no qualms knocking and walking in since that's how they rolled with each other. "I need to borrow some fresh cows."

Levi was in his kitchen drinking coffee. "Nobody *borrows* cows. Forget the liability. It's a logistical nightmare. And I know about logistical nightmares because I run the rodeo grounds, which I rent out to all kinds of organizations, not just rodeos."

"You're tightly wound this morning." Nash slid onto a bar stool and accepted the mug of coffee Levi provided him.

"I could say the same about you." Levi held up a hand. "Isla, I need you downstairs and eating in five minutes."

Nash was gaining a new appreciation for the smoothness with which Helen got Luke out the door each morning. "You saw those cows last night. You know what I need and why I need them."

Levi shook his head. "Other than asking a rancher if you can trailer your horses onto their grazing land for practice, you are asking the impossible."

"I realize loaning cows isn't a thing," Nash said succinctly. "But maybe somebody could. What a novelty. Remember when we used to have to watch TV in real time? Back then, no one ever thought you'd be able to watch whichever shows you wanted to whenever you fancied."

Levi made a show of sipping his coffee. "I might be able to hook you up with a rodeo stockman, but he isn't scheduled to show up until the day before the Holiday Showcase."

"Friday. Friday?" Nash shook his head. "Surely, the retired bull rider is friends with a local rancher who hasn't sold out to Xavier Howard. I need young, rookie cows."

"What you need is a good long look in the mirror." Levi set his mug down hard. "How could you wager our heritage on Helen? We all know she has no chance of placing."

"Don't say that." Nash noticed Levi had a

bottle of whiskey on the far shelf. He looked away. "Can't anyone just accept the fact that I've backed myself into a corner and help me? And Helen?"

It struck him then… It struck him that he'd been feeling the pressure to come through for the family for months, more so than Corliss, who'd made the arrangement to buy the four blue-blooded fillies. It was on Nash's shoulders to make them as perfect as possible, as valuable and marketable as possible. And pulling Helen into this mess had taken some of the pressure off him.

He ran a hand through his hair and realized he'd left his cowboy hat, which was practically a part of him, at home. "I admit it. Accepting the bet was a jerk move. But I can't take it back any more than you can erase your mistakes." Like Levi's disastrous first marriage. "You think I don't die a little to see the fear on her face every day?" Twice a day. "Or to hear the woman I love question herself while she tries to master a skill we've honed over decades of work and practice?" Nash swore. "I know exactly what kind of man I am, Levi. I could lose it all on Saturday. Not just our family ranch, but my family's respect—" if he hadn't already "—and the love of my life." Why would Helen stay with a man who put her through the wringer like he was?

Nash stood. "So yeah. I'm sorry I panicked and made everything worse. I came here this morning because out of all of us, you are the calmest in an emergency." And this was a five-alarm fire, for sure. "But just… Forget I asked." He'd figure something out, even if he and Helen had to burn a day traveling to someone else's ranch.

Levi hadn't moved a muscle while Nash had been speaking. Now, he blinked. "I… didn't know… I'm sorry. Sure. Okay. What do you need?"

"Fresh cows." Why was this so hard to understand?

Levi nodded briskly. "Okay, I'm on it. I can't promise you anything."

"But you'll try. Thank you." Nash came around the kitchen counter and took him by the shoulders. "You are currently one of two of my favorite brothers." He turned and headed for the door, determined to continue his search, at least for another hour.

"Hey! You only have two brothers," Levi called after him.

"That's why you're so special."

ON TUESDAY, AFTER WORK, Helen and Luke met Gwen, her husband Stan, Daphne and Caleb for dinner at Sweetwater Kitchen, ostensibly to make final preparations for the craft fair scheduled for Saturday morning. But Gwen was an organizational queen and had everything covered.

While Stan took the boys to the bathroom to wash up, Gwen took Daphne out of her carrier and gave Helen the third degree. “How are you feeling about this competition?”

“Actually, I might survive.” She still had no delusions of hero-hood. “But I’m also hoping for a Christmas miracle to save the town.”

“You bought lottery tickets?” Gwen settled Daphne on her shoulder.

“Better.” Helen grinned. “I asked my state representative if there were any endangered species in Eagle Springs.”

Gwen laughed.

Luke ran past their table.

“Hey.” Helen turned, curious as to where he was going.

Luke stopped at a corner booth where the elderly cowboy she’d given a ride to a few nights back was dining with someone whose back was to Helen. Although she couldn’t hear what was being said, Luke seemed to be chattering nonstop.

Helen got up and hurried after him.

“And Sneaker is going to be the best horse ever because I come from a long line of horsemen.” Luke thumbed his chest.

"Hi." Helen put her hands on Luke's shoulders. "It's nice to see you again. I've been wondering if you were okay after I dropped you off the other night."

The old cowboy gave Helen a naggingly familiar smile. "I was fine. Thanks for asking. It's hard to ruffle an old bird like me."

Helen turned to his dining companion, smile at the ready and an apology for interrupting on her lips. Only then did she realize it was Xavier Howard sitting there, the man circulating through town making buy-out offers.

Her smile faded.

Xavier looked her up and down, laughing a little and not in a polite way. "You're the Blackwell competing in the Holiday Showcase."

"I am." Helen got her back up. She took Luke's hand. "Not by choice, as you've probably heard."

"Then why do it?" the elderly cowboy asked, looking at her with sincere interest.

If he hadn't been the one to ask, she wouldn't have answered. "This is where my roots are. In the end, even though I'm not the most qualified, I'm the one who was called upon to do it. My father once told me to live without regrets. And I'd regret it if I didn't try."

"Mister." Luke tugged on the old cowboy's blue-checked shirt sleeve. "My Mama gets better every day. That's what Gran says we have to do. Get better at riding. Get better at math. Get better at…" His gaze caught on Wendy Carsden sitting in the next booth over with her mother. "…being nice to folk even when they aren't nice to you."

Helen nearly burst with pride. "We'll let you gentlemen finish your meal." She led Luke back to their table.

"Do you know who that is?" Gwen's husband asked Helen just before she and Luke landed on the booth cushion. Stan leaned forward and whispered as if it was a big secret.

"Yeah." Helen smirked. "Xavier Howard and some cowboy."

Stan remained practically draped over the table. "That cowboy is *Frank Wesson*."

"Frank… Denny's jilted Frank?" Nash's granduncle. The things about him that Helen found familiar clicked into place. His intelligent brown eyes. The strong chin. That almost-lopsided smile. That quiet steadiness.

"Mama?" Luke sat on the outside of the booth, not across from Caleb and not near the cup of crayons and small coloring pages.

Absently, Helen lifted Luke from one side of her to the other.

"Maybe you shouldn't be talking to him,"

Gwen said, ducking her head as well, which was awkward given she held the baby.

People were staring. And Helen wasn't done processing it all.

"Keep your heads up, both of you. It's just Frank Wesson, a lonely old cowboy." She didn't know why she described him that way, but it felt right.

"An evil, lonely old cowboy," Stan said, sitting up slowly.

Helen glanced over her shoulder at Frank, not so sure about the evil part.

"HERE WE GO." Nash tried to sound upbeat. It was Wednesday morning and none of his contacts had found him fresh cows.

He led Beanie into the arena and over to Helen. She stood in the middle of the arena bundled up against the pre-dawn cold.

She turned as they drew near. "You have speakers. I want to listen to Christmas music."

"Why?"

She smiled brightly. "Because you can't be sad or stressed when you sing Christmas songs. And maybe if I sing, I won't be so scared."

Nash was humbled. If there hadn't been a job to do, he would have fallen on his knees and begged for her forgiveness. As it was, his steps felt heavy as he closed the distance to her.

Her smile lost a bit of its shine. “Is there a problem?”

Hold it together, man.

Nash handed her the reins, shaking his head. “I don’t think we’ve ever turned the sound system on.” He couldn’t really remember who had installed it or when.

“All the more reason to use it at least once until…” She caught herself before she said what they both knew was coming—the sinking of the Flying Spur.

“I’ll be back in a few.” It took Nash several minutes to move things in the tack room so he could reach the radio unit. More minutes were required to find a station playing Christmas music and adjust the volume loud enough for Helen to be distracted but not loud enough to spook the horses.

A boy band popular during Nash’s youth sang about the love they’d lost since last Christmas. Their harmonies filled the barn, the arena, probably the entire ranch. The topic was depressing. Where was Frosty? Where was Santa kissing Mommy? Where was Rudolph and his shiny red nose? This song was sure to get the entire ranch up and over to the arena to investigate the tragedy.

Thankfully, the boys wrapped it up and that

candy cane song Luke was obsessed with began playing.

Nash came striding back to the arena only to find Helen singing off-key and riding Beanie slowly back and forth in front of the motionless mechanical cow. He took a moment to appreciate her.

He loved this woman. He loved how she lived without caring much what other people thought of her. He loved her drive and grit. He loved that she wasn't perfect—neither was he. But he was in awe of her courage. What a blessing she was to him and the Blackwell family.

"Music?" Corliss joined him, carrying a mug of tea and bringing the two dogs with her. "What's the occasion?"

"No occasion." Just Helen and Nash wanting to make memories and live life to the fullest here on the ranch while they had the chance. When "Jingle Bell Rock" came on, he sang along.

"What's come over you?" Corliss gave him a suspicious once-over.

"I could ask you the same thing." Nash nudged her. "What happened to the grouchy Corliss that was huffing around the ranch all last week?"

She raised her chin haughtily. "I'm working on something that is none of your business.

And I don't mean the baby." She turned and left him, calling Bow and Arrow to her side.

Nash sang some more, content to watch Helen ride Beanie. She may have been adamant that he wasn't going to give her the joy of riding, but she looked content now.

"Someone's got the Christmas spirit." Gran appeared next to him. "Always liked that about Helen."

"You know—" Big E leaned on a rail nearby "—she just might have a chance."

Nash could hope. Because if he thought about it logically, the way a cutting horse judge would, he knew she didn't stand a shot.

Wyatt ambled over, carrying a coffee mug and looking as if he'd just rolled out of bed. "Is this what we've come to? Early morning singalongs and cheering on rookie cutting horse contestants?"

"Yes," they all told him.

"Okay. Just checking." He drank his coffee and watched Helen.

Gran took hold of Nash's arm. "I'm sorry I upset you."

"It's okay," Nash said gruffly, catching Helen's off-key warble before it drifted off on the wind.

"You know. It's Cal." Gran frowned when they all looked at her sharply. "I mean, the spirit of Cal. Bringing us a wild horse for the first time in years. Having his horse training principles applied to helping Helen overcome her fears."

Big E looked stricken.

"When are you going to put Helen on Rose?" Wyatt asked with a look to Nash that said, *"I don't want to have this conversation again."* He cleared his throat. "And give her live cows?"

"Soon." Nash didn't like to think about how few days they had left.

"What's going on?" Luke stumbled up wearing his dinosaur pajamas, a jacket, his cowboy boots and hat. He rubbed his eyes and then extended his hands to Nash in a silent request to be picked up. "There's never music out here."

"There will be more music," Nash promised. Because that was the key to putting Helen at ease.

That, and kisses.

CHAPTER NINETEEN

"I KNOW I should be thankful for my loyal fan base." Talking to herself, Helen rode Rose across the arena on Wednesday night. Christmas music filled the cold air.

But unlike this morning, Helen wasn't at ease. The closer the Showcase, the more pressure she felt to perform. Maybe she was feeling the weight of Blackwell expectations.

She glanced over at her Blackwell audience. It was larger than ever. Tonight, they'd brought pizza.

Rose whinnied.

"They bother you, too, don't they, girl." Helen gave the black filly a pat on the neck.

"You know, I do tell them it's not cool to come watch." Nash rode Beanie a few feet away from her. It was odd seeing him on the brown gelding.

"It's okay. I understand." And she did. But tonight felt different. She wanted to blame it on the series of instrumental Christmas music the DJ kept playing. But she suspected her problem was with Rose.

Rose was an equine goddess. The black filly was young and well-bred with very long legs. Those long legs made her a fast walker. Those long legs and her good breeding made her a smooth trotter. She was a fast cutting horse, too. And that thought worried Helen more than anything.

But she wasn't trying to think about what lay ahead. Instead, she tried to reconcile black silky ears in her line of vision instead of brown. And how she'd needed an assist to climb in the saddle. The ground was much farther away than when she rode Beanie. And Rose was a talker, keeping up a running commentary—huffs and raspberries and whinnies—rather than just enjoying the slow pace of the ride the way Helen did.

Having Nash and Beanie nearby was comforting as she followed the arching fence line at the far end of the arena and headed back toward the Blackwells.

Rose blew a raspberry.

Further along, Luke scaled the top of the fencing, agile as a barn cat. Not to be outdone, Olivia scrambled up next to him. And then they were joined by Levi's daughter, Isla. Adele's twins poked their heads through the bottom rungs.

"I'll tell them to leave if you like." Nash was

being extraordinarily nice today. The closer they came to the competition, the nicer he seemed to be. It was as if he was walking on pins and needles around her. "Or we could stand in the middle of the arena and bore them to death."

Helen chuckled. "They'd go off to play video games."

"Or put their little ones to bed." He smiled gently as they approached the middle of the arena. "Last chance to make them disappear."

"Don't waste your breath. You Blackwells don't listen very well."

"You're a Blackwell, too, Helen." Nash pointed to her legs. "Be an active rider. Use your legs and your rein."

"I know. I know." But everything she did felt as if she was doing it in slow motion. She moved the hand holding the reins slightly to the left and Rose practically made a hard left. She moved her hand to the right and returned to her line a few feet away from the rail.

Rose whinnied, sounding like she was antsy to do something more than walk around the track. She walked faster. Maybe because she was antsy. Maybe because Luke was calling her.

"How are you feeling? Comfortable? Confident?" Nash brought Beanie into a trot to keep up with Rose. "You look like a Blackwell, honey."

"That's not true and you know it." Helen swallowed thickly. "Honestly, my mind was drifting toward the competition." And riding on Rose. And her insides were turning.

"You got this, Helen," Corliss called. She'd bought another quarter horse today, a big-boned chestnut that she claimed she'd picked up for a song.

"Corliss is right." Nash smiled at Helen in that bittersweet way of his, as if he was afraid to lose her. "You've got this. And just as soon as a sing-along song comes on, we'll put Rose through her paces with the mechanical cow."

Helen felt ill.

And when "Rockin' Around the Christmas Tree" came on, she felt no better.

But Nash was singing, so how could she not join in?

She got so lost in the lyrics that she didn't realize Nash had turned on the mechanical cow until Rose raised her head and whinnied. Helen tried to smile. She probably failed miserably.

Nash brought Beanie next to her, turning the machinery back off and tucking the remote in his pocket. "Can I tell you a secret?"

"Please do."

He reached across the distance between the two horses to take her hand. "I still think you're the strongest woman I know and…"

I love you.

She waited to hear him say the words. And waited.

His smile dimmed. "You should always sing, Helen. Even on Saturday. You look confident in the saddle when you sing."

"And confidence earns points." Helen tried to hide her disappointment.

"As does dancing. You love to dance."

"I love to dance, too!" Luke shouted.

"Are you ready?" Nash asked.

Helen's mind registered black horse ears and her mind went blank. Not blissfully blank, but panicky blank. Her mouth was dry and her cold sweaty palm was still pressed to Nash's warm, dry one. He knew how she felt. And she believed he'd wait forever until she was ready.

But they didn't have forever.

"I can't hear you," Luke called. "Talk louder!"

Someone shushed him.

"Or we could sing," Nash said softly, backing Beanie away from her and releasing her hand. He pulled the mechanical cow's remote control from his pocket.

Helen pressed her riding helmet more firmly on her head and nodded, even though the DJ was reading dedications without playing any music.

The familiar whir of the mechanical cow

coming to life brought Rose's head up. Her ears perked forward, and Helen felt her muscles flex beneath her.

The mechanical cow moved to the right.

Rose zigged so hard it was like being T-boned. Helen barely had time to recover before the mechanical cow slid along the pulley system to the left. Rose zagged to the left fast as lightning.

Helen didn't zig or zag. And then the world went dark.

"Helen." Nash's voice. Anxious. "Honey? Talk to me?"

Helen opened her eyes. Her ears were ringing, and Nash's face was a blur. But she felt his fear in the way he held her. And then his face came into focus, pale and tense. "What happened?"

"Nothing." He helped her to her feet, brushing dirt off her. "Do you hear what I hear?"

"That ringing in my ears?"

"The song," he prompted.

Rose ambled over, nuzzling Helen's shoulder as if ready to try again.

Applause cut through the ringing in her ears. The Blackwells all stood at the railing near the barn.

"Everybody is so nice to me," she all but whispered.

He wrapped his arms around her and gave her a tender squeeze.

And when he loosened his hold, she said, "I'm ready to go again." She wasn't anywhere near ready, but she had to push through. So many people she cared for were relying on her.

"You don't have to," Nash said, but she didn't believe him.

She gathered Rose's reins.

Nash cupped his hands to give her a boost up. He stared up at her. "Sing for me this time, okay?"

"Mama, the candy cane song!" Luke hopped down from the rail and started dancing as the words kicked in over the easy melody.

Helen dutifully waved a hand back and forth above her head to the beat.

Nash grinned. "What is his fascination with that song?"

"I think they taught the kindergarten class a dance to perform at the craft fair. Prepare yourself. You won't be able to get the song out of your head."

"That's Saturday?" His brow furrowed. "Morning, right?"

"Yes." She urged Rose forward to the start position. "I put the flyer on the fridge."

Nash nodded, clearly not having noticed anything. Not that she could blame him. He trained horses twelve hours a day.

The song launched into the cheery chorus. The other kids caught Luke's enthusiasm.

Luke danced in a circle, spinning his arms like a windmill.

"I'm ready." Helen nodded toward Nash. She gripped the saddle horn and sang under her breath.

The whir of the mechanical cow became the rumble of a freight train in her head, drowning out the music and Rose and Nash.

"Helen. Helen." Nash was leaning over her again. "How many fingers am I holding up?"

Helen didn't bother opening her eyes. "I hope it's the number of cuts I lasted on Rose."

He sighed. "I think we've had enough for one day."

Helen sat up slowly, letting the world come back to focus. "Isn't there a horse around who's faster than Beanie but slower than Rose? Nosey? Starling? Whirligig?"

"You're not riding any more tonight." There was a hard note in his words she'd never heard Nash use before. He helped her to her feet.

"Nash. I know I can't seem to stay on but I'm tougher than I look. We don't have that many more tomorrows to get me up to speed. Literally."

"Enough. Enough." He collected the reins of both horses and led them away. "I can't watch you fall anymore."

He left her standing in the midst of the empty arena.

Even her so-called fan club had deserted her.

"HELEN, DO YOU have a moment?" Denny flagged Helen down Thursday morning.

Helen had been about to climb into her blacksmithing van to start her work day. She'd already taken Beanie into the arena and tried to ride him while operating the mechanical cow remote. Multi-tasking on horseback hadn't resulted in her best effort, but at least she hadn't taken a tumble.

Nash had gotten up earlier than she had and left. They hadn't spoken about her attempts to ride Rose.

In short, Helen wasn't having her best day and it wasn't even half-past eight.

But she put on a brave front, closing the van's door and turning toward Denny, mustering a smile. "You're out and about early." With every word spoken, her breath made puffy little clouds that tried to make light of her mood.

"I wanted to ask you something." Denny linked her arm with Helen's and led her toward the south pasture. "Last night, Nash reminded you that you're a Blackwell, too."

"In name only." Helen heaved a sigh. "I'm not a natural when it comes to horses, like the rest of you."

"It takes all kinds of fruit to make a good fruit salad." Denny stopped looking ahead toward the white filly and turned an inquisitive eye on her. "Pardon me for saying this, but you don't have any other family. Does it make you feel better to be considered a Blackwell?"

What is happening?

Helen had no clue how to answer and given the demoralized way she was feeling this morning, she didn't try to be political about her feelings. "It does and it doesn't. Since I'm not married to Nash anymore, I feel more like a distant relation."

The old woman's gaze drifted back to the filly. "But when you were married to Nash..."

Clouds gathered on the western horizon, promising overcast afternoon skies and snow.

"Back then—" Helen drew a fortifying breath "—I felt so lucky to be included as one of you, as part of the family. I felt comfortable walking into your kitchen without knocking. I pitched in without asking whenever you needed me."

Denny nodded slowly. "I thought so."

Still in the dark as to where the conversation was going, Helen checked the time. "I really need to be leaving." Her first appointment was about ten miles out.

Denny continued to hold on to her arm. "And what was Christmas like for you when you dropped Luke off with us? You know, after you and Nash broke up."

Lonely. She didn't want to admit that. "It was…just another day." Last Christmas, she'd taken down the holiday decorations while Luke celebrated with the Blackwells. It had felt very gray and depressing. There'd been no one to sing with. No one to dance with. No one to tell her it was okay to have a second piece of pumpkin pie.

"I'm sorry, Helen. You are family to us and we haven't held up our end of the bargain. That's sad."

"It is," Helen agreed. She gave her arm a tentative, ineffectual tug. "What's this about?"

"I had a failed relationship, too," Denny admitted, facing Helen and rolling her shoulders back as if there was work to be done. "And I've been thinking about how that man I left must feel."

"You mean, Frank Wesson?"

Denny nodded. "His parents are dead. He never married. He must be lonely, especially at the holidays."

"I think he is. I've met him." Helen explained about coming to his rescue and seeing him again at Sweetwater Kitchen. She could see where Denny's thoughts might be going now. "You aren't thinking of inviting him for the holidays." Because the holidays came after Helen competed in the Holiday Showcase. And based on her performance last night on Rose, a gathering that included Frank might involve an unfortunate scuffle.

Denny tsked, as if she disagreed. "I want peace, but not just at Christmas. Peace in our little corner of the world."

Helen hoped she'd get it. Really, she did.

But Helen didn't think inviting Frank Wesson to a Blackwell family holiday was going to result in what Denny was wishing for—a Christmas miracle.

CHAPTER TWENTY

"WHATCHA DOIN', GREAT GRAN?" Luke sat on a bench near the south pasture gate.

After an hour of light snow showers Thursday afternoon, the sun was out and sparkling on the white hide of the wild filly. Corliss and Ryder were in town picking up groceries with Mason and Olivia. Elias was on some video chat, whatever that was. Nash and Helen were training in the arena to blaring Christmas music. And Denny had seen Wyatt and Harper drive off earlier, most likely to find one of those hidden treasures, otherwise known as undiscovered places, that Harper got so excited about.

Denny smiled at Luke. Now was the time to prove she wasn't dead weight.

"You wanted to start training Sneaker, didn't you?" Denny carried a training flag, a lightweight rope halter and a lead rope with a breakaway clasp. "Well, let's get to work."

Luke bounced to his feet and ran to Denny, reaching for the equipment. "I'm ready, Great Gran. You know I am."

"Not so fast." Denny held everything out of reach. "We're going in as a team. And teams have rules."

Luke's shoulders slumped. "I hate rules."

Denny bit back a smile. She didn't like rules much either, not unless she made them. "First rule. Do as Great Gran says."

Luke's gaze shifted toward the horse in the pasture, his mouth pulled to one side, as if considering whether or not her terms were worth it.

"Are we agreed on rule one?" Denny bent at the waist. "Or I can leave you out on this bench if you prefer."

"Okay." Never had such agreement sounded so reluctant. Luke compounded the impression by scuffing his boots in the snow.

"Second rule. We don't know if she's going to charge, rear, bite or kick so—"

"Oh, Sneaker isn't like that." Luke grabbed on to Denny's black jacket and beamed up at her. "She's a good horse. The best horse."

"You don't know that." Although Denny tended to agree.

The filly had been calm in her confinement, keeping away from humans who came to look at her rather than charging or racing by, teeth bared, hooves flashing.

Denny went over other rules, including the one about Denny always taking the first step in putting the filly through her paces. "I'll give you a chance after I see how she reacts."

"I know what I'm doin'." Luke thrust out his jaw.

"Don't forget rule number one," she reminded him. "Do as Gran says."

Luke heaved a sigh. "Okay."

They entered the pasture, closing the gate firmly but softly behind them.

The filly's head was raised, ears forward.

"That there is a good sign." Denny took Luke's hand. "Stay by me. We're going to the middle just as if this was a round pen."

"And then we use the training flag." Luke hopped like a bunny, staring at the ground. He was moving too quickly and not paying attention.

Denny felt the first twinge of remorse that comes from pursuing a bad idea. "No hopping. Eyes on the filly at all times."

"Okay." Luke straightened and walked next to her, little shoulders back.

He looked so much like Cal, and her son Hudson, and Nash.

For a moment, Denny blipped, at a loss as time and events from the past tumbled about her brain.

"I know I'm not s'posed to love you," Cal

had told her, a pained expression in his deep brown eyes.

"Give her space," she'd told Cal as they entered a pen with a white filly. "She's got to trust us as well as we trust each other."

"I was this close to winning it all, Delaney," Cal whispered, words slurred by whiskey. "This close."

The brisk winter wind on her face brought her back to the Flying Spur. To…

"She's a good horse," Luke crooned by her side.

Reminding her of her purpose.

She assessed the situation, the filly, her plan. "We work on circles and direction changes in the round pen," Denny said, more to herself than Luke. She set the halter down and made a small circle with the lead rope for them to stand in. "You stay in this circle until I say otherwise."

"Okay." Luke hopped inside the circle with her.

The filly took a few nervous steps to one side. So did Luke.

"Easy, girl. You have to move slowly, Luke, or you'll be benched." Denny moved forward, raising the training flag with her right hand. *Kiss-kiss.* She made the kissing sound. The noise, combined with the movement of the training flag, sent the filly trotting to her left.

"Great Gran, why do you kiss instead of cluck?" Luke made the clucking noise with his tongue. "Daddy clucks."

Denny drew a relaxed breath. "Some people are kissers and some are cluckers. Someday, you'll decide which you are."

Sneaker trotted around the perimeter of the enclosure. Denny kept making kissing noises and waving the flag to keep her moving a few times around. The filly came to a stop at the farthest corner, turning to face them directly.

"Good girl." Denny lowered the training flag. "See how she stopped and is looking at us. If she would have stopped and turned away, I would have waved the flag to keep her going. Now you try to send her the other way." She helped Luke position the flag in his left hand, keeping him in the makeshift circle.

The filly obediently trotted in the other direction.

Maybe this wasn't such a harebrained idea after all.

"We're tiring her out," Luke noted after she'd done a few more laps and had slowed her pace. He was a clever child. With Denny's help, he brought her to a halt.

Again, the filly stopped and faced them.

The boy and the filly have promise, Cal.

He'd be so proud.

"The more tired she is, the closer we're going to move to her." Everyone was going to be impressed at the work she and Luke were doing.

A noisy black bird swooped around the pasture, fluttering over a sprinkling of hay on the snowy ground, flapping its wings and chastising the world.

The filly spooked and ran directly at Denny and Luke.

CHAPTER TWENTY-ONE

"DADDY! DADDY! COME QUICK." Luke slid between the arena rails, rolled in the dirt, and came running toward Nash.

"Luke, lower your voice, please," Nash said automatically.

Helen rode Rose around the perimeter of the arena. They were practicing balance in the saddle. He'd looked up some tricks to help riders develop a firmer seat. She had a foam ball tucked into her shirt at the small of her back to encourage a taller posture and rode with her weight pressing through the balls of her feet to the stirrups. She needed to use more than a one-handed grip on the saddle horn to stay in the saddle when she set Rose free to cut.

"But it's Great Gran." Luke skidded into Nash's leg. "She fell and I can't get her up."

"Where?" That was Helen, kicking Rose into a lope and heading for the open gate.

Luke trotted after them. "In the south pasture."

Nash bit back a curse and raced through the barn.

Helen reached the pasture first, flipping

Rose's reins over the rail and slipping through the gate as Nash ran up.

"Move slow, Helen," Nash cautioned, heart squeezing painfully when he saw his grandmother on the ground. "You don't know what that filly will do if she's startled."

Helen froze just inside the gate, glancing around to locate the filly, who was as far away from her as she could be. The filly sniffed the air but continued to look alert, not angry or threatening.

"Sneaker won't hurt you." Gran lay flat on the ground as if she'd been making a snow angel. "I'm fine, by the way. Just can't get up."

Helen moved slowly to Gran's side.

Nash eased into the enclosure and joined them. He glanced down at his grandmother's face. Her expression could be fiery and intense when she was passionate about something. Or it could be open and cheerful when she was in a good mood. Right now, she looked lost and frightened.

"What in the world were you thinking, Gran?" Nash blew out a frustrated breath. "No. Don't answer that. Tell me where you're hurt."

"You've always been the strangest boy," she said, recovering some of her spunk even as she lay in the snow. "Most folk would demand to know what happened."

"I know what happened," Nash said in a near-growl. "I'm not the only Blackwell to make rash decisions."

"Can we have this conversation elsewhere?" Helen had her hand beneath Gran's head. "I don't see or feel blood anywhere. I think we can try to move her."

"I can sit up." Although Gran struggled to do so without their help. "It's the standing that flummoxes me."

They got her up and moving toward the gate, but her shoulder didn't seem right, and she kept sucking in a breath as if something hurt.

Luke opened and closed the gate for them, serious for once. He'd probably had a good scare. Nash hoped it was something that would serve him well moving forward.

"I can make it to my room." Gran wheezed, trying to steer their three-person ship toward the house.

"We're going into town to the medical clinic," Helen said before Nash could, keeping her on course for the truck.

Nash nodded. "Luke, take Rose back to her stall. Once she's inside, take off her bridle. Then get my phone from the tack room and bring it to my truck."

"Oh, I don't want to see the doctor." Gran's voice sounded like an old-fashioned fire siren, winding up from a thin thread to a loud, angry shout. "I'm fine, I tell ya. You've got more than enough on your plate than to be wasting time with me when all the doc is going to say is take two pills and call me in the morning."

They ignored her complaints. They ignored them all the way into town and all during the visit with the doctor.

And it was a good thing, too. She'd bruised her shoulder badly and needed a sling.

But she did get the prescription for two pain pills and the recommendation to call the doc in the morning.

Once they got her back home and safely tucked in bed, once they'd heard Luke's version of the story and Gran's and told all their tales to everyone else, Nash returned to his place with a slumbering Luke balanced on his shoulder and Helen's hand clasped with his. This was when he started to feel the first beginnings of loss.

Grief, if you will.

Because someday soon, he'd lose his once invincible grandmother and someday sooner, he'd lose the only place he'd ever called home.

"I WAS NOT meant to be a cowgirl." And although Helen said that statement out loud on Friday morning, the only living being who heard her was Beanie.

Fresh cows lowed on the other end of the arena. They'd been delivered by some cowpoke Levi had found and Nash had scolded him because they'd taken all week to get to the Flying Spur. Wyatt was on horseback, riding the newest addition to the Blackwell stable, Bubs, the second horse Corliss purchased recently, keeping the group together. Beanie had been watching those cows like a hawk.

Nash trotted over on Rose. "Mount up, Helen. Beanie's waiting."

She drew a deep breath as "Jingle Bells" played on the speakers. She'd taken a day off from work on this, her last practice day before the competition.

Behind her and several feet back on the other side of the fencing, in what was now lovingly being dubbed "the good seats," Adele sang along, dancing with her little girls. She'd been recruited to keep an eye on Denny while Corliss and Ryder went to their first pre-natal doctor's appointment.

Denny sat in her usual chair, foot tapping to the beat, arm still in its sling. "You can do this, Helen."

"She means *you* can do it with me on your back, Beanie." Helen climbed into the saddle and before she had a chance to loosen the reins, the gelding had his ears up and took her at a trot to the herd. "Okay, then."

"I'm timing you." Nash had to work to bring Rose to the outer edge of the herd. She wanted her turn at the cows, too. "Two and a half minutes." That was all the time she'd have in the competition. "Two cuts. One has to be deep." Meaning through the bulk of the herd.

"Plenty of time," Wyatt said and gave her a thumbs-up.

And it appeared it would be more than enough time because Beanie was determined to rush right through the herd.

Helen sawed on the reins, having watched Nash compete enough times to know that was unwise. But if she didn't, he'd startle the entire herd, scattering them, which would cost her points in a real competition.

Choose your battles, dove.

Where was Dad's voice when she needed it?

"Good. Good. Look at what you've got." Nash was full of advice from his position thirty feet away.

What I've got... What I've got...

The herd felt claustrophobic. Helen's mind blanked, dropping into panic mode, because after a cow was selected, the scary part would begin.

Good thing Beanie remembered what to do.

A cow made eye contact and the gelding quickened his walking pace. That made the cow nervous. The cow separated from the herd.

Beanie's a rock star!

"Lower those reins," Nash cautioned. "Let him do it. Your job is to ride tall. Square your shoulders. Push your balance into those stirrups."

She did, tightening her grip on the saddle horn.

The cow darted to the right.

Beanie spun on a dime. Helen's center of gravity didn't spin quite the same.

"Hold your line," Nash said, meaning she needed to stay upright in the saddle.

"Easy for you to say." She barely got the words out before the cow *and* Beanie were darting back the other way. This was what it felt like right before she fell off Rose. Blood roared in her ears. She was either going to fall off or vomit.

Or both.

"Stop." She pulled on the reins.

Beanie blew a raspberry, tossing his head.

"Oh, you almost had him." Wyatt trotted over on Bubs. "He was about to give up."

"I am, too." She took deep breaths, falling forward until she rested on Beanie's neck.

"Hey." Nash approached, concern rimming his eyes. "You looked great. Are you okay?"

"No. Yes. Maybe?"

Nash smiled a little and cocked his head. "Do you hear what I hear?"

Helen shook her head, not hearing anything…except… "Winter Wonderland"?

"It's one of your favorites." Nash gave her a soft smile. "Have you forgotten? Singing puts you in the zone."

Helen sat up and drew a deep breath, and then another, joining in the chorus.

"The herd is all set." Wyatt left them to take his position.

"Okay. We'll try it again." Helen turned Beanie toward the herd and sang under her breath.

"When you're ready, Helen, I'll start the clock." Nash and his clock.

Beanie was ready. It was almost like the gelding bounced on imaginary toes. He stood in place, but he leaned forward, extending his neck and flicking his ears.

She gave the gelding some rein, pointing him into the herd.

"That one," Nash said softly, seeing opportunity before she did.

Helen mouthed the lyrics and scanned the crowd, not seeing which cow he meant. No cow was looking at her.

It didn't matter. It was as if Nash and Beanie

were on the same wavelength. The gelding veered left, easing forward in a smooth, intentional gait.

Bile rose in her throat and Beanie hadn't even begun to dance with the cow.

"Isn't that 'Carol of the Bells'?" Nash asked.

Music. She needed to focus on the music. Helen lowered the reins, white-knuckled the saddle horn and focused on the music. What was playing? Oh, yeah.

"He's given up," Nash pointed out. "Great job but the clock is still ticking."

Helen realized the cow was holding still and staring at her. "Okay, okay. Let's go get another one." She turned Beanie around. She'd promised Nash she'd cut a dozen cows today.

He'd offered her a kiss if she rode Rose for at least one round.

That was still under negotiation.

"Deep cut, Helen," Wyatt reminded her. She needed to walk Beanie through the thick of the herd and cut out a cow, just as if she was singling out a cow that needed medical attention.

The chorus rang out. Helen guided Beanie into the herd.

"Look for the twitchy ones." Nash's voice drifted past the music, shutting it down.

She heard the chuffing of the herd. The slap

of swishing tails. The jingle of a bit. Ivy or Quinn asking their mama if she had snacks.

"Stay with it, Helen. Beanie's doing his job. You need to help choose one for him." Nash again.

Helen gritted her teeth.

"'Jingle Bell Rock,' Helen," Wyatt said, bringing her back to the center.

She hummed along with the music coming through the speakers, made eye contact with a cow and turned Beanie in that direction.

The gelding lengthened his stride. In no time, they'd pushed the cow out of the herd and were dancing.

She paused, forgetting about music.

Someone was singing and it wasn't Helen.

Nash.

She held onto the saddle and joined in, softly at first. Then louder when she didn't fall out of the saddle before Beanie caused the cow to give up. Was she getting better? She was concentrating so hard she couldn't believe it.

"Time," Nash called.

"You weren't timing me." He couldn't have been, not if he was calling out instructions *and* singing.

"I was." He nodded toward the center of the arena. "Let's reset and go again."

"How are you feeling, Helen?" Denny called from the good seats.

"Yes, how are you feeling, Helen?" Nash took the cue from his grandmother, giving Helen an apologetic smile. "Ready to go again?"

"Nice save, handsome." Helen turned Beanie around, marveling a little that she was on horseback and cutting cows from a herd. "I'm going to need chicken noodle soup after this."

"After a couple of runs, maybe we'll switch horses."

"No!"

Beanie's ears flicked back, and he swung his head around, checking on her.

"Ask me later. We've only cut two cows."

"Helen…"

"Ask me later…"

"We need presents under our tree." Luke sat at the dining room table in the mobile home. He was shoveling food, trying to eat quickly so he could take a bath and practice his candy cane dance for tomorrow.

Nash sat at the table, half listening to Luke, half reviewing Helen's progress today. She'd been a trooper on Beanie. But she'd refused to ride Rose. After much negotiation, she'd agreed to give Nosey a go. They'd done well. But her time was better on Beanie.

The problem was she had a real chance at winning on Rose. *If* she could stay in Rose's saddle and *if* she could set her hesitation aside and remember to sing.

"Did you buy me any presents yet, Mama?"

"Yes. Chew your food, please." Helen tried to make a funny face to get Luke's attention. "Slow down, cowboy. There are plenty of days between now and Christmas."

"Christmas isn't until forever." Luke chewed and swallowed. "It's not close until we have presents under the tree. And our stockings hung." He sat up taller. "Where are our stockings?"

"Back at our place." Helen pushed bits of cheesy rice around her plate.

"*This* is our place." Nash sounded sterner than he should. But one look at Helen's wide-eyed gaze and he quickly added, "Or it will be if we save the ranch."

That addendum did not go over as planned. It was met with silence.

Nash pushed on to the real elephant in the room. "Tomorrow morning, we'll work with Rose."

Helen mashed the last of her rice with her fork. "Tomorrow morning is the craft fair. Luke's going to be performing."

"You're a quick learner, Helen. Your balance

has improved. We should give it another try. Just one."

She shook her head. "Beanie is plenty fast for me."

"But Rose is—"

"You could ride Sneaker," Luke said brightly.

"No, I can't." Helen brought her plate to the sink and turned on the radio, filling the house with holiday music.

Nash cast about his brain for an argument to convince her to give Rose a go.

While he was thinking, that familiar, hokey song about candy canes came on.

Luke's head shot up. "Mama. Do you know what time it is?"

Helen spun at the sink, playing into Luke's hands. "Time to dance."

"The candy cane dance." Luke dropped out of his chair and started cutting a rug. "Come on, Daddy."

"I'm not finished eating." Or sulking. Or trying to find a solution to this no-win situation they were in.

"Everybody needs a dance break." Helen danced over to the table, holding out her hands toward Nash. "You used to dance with me. Show Luke what you can do."

Without meaning to, Nash's hands found hers. He got to his feet.

Luke sang to the music, dancing up a storm.

Helen danced that way, too. And she smiled at Nash as he danced, as if Nash had rhythm to spare.

They danced and danced, the silly song about candy canes went on. They danced the way they used to when they were dating and frequented the Cranky Crow, feasting on burgers, quenching their thirst with beer.

Beer…

Nash could almost taste it.

The song ended on a sour thought.

Nash returned to his seat at the table, out of breath but not because he'd been dancing.

He washed a hand over his face.

Helen stared at him, waiting for him to explain. He could feel her questions without even looking at her. But how could he tell her that he was having a low moment? She'd think he was weak. She'd say something the way Gran had about pressure and temptation.

Nash needed to think. He needed air.

Luke carried his plate to the kitchen. Reaching up to slide it on the counter, giving up before it was fully landed. The plate slid to the floor and broke, sending crockery and food scraps everywhere.

"This is why I can't have nice things," Nash said, heavy on the sarcasm.

"What did you say?" Helen's stare was cold. She guided Luke carefully away from the broken bits on the floor. "Go to your room, sweetie. I need to talk to Daddy alone."

With effort, Nash waited for Luke to close the door. He was still breathing hard, still reliving the taste of beer on his tongue. "I don't care about the plate. I'm talking about…" *Don't say it.* "…about…" *Just apologize.* "…when we're being silly, I…" *Want to drink.* "And you…do."

Somehow she knew exactly what he was trying so desperately not to say. "I don't drink anymore, Nash. I haven't had a drink since I lived here and realized you were an alcoholic. If this is one of your plays to stay sober… If I make you want to take a drink… Luke and I should leave."

There. Those words. It was what he feared all along. That he'd falter and she'd run.

"That isn't what I want." But there wasn't enough oomph in his statement. He was scared to death of taking a drink once more. Especially now, with the Blackwell ranch at stake. "I didn't want to dance."

Helen's expression immediately softened. "Do you want to talk? Would it help?"

"No." He hated talking. He hated admitting weakness. He hated looking weak to her. He hated. He hated. He hated himself.

She stood still for so long, he thought he'd spoken those last words out loud.

And then she was a blur of movement, taking her cue from the best cutting horses. "I can't stay here."

"Hey, hang on." Nash gathered the pieces of broken dish and dumped them in the sink. "Is this because you have to ride Rose tomorrow?"

"No." Helen was in the bedroom, stuffing her things into a suitcase. "Luke, we're leaving."

"*Why* are you leaving?" Nash could barely get the words out. "Don't go."

She stopped moving, hands freezing mid-air. And then her gaze lifted, meeting his. "Have you learned nothing from being a cutting horse trainer? If you don't communicate with your team, you can't win. And if you can't trust your team, you can't win."

"I… I don't understand." Oh, he understood, all right. He wasn't good enough for her. And maybe it was better this way.

"You can't talk to me." She was whispering, probably because Luke was in the next room. But even though she was whispering, her words struck him louder than a scream. "You can't even dance with me. Not without associating it with drinking. And until you can trust me—*no*—until *you* can trust *yourself*, we can't live like this and pretend things can be like they were." She started moving again, shoving things in her suitcase faster than before.

This was real. This was happening. And he wanted it to stop. He wanted to rewind the night, the day, the past two weeks.

He moved closer, slowly so as not to startle her. "I admit, things have been intense since you and Luke have been back. Take a beat and return in the morning. Luke can stay here. A little break and you can try Rose before we leave for the competition."

"I'm not riding Rose."

Nash shook his head. "You have to compete on Rose. That's our best chance. And you know it."

"My best chance..." Helen closed her suitcase and picked it up. "You can hide behind a lot of things, Nash, but you can't hide from what I'm fighting for or we'll lose each other for good." She walked past him. "Luke, we're leaving," she called.

"I said he can stay."

She stopped in the bedroom doorway, not turning. "He's not staying. He might dance, Nash. I wouldn't want him to make you feel bad." She closed the door behind her, shutting him in his bedroom.

And Nash didn't fight for her or his son.

Because she was right.

CHAPTER TWENTY-TWO

"SHE'S A FINE HORSE." Big E walked into the arena where Nash was putting Rose through her paces an hour after Helen and Luke had gone. "And you look good on her."

Nash powered down the mechanical cow and dismounted, leading Rose over to his granduncle. "She was never meant for me."

"Ah." The old man walked up to the filly and stroked his hand around her cheek to that spot where she always seemed to have an itch. "So, she was always meant for Helen."

"No." Nash felt heat flush up his cheeks. "She's a champion. She has the potential to earn millions." As soon as the words left his mouth, Nash was consumed with shame. He hung his head.

"Chin up, boy. That's the Blackwell motto." Big E bent until Nash did as he asked. "People of honor don't just pick words out of the sky to guide them. They embrace something because it helps them get through hard times. Bad times. The worst imaginable times."

Nash nodded. "I came to the arena tonight

after Helen left…me. And after making a few phone calls, including to my sponsor, I came here to…"

Rose nudged him, huffing a little, as if to say that Big E was smart enough to know why he was here so late at night.

Nash tried to smile and keep his chin up, the way a long line of Blackwells had done. "It's easier for me to work through the hard emotions and dark temptations when I'm on a horse. Helen would prefer I talk things through with her."

"A tough lesson even I struggled decades to learn," Big E admitted.

"But it always seems like she sees me through a gilded lens."

"Like she doesn't see your flaws?" Big E smiled as if this was a loaded question.

"Oh, she sees my faults. Quite easily." Pride being chief among them.

"Then you don't want her to see your fears." The old man nodded.

"I don't think you ever met my father." Nash stroked Rose's sleek black neck. "He was the doctor in town. And because he was the only doctor for thirty miles and we live in a rural county, there are sometimes accidents." Nash felt his chest tighten, the way it did when he discussed his own car crash. He took a slow breath. “He’d come home some nights quiet. Somber. And Mom would ask him what was wrong. And as I grew older, I knew that something bad had happened. Something he couldn’t talk to anyone about. But then I’d see him riding later.” Back then they’d only had the arena with lights, not a roof. “He’d be out here for hours working through what he’d seen. What he…hadn’t been able to prevent.”

“Your father sounds like a fine man. I can’t wait to meet him.”

Nash wiped at his nose. “He’d like you. He’d like that you showed up when Gran needed you most.” He’d respect that Big E didn’t back down from the strong woman who had shaped this valley, this ranch and her own legacy of Blackwells.

Big E cleared his throat. “I need to ask. What would he think of your wager with Phil?”

“Ah, going for the low blows now, are we?” Nash shook his head.

“Whoa.” Big E laid a hand on Nash’s shoulder. “I’m not taking a shot at you, Nash. What’s done is done. But let me impart a little wisdom that I’ve only learned in the past four or five years.” He waited until Nash nodded. “When I’ve been backed into a corner—and I’ve backed myself into a corner far too many times from far too much foolishness—lately, it helps me to think of what my mother would do in the same situation."

Rose stomped her front hoof, as shocked by Big E's statement as Nash was.

"Your mother. Not your father?" Hadn't they just been talking about Nash's dad?

"My mother was the rock in the house when my father blew his stack. If she'd had her way, we would have gone after Delaney, brought her and Cal home, sobered that man up and welcomed them back into the family fold."

"Yeah, that didn't happen."

Big E let his arm drop to his side. "And look at the fallout. I had similar family strife of my own. All because I learned too late that family is what matters. Oh, you can demand that your family respects you. And you'll most likely find that drives most away. It's not being right that matters." His voice had turned to a rough rumble rife with emotional speed bumps, a testament to his rocky past. "It's not winning that matters. It's showing up and staying there that matters, through thick and thin, through arguments and happiness, through good times and bad."

Nash agreed, feeling the cold of the winter's night seep into his boots and into his bones. It was time to get Rose inside where it was warm.

He led the horse toward the gate, content that the old man walked along with him.

"Yes, Rose is a fine horse that could be a champion. And you're a man with a solid reputation as a skilled horse trainer, Nash. Not only that, people come from miles around to pay to have you coach them, even for an hour." Big E chuckled. "What I can't understand is why you're so dead set on making Helen ride a horse that is beyond her capability?"

"You know..." Nash sighed. "I asked myself that the moment she slammed the front door."

"WHAT ARE YOU doing here?" Gwen asked Helen pushing her behind the table set up by the vocational studies program at Eagle Springs' annual craft fair Saturday morning.

And Helen, who was knee-deep in heartache and determined to support Luke through today's event with a smile on her face, was more than happy to take in what one of her favorite groups had to offer.

Their members had cut four-by-six boards into triangles and for five dollars you could paint Santa Claus or a gnome hat on the pointed end, and glue on a beard on the wide end of the base.

Helen admired some of the samples, which

looked adorably distracting. "These turned out really well."

"Helen." Gwen shook her arm a little when she didn't answer. "You should be home. I told you to drop Luke off backstage and I'd take care of him."

"I can't stay at home by myself." Helen might not know what she was doing today—compete or not—and she might not know what she was going to do about Nash, but she knew she had to show up for Luke. "I'll just sit over by the stage and watch the performances." She felt calmer already because they were playing Christmas music in the cafeteria. She unzipped her jacket. "No one will notice me."

"You're already being noticed." Gwen glanced around and tugged Helen across another row of craft stations to the choir's table. Their members were stenciling T-shirts with glitter paint. They had stocking stencils, holiday bulb stencils, shining star stencils.

"Oh, these are cute." Helen sifted through the options. "I bet Luke would enjoy doing this."

"Helen. Focus." Gwen took a step closer. She was wearing cute black suede boots with fringe and a red and white Mrs. Claus dress, the shorter, sexier variety. It was distracting because it was completely out of character.

So much so that Helen lost track of whatever words Gwen said after *focus*. "Did I forget something? Why are you dressed like a marching band majorette?"

Gwen scanned the room and pulled at the hem, muttering about busybodies, and then they were on the move again, stopping at the kindergarten table where children could make a reindeer or Santa from plastic spoons.

Mrs. Carsden stood behind the table, wearing a plastic apron over her gray business suit. She didn't look at all welcoming.

Still, it was good to support the class and perhaps smooth the waters with Wendy's mother. Helen inched forward.

"No." Gwen knocked away Helen's hand before she could so much as touch a plastic spoon. She sought refuge behind the parent-teacher association's table.

Their craft was a personalized ornament made from thick tree branches they'd sliced like cookies. They had glue, glitter and glitter pens. It looked like a lot of fun, especially since the table was located in the corner of the cafeteria away from the active flow of traffic from participants.

She scanned the wood cookies, looking for one that was perfectly round.

"Helen, come on. Forget about crafting." Gwen pulled Helen back to the glass-encased fire hose in the corner. "Listen to me. You walked away from Nash. You are in mourning. All these bright shiny baubles and all these mindless little projects are not going to help you clear your head. And you need a clear head, Helen, today of all days."

Helen swallowed past the lump that refused to go away in her throat. "I hear you. That's why I..." She gestured toward the rows of chairs set up in front of the stage.

"Not a chance." Gwen planted a hand on either side of Helen. "Can you please just listen for ten seconds to what I have to say?"

Helen nodded, because Gwen seemed so intent.

"Corliss Blackwell has been looking for you." Gwen glanced over her shoulder toward the refreshment counter where Helen knew Corliss and Mason were volunteering.

"She probably wants to know if I'm going to show up tonight." Helen hadn't decided. She knew she should, but every time she thought about seeing Nash, she teared up, and every time she thought about having to ride Rose, she froze.

"Earth to Helen." Gwen waved at her. "Speaking of that competition, everyone is excited about your performance. They're all asking for you, too."

"Who is?" Helen took some tentative peeks over Gwen's shoulders.

"Everybody." Gwen closed her eyes and shook her head. "You won't find any peace here, Helen."

Peace. That reminded her of Denny. And of Frank. And of Nash.

"Ugh." Helen covered her face. "My head is just one giant mess." She dropped her hands to her sides and squared her shoulders. "All right. I'm going to lurk outside until it's Luke's turn to perform. Just tell me one thing."

"Yes." Gwen lowered the arms.

"Why did you come here as Mrs. Sexy Claus?"

Gwen drew herself inward with a shudder. "Helen, I know you've had a bad stretch, but you don't own the market on bad days. I was supposed to show up as Mrs. Claus to run the kindergarten craft table. I have that lovely Victorian dress. You know the one. Antique. Red velvet. Dainty white fur trim. Floor length."

Helen remembered the dress. "It really flatters your figure."

"I know, right?" Gwen almost smiled. And then the cloud descended over her again. "I steamed it last night and hung it up in the hall bathroom on the shower curtain rod on that slender little hanger it came on. I can see it now..."

Helen glanced at Gwen's current dress, which wasn't Victorian or figure-flattering, waiting for further explanation. When none came, she prompted, "And then…"

Gwen gave a little groan. "Sometime during the night, the cat must have decided my dress would make the perfect birthing bed." Gwen's eyes filled with tears. "When I got up this morning, the dress was in the bathtub and was home to four newborn kittens. They're so cute and adorable that I couldn't even hold a grudge."

"I'm sorry, Gwen." Helen slipped an arm around her friend's shoulders. "And this dress?" The one that seemed a bit snug.

"The second thing I did this morning after wailing, and waking the entire household, was to call my mama, because you know she never throws away anything."

"Oh." Helen saw where this was going. Gwen's mother and father had once played Mr. and Mrs. Claus in a community production of something Jackie Youngblood had written. The girls had been teenagers and the show had been mortifying both because of how bad it was, and that Gwen's parents were in it. "That explains…" Helen made a circular motion with her hand, one that encompassed the unfortunate dress. "But not why you're here wearing it."

"My mother assured me the dress was fine and that I'd fit in it. And you know me and my memory. I didn't remember it was—*oops, this high*—and—*oops, this low.* I was running late, so I didn't even change. I had Stan drive me to Mama's in my pajamas. He left me to go buy diapers—'cuz he's a gem—and I was left at Mama's mercy. And you know my mama. She was adamant I wear this dress or she'd throw her car keys somewhere no one would want to retrieve them." Gwen shivered. "And then, when I got here, Mrs. Carsden said I wasn't dressed appropriately enough to work the kindergarten craft table. And I was so annoyed that I told her there was nothing wrong with this dress or me wearing it and that I wasn't going to leave. So, there you have it. I'm shamed by my own darn pride."

"Wow. That makes me feel a little less sad about my broken heart." It did. It really did.

Gwen nudged Helen's shoulder. "I'm going to remind you of that someday."

"Helen?"

Gwen and Helen both froze at the woman's voice.

Slowly, Helen poked her head up high enough to see over Gwen's shoulder, which had linebacker shoulder pads. "Hey, Corliss."

Was it too much to hope that Nash's sister

wasn't here to try and talk Helen into…something?

Corliss joined them in the corner, a dry cleaning bag draped over her arm. "I thought I saw you come in. I wanted to apologize for whatever my brother said. Or did. Or didn't do. He's going to be here soon to watch Luke." She tried to smile, not doing a good job of it. "Yeah, this is awkward. I'd been planning on giving this to you, and this morning when he broke the news that you left, I wished I'd done it sooner." She held up the dry cleaning bag, revealing a black button-down blouse with pearly snaps and embroidered with big red roses. "I didn't win many cutting competitions, but I always felt better wearing it."

"It's beautiful." Helen worked in the most boring clothes. She was a lover of fashion from afar. And this was a Western show-stopper. "Thank you so much."

"That was real nice, Corliss," Gwen said, dishing on the disdain. "You didn't even put in a plug for Nash or pressure my girl into showing up tonight."

Corliss handed the blouse to Helen, chin in the air. "This is not some ploy to get Helen to compete. I have a back-up plan to handle Phil."

Gwen crossed her arms over her chest and

arched her brows, apparently not believing a word of it.

"Testing-testing." Someone tapped a microphone.

Helen of Old decided to make an appearance. "Ladies, my son is about to perform his little heart out. I thank you both for your support, but I can't hide in a corner just because life gets hard sometimes."

CHAPTER TWENTY-THREE

HELEN WAS LATE. Really late.

The cutting horse competition had started. Or so she'd been told by the man who'd said she was the last contestant to check in and her event began in less than thirty minutes.

Helen would have liked to have blamed her tardiness on Gwen, who'd given her a ride and was going to sit inside with Luke, Caleb, and Stan. Gwen always took forever to do her hair and make-up. But that hadn't been the case tonight. Stan had gotten them here on time. But then Helen had gotten lost trying to find where to check in.

And now, looking for the Blackwells, she was lost in the pasture the contestants had parked their trailers in. She'd been wanting to avoid texts or phone calls, but it looked like she wasn't going to have the option of facing them all when she told them, *"Ta-da. I'm here."*

Two very familiar twin toddlers ran past Helen in their very familiar pink snowsuits.

"Hey. Come back here." Adele jogged up next to Helen.

They looked at each other for a moment. It was one of those I-know-that-you-know-that-I-left-your-brother moments. And there might have been an over-abundance of surprise in Adele's eyes that Helen had shown up at all. But that was moot.

"Did you see where the girls went?"

Helen pointed toward a large trailer. "That-away."

"Come on, then." Adele ran ahead, leaving Helen no choice but to follow. "Quinn? Ivy? You know you aren't supposed to run out of my sight."

"That's a two-year-old thing," Helen said.

"I'll take all your sisterly advice later," Adele sing-songed, darting around another long horse trailer. "There are my babies."

Helen rounded the corner and nearly bumped into Harper, who wore a magnificent red and black buffalo jacket. "Sorry."

"Don't apologize." Harper steadied her. "We've all been worried sick about you."

"Sorry," Helen said again. "I turned my phone off." A cowardly move.

"The guys have the horses ready." Harper turned Helen around and removed her jacket. "Now it's your turn. Nice shirt."

"Thanks." It was the one Corliss had given her this morning. She smoothed out the wrinkles and glanced down because she was dressed all in black. It was her ode to Blackwell.

"Now that you're here, I brought you this." Adele handed Helen a riding helmet fitted beneath a black cowboy hat. "I found it in an estate sale last weekend. I think it makes you look the part while keeping your noggin safe, just in case..." She trailed off.

"It's perfect." Helen strapped it on her head. "How do I look?"

"Adorbs," Harper said, snapping a picture with her phone.

Denny tottered up. Her arm sling had been decorated with sparkles, most likely by Olivia and Isla. She held up a squashed penny. "I got this at the state fair the year I placed in the cutting horse competition." She tucked it into Helen's jeans pocket, the same one that Luke had tucked a small candy cane into when they'd parted earlier. "I wanted you to feel you weren't alone out there."

"I won't be." In reality, she'd be out there with four Blackwell family members—Levi, Ryder, Wyatt, and Nash. They'd be her herdholders, making sure the cows didn't scatter or run for the opposite side of the arena and blow all her precious two and a half minutes. "But this is special. Thank you, Denny. Really."

Helen was beginning to feel as if she was

about to blast off into space on the first manned trip to Mars and her loved ones were giving her their special finds and lucky charms.

"I'm gonna put a little silver conch on your saddle." Levi showed her the quarter-sized, decorative piece. "It was Grandpa Cal's. Gran gave it to me when I first started to ride. She said it would bring me luck if I carried it. I used to put it in my crash vest before every bull ride."

Helen thanked him as he disappeared to the other side of the Blackwell horse trailer.

The announcer called her event. Helen felt a little numb. She had yet to see Nash or Rose.

"I tested all your straps and stirrups." Wyatt came out of the shadows and handed her the reins. Instead of Rose, Beanie pranced behind him, not looking like the dear old gentleman who'd helped her overcome her fears of the saddle. He had a bounce to his step and glitter on his hooves. "Everything is right and tight. And Harper added glitter to Beanie's hooves."

Holding Beanie's reins, Helen thought she might cry. The Blackwells were her family. She'd never felt more like one of them. But after tonight, she knew she wouldn't see them every day. Her time as a Blackwell was coming to a close.

She turned toward the doors leading inside the facility.

And there was Nash, standing right in front of her, dressed all in black. "Helen, I…" He wrapped his arms around her and crushed her to his chest. "I'm sorry I got you into this. I'm sorry we argued. I…" He held her away from him. "Don't ride."

"Nash." Helen clung to his waist when he would have pushed her away. "I have to do this. For me." She'd thought a lot about this once Luke had performed his beloved dance at the craft fair and gone home with Caleb, giving her time to think. "And for you. Sometimes the best victories are the moral ones."

And in that moment, she knew it was true. She had to quit complaining and be the courageous little dove her mother had raised, and her father had nurtured. She had to ride for her honor and the rest of Eagle Springs. She had to stay in the saddle and ride tall for the Blackwells.

Nash's gaze swung slowly over her face. "I don't handle stress well. I either leap before I look or I hunker down and do nothing. This isn't your fight. You shouldn't be cleaning up my mess."

"Too late, Nash. I'm going to finish what we started. *We*." She grabbed hold of his hand. "I could have spoken up that night on Lander and told Phil there was no bet. But a part of me wanted to be in this with you. A part of me dreamed of a second chance. And earlier that day, you'd told me that couldn't happen. I'm just as much to blame as you are."

He shook his head. "You always were too willing to forgive my mistakes."

"That's because I love Christmas, the season of forgiving."

He sighed.

"Anyway, I'm doing this, Nash. It's too late to stop me." And with that, she led Beanie toward the doors to the competition ring.

CHAPTER TWENTY-FOUR

DENNY WALKED AROUND Nash's horse trailer and confronted the man at the root of all their troubles. "What are you doing lurking back here?"

Frank Wesson didn't flinch. "I'm curious." He gave her sparkly shoulder sling a derisive look.

Her gut reaction was anger. "My girl's going to give you a run for your money."

He scoffed. "She's not your girl."

"But she is, Frank. She's family." And Denny loved Helen as if she'd been born into the fold. "She's family the same way you and Cal were my family back in Falcon Creek."

He said nothing. But there was longing in his eyes as he watched the five Blackwell competitors, dressed in their namesake black, heading toward the final showdown.

And in that longing, she found a sudden certainty, one fostered by her conversations with Helen.

"I'm tired, Frank. And you've won this fight. But I'd like you to know Cal's family. And I'd like them to know you. Come by the ranch tomorrow around noon. We always gather two weeks before Christmas and have a big feast."

"Is this a joke?" Frank's voice was hard, but he was no good at poker and never had been. The truth was always to be found in his eyes. He wanted to come. And yet, he shoved his hands in his pockets. "Have you devised some kind of clever trap? If that's what this is, it won't work."

"It's Christmas," she said gently. "That's all. And Christmas is for family, a time to set aside differences and be at peace."

"There can be no peace." But the bitterness and anger that had filled his voice at Thanksgiving were conspicuously absent.

Frank was like that wild filly—calm one minute, frantic the next. She knew how to tame wild horses. And suddenly, she knew how to tame a lonely old man.

"Maybe Cal's grandchildren won't find it in their hearts this Christmas to forgive you. But I've found it in mine. Show our family what kind of a man you truly are, Frank. Show up for our annual Christmas feast and let them show you who they are, too."

"Delaney?"

Denny turned at the sound of her brother's voice. "Coming."

And when she turned back, Frank was gone.

CHAPTER TWENTY-FIVE

HELEN'S PALMS WERE SWEATY. Her fingers shook. She was next.

They'd open the gates and let her and Beanie in just as soon as the previous competitor's score was announced.

"You've got this, Helen," Levi said from her right.

"Trust Beanie," Wyatt said to her left.

"You can do anything for two and a half minutes," Ryder said from her left flank.

"Cut deep and sing a Christmas carol," Nash said from her right flank.

A score was announced. The gates were opened.

Beanie pranced forward proudly, like the veteran he was.

Helen raised her shoulders and smiled, knowing she was being judged on her confidence and knowing Beanie deserved a good performance from her just as much as the rest of Eagle Springs.

They entered the arena on a big round of applause.

Helen hadn't been inside until now. She was surprised at her reception. The audience clapped hard and long.

Beanie pranced out to a location beyond the herd of young cattle. Herefords, their white faces looked gentle and kind. The Blackwell crew positioned themselves at the virtual four corners of the herd. Helen moved the reins, signaling to Beanie to turn and face the herd. His ears perked up and he fidgeted a little.

"This is Helen Blackwell riding Beanie. Her time starts *now.*"

"Dashing through the snow." Someone up in the stands started to sing. *"In a one-horse open sleigh."*

"O'er the fields we go," Helen sang under her breath as she guided Beanie into a deep cut of the herd, looking for a cow nervous enough to make eye contact.

A small cow stared at Helen and then turned, nervously hurrying to try and disappear into the herd.

Helen cued Beanie with leg pressure and lowered the reins, her signal to him to go for it. And then it was just a matter of dancing with the cow following Beanie's lead, singing under her breath. The gelding made some nice deep sweeps to keep the cow from returning to the herd. And Helen did her best to hold on and not do her impression of a rag doll. And after what seemed like a lifetime, the cow stopped and stared at them, giving up.

Time for another cow.

While Nash encouraged the first cow to rejoin the main herd, Helen and Beanie made a second foray into the group. That's when Helen noticed that practically the entire arena was singing "Jingle Bells."

She had no time to wonder at it because a cow lifted its head and stared at them.

Almost before she knew what was happening, Beanie was giving chase.

It was all Helen could do to stay on this time.

The cuts Beanie made were deep and sweeping. He stopped on a dime and nearly threw her.

The crowd gasped.

"...in a one-horse open sleigh," Helen murmured, hanging on.

Beanie wore the cow down. It stopped and made eye contact.

"Good work," Nash told her, their signal for the competition to be over, even if she had more time, which she did.

She and her crew rode toward the gates with fifteen seconds to spare. The crowd was applauding and hollering and…

Helen glanced up.

They were giving her a standing ovation.

She held up a hand, waving, acknowledging her hometown crowd's support.

And then they were through the gates, dismounting. Hugs. So many hugs, including from Nash, who spun her around before depositing her on the ground.

"I'm sorry. I lost balance that one time."

"Who cares? I'm so proud of you," he told her. And then he draped his arm over her shoulders and turned them toward the arena. "Now for your score."

Helen didn't want to hear it. "No matter what, we won."

"Right," Nash said, but she knew he hoped for more.

She glanced at the others. Her crew. Her family. She could see they hoped for it, too.

"A score of seventy for Helen Blackwell. Seven-zero."

Nash's arm fell away. He'd told her she needed at least a seventy-four to have any hope of placing. He led his horse out.

The crowd booed.

"You were robbed," Wyatt told her before turning and taking his horse and Beanie out.

The others followed him, until it was just Helen, standing alone, trying to catch her breath and swallow back the overwhelming feeling of loss.

"Helen." Phil appeared next to her, a literal thorn in her side. "What a ride. I'm so proud of you."

"Which means nothing to me, Phil." She spun on her boot heel and marched off to find the Blackwells.

"Excuse me." A middle-aged woman shepherded a teenage girl forward, blocking Helen's path. "I'm Madeline and this is Sylvie."

"Hi." Helen glanced past them but couldn't see any of the Blackwells. Other groups with horses were coming in.

"I mean… I guess you don't know…" Madeline smiled harder. "Nash has been training Beanie for us. For Sylvie."

The air left Helen's lungs in a rush because here was another loss. Beanie wasn't hers. She'd known it all along, but still…

The teenage girl smiled, revealing braces. She had dark brown pigtails hanging over each shoulder and was wearing a brown button-down shirt embroidered with yellow daisies. She seemed cute and bright and perfect for Beanie.

If Helen hadn't loved the gelding head-to-toe, she'd have been ecstatic for her.

Madeline and Sylvie's smiles fell.

Helen realized it was her turn to say something. Her turn to be gracious and giving. "He's a wonderful horse. Patient and… Well, he goes at his rider's pace. At least, until you get him to cutting cows. Then it's like he's a frisky, young colt."

"He's fabulous," Sylvie gushed, awkward silence apparently forgotten. "He was supposed to be a surprise for Christmas."

"But Nash called yesterday morning to ask if we'd mind him competing today."

Nash.

He hadn't decided to put her on Beanie at the last second. Helen's heart ripped a little further.

"I was leery about having Sylvie compete in cutting—"

"She thinks I'll get hurt." Sylvie rolled her eyes.

"—but hearing you praise him…knowing what you've overcome…" Madeline gave her daughter a significant stare. "I'm sorry if this is getting too personal. You just reassure me."

Sylvie rolled her eyes again. "I lost part of my leg in an accident. And Mom thinks I should live my life in a bubble. But that would be boring." She softened her words by taking her mother's hand and swinging her arm. "My new motto is: *If Helen Blackwell can do it, I can do it.*"

Blinking back tears, Helen spread her arms and enveloped the pair in a hug. "I couldn't think of a better rider for Beanie." It hurt to let him go, but it was true.

Just like it probably hurt for Nash to let Helen go. But he didn't have to. They made each other stronger when they were together. Or they could if Nash would be honest about moments when things became hard for him. He could reach out. He could speak out.

"Okay..." Sylvie laughed self-consciously.

"Oh. Hey. Sorry." Helen stepped back, having held on to them too long. "I'm a hugger." She waved and moved toward the stock exit.

"Helen." A woman stepped out of the shadowy hallway. Her hair was blond and a little tired, and her face was gauntly hopeful. *"Dove."*

Big E stood behind Helen's mother, nodding encouragingly.

"Mom?" Helen nearly collapsed. And before she could process how she felt about seeing her mother again, they were hugging.

"I'm so sorry," her mom said, sobbing. "And so proud." She held her at arm's length. "You're beautiful, capable, and so strong. But you always were."

Helen tried to tuck a lock of her hair behind her ear and realized she still wore the riding helmet. She took it off.

"I found her." Big E came forward. "She's been living in Idaho."

"Working on a ranch." Her mother sniffed. "Seventeen years sober."

Seventeen years. "You stopped drinking that year..."

She nodded, her movements jerky and self-conscious. "Checked into rehab once I'd realized my mistake."

"There's a lot to unpack here," Helen said diplomatically, gaze seeking Big E's. She had so many conflicting feelings. And right now, her priority was Nash. "Can we talk tomorrow?"

"I'd like that." Her mom started to cry again.

Big E drew her away, assuring Helen that he'd bring her to the Christmas feast.

Helen marched on alone.

The Blackwells had the horses haltered, unsaddled and loaded in the trailers.

Helen glanced around, a bad feeling knotting between her shoulder blades. "Where's Nash?"

No one would look at her.

No one except his grandmother. Denny grabbed hold of Helen's hand. "We told him it didn't matter. We told him we didn't blame him."

"But he blames himself." Helen spotted Levi headed back toward the facility. He was running the show and wouldn't be leaving soon. "Levi, can I borrow your truck?"

He stopped, turning slowly. "What for?"

She marched over to him, moving like a general about to issue new orders. "To find Nash and stop him from doing something foolish."

Like take a drink.

NASH SAT AT the bar of the Cranky Crow, head in his hands, staring at a shot of whiskey.

"Let me take that back." Harriet reached for the shot glass.

Nash held out his hand. He deserved this drink for all he'd been through. He deserved to savor the taste of whiskey on his tongue for all he'd put Helen through. And his family. And Eagle Springs.

But he just couldn't do it.

He washed a hand over his face, remembering how Helen had broken down just sitting on Beanie two weeks ago. How her hands trembled and her face turned green.

I did that to her.

The whiskey glass was whisked away by a familiar feminine hand.

"That's enough of that." Helen crowded into the space next to him, in between the bar stool he sat on and the empty one next to it. She wrapped her arms around him. "Thank you."

"Thank you?" He closed his eyes, wishing she'd hold him forever. "Thank you for what?"

"Thank you for coming to the first place I looked for you." Helen wasn't wearing a cowboy hat. She bumped his off his head.

"Hey."

Before he could reach for it, she kissed him.

And before he could unwind all the tension inside him, she ended that kiss.

She grinned. "You owe me that for staying in the saddle tonight."

He wanted to smile. He wanted to believe everything was all right. But the truth… The truth was so much worse. "Let's not do this."

"Nash Blackwell." She cradled his face in both hands. "You honestly think that either one of us is ever going to find someone brave enough to love us the way I love you and you love me?"

On the other side of the bar, Harriet snorted.

Helen wasn't having it, she snapped toward the woman. "Harriet, unless you want me to give you a piece of my mind for pouring Nash that drink, you need to head on over to the end of the bar and mind your own business."

With her eyes flashing and her voice commanding, Helen was the most beautiful woman Nash had ever seen.

Suddenly, she turned all that passion and heart toward him. "You aren't off the hook, not by a long shot. You took me for granted after the crash. You thought you could just hide away from me."

"I'm sorry, but—"

"And I thought I was to blame because you'd never told me you loved me, not without being prompted. So I tried to be someone else. Someone who didn't make waves or dance in public. And tucking myself away, along with leaving you, nearly ended me."

"I'm sorry, but—"

"It's not fair. I want to be me." She speared her fingers into his hair and took hold. "And I want you to be you."

Nash didn't know what to say to that, mostly because he didn't know who she wanted him to be.

"You are all the Blackwells rolled into one. Stubborn like Denny. Kind like Adele. Driven like Levi. Clever like Wyatt. And bossy like Corliss." She drew a breath because apparently, she wasn't done. "You are predictable, until you aren't. And lovable, until you clam up. You make me want to dance and sing and feel everything that makes life worth living." She laughed. "You forced me to face my fears, openly for everyone to see. But you were there by my side. And now, I want to do the same for you."

Nash shook his head. "I'm here. In a bar. Clearly, I was about to let you down."

She huffed and waved to Harriet. "How long has he been sitting here staring at this shot of whiskey?"

"Twenty-eight minutes."

Helen put her forehead to Nash's. "You were waiting for me. You were waiting for me to come and talk about how we gave it our best shot but we lost. Tonight, we'll be down in the dumps. But tomorrow, we're going to begin making a new plan for the future. Together."

He blinked at her. At green-eyed determination. She deserved…so much more.

"Just admit that you were waiting for me," she said softly, pleadingly. "That's all, Nash. Admit it. And we can try this crazy thing called love one more time."

Nash opened his mouth. He should tell her he'd been waiting for her, all right. Waiting for her to bear witness when he took that drink. Then she'd go her own way. Then she'd find someone to love her how she should be loved. Except…

The truth was, he had been waiting for her, hoping that she'd come and tell him not to give in or give up hope. The way she just had.

"I was waiting for you," he said on a weighty breath of air. "I will always wait for you."

CHAPTER TWENTY-SIX

"THIS IS IT, THEN." Denny stepped out on the porch and took in the snow-blanketed ranch that she'd built from scratch in honor of Cal's memory. "If it has to end, at least it looks beautiful."

"There are still two weeks." Elias stepped up next to her. "Anything could happen… *Denny*." He rocked back on his heels and gave her a teasing glance.

"Let's not sugarcoat things… *Big E*." She glanced up at her older brother. Despite his age, despite the years of a life built outdoors, she could still see the strong, handsome features of his youth. "My family needs my acceptance this morning."

This, the morning after the Holiday Showcase. It was also two weeks before Christmas, the date all the Blackwells traditionally gathered for the annual family Christmas photograph and feast. There'd be tears, no doubt. But there would be laughter as well. Food. And horse talk. There was always horse talk.

Already, trucks were rolling in. Levi with his

small family. Adele with hers. Wyatt was busy with Mason, setting up the smoker and grill. Harper was nearby, snapping photos with her phone. Ryder and Corliss were in the kitchen keeping an eye on the buns in the oven while preparing salads and side dishes. Nash and Helen emerged from the barn, each holding one of Luke's hands.

"Do you think he'll come?" Elias headed for the stairs, lingering at the top until Denny joined him and they could go down the steps together.

"He'll show." If there was one thing Denny knew about Frank Wesson, it was that he'd grown up in a loving family. "Now that he has what he wants, he's going to start realizing it isn't what he needs." If he hadn't begun already.

"You're a bigger person than I am." Elias walked next to her, modulating his steps to her pace. "I've lived most of my life with a tit-for-tat motto."

"My way or the highway." Denny smiled. "You were always determined to have things just as you wanted them."

Elias spread his arms. "I'm living proof that no man is a lost cause." He'd spent the last four years mending bridges and making amends.

"Don't you go preaching about your journey

if he shows." Denny huffed. "Everything isn't all about you, *Big E*."

He chuckled. "Nor you, *Denny*."

"This is going to get old fast," Denny grumbled. And then she took hold of his arm. "Today is about family and fun. Smiles ready?"

He nodded. "Smiles ready."

CHAPTER TWENTY-SEVEN

"THAT'S IT, LUKE." Nash stood with their son in the middle of the partitioned south pasture. They were working well with Sneaker.

"I'm the best horse trainer ever." Luke's face was scrunched intently, shaded from the sun with the bent and dirty gray felt hat. "Mama, look at me."

"I have been looking." At Luke and Nash while she counted her blessings. Family was more important than any one roof over their heads.

Helen turned as a truck rolled slowly up the driveway. She glanced back toward the main house, but no one stepped outside. There was a poker game going on inside along with too many cooks in the kitchen. Her mother was among the poker players.

That was going to take some getting used to.

Frank Wesson parked near her.

"Wow. Denny was right," Helen murmured.

Nash gave Helen a questioning look. She

waved, indicating she was fine. Maybe they'd all be fine.

Nash continued to help Luke work the white filly.

"Merry Christmas." She greeted the old cowboy who'd engineered the end of the Flying Spur and Eagle Springs as if he were a long overdue and welcome guest. "We've never been formally introduced. I'm Helen Blackwell."

"Frank Wesson." He tipped his hat with one hand, holding something else behind his back. "I thought you'd judge me if you knew my name."

"Well..." Helen hedged. "One thing I know for sure is that I wouldn't have left you stranded on a dark and deserted, snowy highway whether I knew who you were or not. That's just not what we do around here. What we did..." she added half-under her breath.

"You don't seem surprised to see me."

Helen shrugged. "I heard a rumor you might show. And as long as you didn't come with Phil, I'm okay with you being here."

Frank smiled, glancing toward Nash and Luke for the first time. He reached for the fence post, leaning heavily on it.

"Are you all right?" Helen moved closer,

glancing up at Frank's face, which was pale. "Should I call someone?"

In the pasture, Nash directed Luke to lower the training flag. He walked over to join them, followed by Luke and Sneaker. The filly was going to be a good horse someday. Helen just wasn't sure if she'd be Luke's horse.

"No. I'm… It's just…" Frank straightened. "They—Nash and Luke—look so much like him. Cal, I mean. It's like seeing him as a child and…as the man he would have become."

"Haven't you seen Nash before?"

Frank shook his head. "He doesn't come to town much and neither do I. I've been staying at a friend's ranch."

"Hey, Mister." Luke ran ahead of Nash, smiling. "Mister, it's you. Did you see me training Sneaker? She's going to be a champion someday. And so am I." He tipped his hat back as he gazed up at his granduncle. The hat fell off, of course. It had never fit right.

Nash scooped it up, frowning at it.

"Here." Frank extended his hand over the gate, revealing a small straw cowboy hat he'd been carrying. "I think that hat of yours lived a good life, Luke. But a fine horse trainer needs a hat for the daily grind."

"Thanks!" Luke accepted the gift and

plopped it on his head. He turned, distracted by Sneaker blowing out a breath behind him in an unashamed play for attention. "Do you like my hat, Sneaker? I bet you could wear my old hat, girl."

"No, she can't." Nash handed Helen the stained gray one before Luke had a chance to get his hands on it.

Helen took it graciously, the same way she had when Phil had first gifted it to Luke. And then she placed it on the ground and stomped on it.

"Here's to happy endings." Nash grinned. He extended a hand over the gate. "I'm Nash."

Frank hesitated, moving slowly to accept the gesture. "I'm sorry, but I… You sound just like my brother. Like…like Cal."

Nash shrugged, looking a little awkward, but he smiled with that endearing, almost-lopsided expression of his. "I hear I'm similar to him in more ways than one. But I'm my own person and we'll be following our own path from here on out."

Helen nodded and took Frank's arm. "You should come inside and meet the rest of the family. Nash and Luke need to clean up for supper and pictures."

"Pictures?" Frank allowed her to lead him

away. His steps were sturdier than Denny's, but he still moved at a measured pace. He had to be around eighty.

"Every year, the Blackwells take a picture to celebrate this time of year," she told him. "Before the holidays, since they all have such busy schedules."

Frank dug in his heels.

Helen gently pressed him forward. "Don't be camera shy."

"These people hate me."

Helen tsked, propelling him on. "Families get into disagreements all the time. They get their backs up. They might not talk for years..." Helen patted him on the arm. "I hadn't talked to my mother for nearly twenty years until last night. And if I've learned anything from all of this, it's that I need to be the bigger person and forgive."

"The bigger person..." Frank nodded. "In my situation, that'd be you and your Blackwells."

She looped her arm through his. "They're your Blackwells, too. Or Wessons, if you prefer. Come on. A man who buys up a valley and reshapes the lives of thousands of people shouldn't be afraid of his own family gathering."

Frank cleared his throat. "Right."

They climbed the porch steps and came in through the mudroom to the kitchen. While they were removing their boots, jackets, and hats, boisterous voices and joyful laughter could be heard filling the house.

When she would have entered the kitchen, Frank held on to Helen's shoulder. "I don't belong here. They sound so happy." He glanced down at her, silver brows knitting. "What do they have to be happy about? I've taken just about everything they hold dear."

"Happiness isn't measured by the place you call home, Frank. It's measured by the love you find within the family you have and the family you create."

"I thought…" He glanced toward the door, as if considering his escape. "I thought I was ruining their holiday."

Helen smiled ruefully. "I think that's pride talking. You can take away all of their things, but they'd still be Blackwells. They'd still revel in each other's company, cheer on their successes and comfort each other through their losses."

"You're lucky to be a part of them." Frank eased back toward the bench where he'd left his boots.

"You're part of them, too."

He shook his head.

"Is that you, Frank?" Denny, her arm still in its sling, tottered into view, smiling a little. "Don't just stand there. Come on in."

"What is happening?" Frank whispered.

"Go with it," Helen advised. "You'll sleep better at night."

And the rest of them would, too.

LONG AFTER THE food was gone… Long after his siblings and their families had retreated to their nests… Long after Denny had made up with Frank… And long after Helen had gone to put Luke to bed…

Nash wandered through the barn, saying goodbye to the horses he'd been training, whether it had been for months or weeks or days. He stopped at the empty stall that used to be Beanie's. Madeline and Sylvie had picked him up this morning, eager to start their journey with the wise and loveable gelding.

The barn door opened.

Nash turned, smiling because he was expecting Helen to join him.

Instead, Frank entered the barn, closing the door behind him.

Nash's smile became harder to hold on to. He knew Gran wanted him to forgive what Frank had done but it was tougher for him to let go of the resentment. And he knew that was because he hadn't let go of his own guilt and the belief that he had let the family down.

Frank joined him at the stall door. "So this is where the infamous Beanie used to reside. I think he stole the heart of everyone last night."

"Yeah." Nash tapped the top rail of the stall door. "He should win comeback horse of the year."

Frank glanced inside the empty stall. "There's room for Sneaker in here now."

"That hardly seems fair. We'll be moving soon, most likely renting a place that doesn't have a warm stable."

Frank looked away, nodding.

Silence fell in the barn. Nash wished he had put Christmas music on the speakers. Or that Helen would join them.

Frank cleared his throat. "I…uh… I'd like to buy Sneaker for—"

"She's not for sale." If there was one good thing that would come out of this mess—besides winning his family back—it would be that Nash could give his son a horse. "Every horseman needs a good horse. She's Luke's."

The older man glanced at Nash, nodding again. "What I meant was that I'd like to buy her for Luke."

"I'm not following." Nash shook his head. "We already own her." Adele and Grady had found no record of her in the lost or stolen database. She wasn't microchipped and didn't have a lip tattoo.

"What I meant is that I'd like to buy her and give her to Luke." Frank's voice filled the barn.

Several horses poked their heads out, curious as to what the ruckus was.

"But…" Nash was at a loss. "Why?"

"I'd like to pay you forty thousand dollars for her."

Nash's mouth dropped open. With this sale combined with the sales of Queenie and Java, they'd have more than enough money to pay off the bank loan and Big E. To avoid foreclosure. To save the town.

To thwart the villain. Frank Wesson.

Nash put a hand over his chest, over his heart which was beating double-time. "I still don't understand. With that money—"

"You can save the Flying Spur." Frank ran a hand around the back of his neck. "And Eagle Springs."

"Yeah," Nash breathed, still unable to believe it.

"All I ask is…"

Nash drew back, preparing for the worst.

"...that you allow me to visit. I'd like to be a part of Luke's childhood and your...you..." he swallowed, visibly out of sorts. "I want to be a part of your lives. All of your lives. Denny was right. You're all the family I have left." His composure crumbled.

And suddenly, Helen was there, wrapping her arms around both of them, mending the chasm between them, bringing them together. Wesson and Blackwell.

"It's all right," Nash said. "It's all going to be okay."

And for the first time in months, Nash actually believed it.

HELEN AND NASH waved as Frank drove off.

Nash's arms were around her. Christmas lights were sparkling from one end of the ranch to the other. The sky was clear and the stars above glowed. Everything was perfect.

But she was wise enough now to know it wouldn't stay that way.

Helen turned in Nash's arms. "We need to go tell everybody. You saved the ranch."

"I didn't save anything," Nash said in a humble, aw-shucks voice. "It was all you and Denny."

"Well..." She ran her palm over his stubbled

cheek. "We couldn't have done it without you and Luke being doppelgängers for Cal."

Nash smiled. "Finally, this mug is good for something."

"Come on." She took a purposeful step toward the main house.

"Wait." Nash held on to her. "I have something for you."

"Did I earn more kisses?" She smiled up at him, her handsome cowboy.

Nash dug in his pocket and brought out—

A ring?

—a wilted clump of mistletoe.

He held it over her head. "Merry Christmas, Helen."

She laughed and planted a quick kiss on his lips. "It's still two weeks away."

"I know." He continued to hold the mistletoe above her head. "And I also happen to know that Christmas is your favorite time of the year. Let's get married again. On Christmas. This Christmas. I love you, honey," he said gruffly. "Say you will."

"I love you, Nash Blackwell!" She threw her head back and laughed at fate and the stars and hard lessons.

Nash swung her around and held her as if

dipping her in a tango. "You'll marry me? On Christmas?"

"I will. Of course, I will."

"Helen Blackwell." His lips moved closer to hers. "You always were the best part of me."

EPILOGUE

IT SNOWED ON Christmas Day.

On Nash and Helen's wedding day.

Helen couldn't have been happier.

They were getting married in the arena. Christmas trees had been put up in a half-circle on the far end to create an altar. Chairs had been brought in for guests, which included all the Blackwells—both Denny and Big E's branches of the family—and close friends.

They were also getting married on horseback. One of Big E's granddaughters had recommended it. And Helen was up for it, but only if she could ride on Beanie.

Madeline and Sylvie had been happy to bring her their treasure, including allowing Helen to apply glitter to his freshly shod hooves and weave roses in his mane and tail.

"I'm up for being your surrogate," Gwen told Helen as they waited in the barn for the signal to mount up. "If you decide you want more kids."

"We're happy with Luke." It was true.

"You could have really cemented your relationship with Frank," Gwen continued pushing. "Named your next kid after Cal."

"She can't." Corliss came out of a stall leading her beloved Skyfire, the horse they'd used as collateral to buy the horses Nash had been training all these months. "Ryder and I are beating them to the punch. It'll be Callie Wesson Blackwell Talbot if it's a girl. Or Calvin Wesson Blackwell Talbot if it's a boy. But you can't tell anyone, Gwen," Corliss cautioned. "This is Helen's big day. It's just… I couldn't keep it in with you going on and on."

"I know when to quit, Corliss." Gwen sniffed.

"Sure, you do." But Corliss laughed. "Time to mount up."

Helen swung up on Beanie's back and adjusted her outfit, smoothing the wide-legged white velvet slacks and matching white sweater with all its fancy beads and sequins. She settled the white cowboy hat on her head, short veil trailing over her shoulders.

Corliss came around and fluffed out her white duster. "You look like a throwback to a simpler time."

"You can thank Adele for finding our wedding clothes online." At first, Helen had thought Adele had been joking. But there was a charm and casualness to their wardrobe. Nash would look even more handsome—if possible—in a traditional black Western suit and a black duster.

"And don't forget to thank Levi for loaning you the chairs and Wyatt for rigging the special lights."

Helen assured Corliss she wouldn't.

"And my wedding gift to you…" Corliss said slyly, "…is the besting of Phil. I beat him at his own game when I bought those horses on the cheap and had Nash train them. For two weeks." She laughed. "He wanted two Nash Blackwell horses and he got them. Whirligig and Bubs."

"They're good horses now." Helen had been sorry to see them go. Except Phil had refused to pay forty thousand dollars for two horses worth about a thousand dollars apiece. So they were still in the Blackwell stable. And there they would remain.

Denny entered the barn. Her shoulder no longer bothered her and without the stress of losing the ranch, there was color back in her cheeks. She wore black boots, black jeans and a silver button-down. "They're ready."

Corliss came to her side. "Gran, are you sure you don't want to wear a jacket? It's cold."

Denny brushed her concerns away. "Little miss, I'm more than capable of sitting a horse for a five-minute ride before I freeze to death."

And then they were mounted up and heading off.

Corliss rode next to Gwen, who was a nervous rider and not likely to last the entire ceremony in the saddle.

Denny rode next to Helen, being the one Helen had chosen to give her away.

She then spotted Nash, sitting on Rose and waiting for her at the half-circle of sparkling Christmas trees. Jake Gallagher was next to him on horseback.

Luke sat in the front row on the bride's side next to his granduncle Frank, who was fast becoming one of his favorite relatives.

Blackwells filled Nash's side. Faces and names flitted through Helen's head. Familiar ones, like Nash's parents, his uncle and cousins. And new to her—the Montana Blackwells—Ben, Lily, Ethan, Georgie, Peyton, Chance and… There were too many to name. Her family was growing. Levi sat with his arm around Isla and Summer. Harper was holding hands with Wyatt. Adele sat with Grady, a twin toddler girl in each of their laps.

And at the far corner, sat Helen's mother with glowing features and recently highlighted blond hair, thanks to Gwen. Helen and her mother had begun talking in fits and starts. It might take some time, but she wanted Luke to know his family history—both sides of his family history.

Helen stopped several feet from the altar, heart bursting with love for all the blessings this holiday season had given her.

"Who gives this woman away?" the minister asked, feet firmly on the ground.

"I do," Denny said in a strong voice, reaching over and patting Helen's hand. "She's a Blackwell, through thick and thin."

"I am." Helen blinked back a well of happy tears.

Corliss led Gwen's horse into position, while Denny rode slowly to the far side of the altar. And then Corlis dismounted and tied her horse and Denny's to the arena fence. She helped Denny down and to a seat where a coat and blanket awaited beside Ryder.

Finally, Helen reached the altar and the man who'd had her heart since the moment she'd laid eyes on him at the Cranky Crow.

Nash moved his horse next to hers and took her hand. "Merry Christmas, love."

"Merry Christmas." And a happy-ever-after.

* * * * *

If you missed the first romances featuring the Return of the Blackwells or the follow-up miniseries The Blackwell Sisters from the same authors, please visit www.Harlequin.com today!

Get 4 FREE REWARDS!
We'll send you 2 FREE Books plus 2 FREE Mystery Gifts.
MONTANA MAVERICKS
The Maverick's Marriage Pact
STELLA BAGWELL
Secret under the Stars
ELIZABETH BEVARLY
FREE
Value Over
$20
The Cowboy's Ranch Rescue
Lisa Childs
His Partnership Proposal
Both the Harlequin® Special Edition and Harlequin® Heartwarming™ series feature compelling novels filled with stories of love and strength where the bonds of friendship, family and community unite.
YES! Please send me 2 FREE novels from the Harlequin Special Edition or Harlequin Heartwarming series and my 2 FREE gifts (gifts are worth about $10 retail). After receiving them, if I don't wish to receive any more books, I can return the shipping statement marked "cancel." If I don't cancel, I will receive 6 brand-new Harlequin Special Edition books every month and be billed just $5.49 each in the U.S. or $6.24 each in Canada, a savings of at least 12% off the cover price, or 4 brand-new Harlequin Heartwarming Larger-Print books every month and be billed just $6.24 each in the U.S. or $6.74 each in Canada, a savings of at least 19% off the cover price. It's quite a bargain! Shipping and handling is just 50¢ per book in the U.S. and $1.25 per book in Canada.* I understand that accepting the 2 free books and gifts places me under no obligation to buy anything. I can always return a shipment and cancel at any time by calling the number below. The free books and gifts are mine to keep no matter what I decide.
Choose one: ☐ Harlequin Special Edition (235/335 HDN GRJV) ☐ Harlequin Heartwarming Larger-Print (161/361 HDN GRJV)
Name (please print)
Address
Apt. #
City
State/Province
Zip/Postal Code
Email: Please check this box ☐ if you would like to receive newsletters and promotional emails from Harlequin Enterprises ULC and its affiliates. You can unsubscribe anytime.
Mail to the Harlequin Reader Service:
IN U.S.A.: P.O. Box 1341, Buffalo, NY 14240-8531
IN CANADA: P.O. Box 603, Fort Erie, Ontario L2A 5X3
Want to try 2 free books from another series? Call 1-800-873-8635 or visit www.ReaderService.com.
*Terms and prices subject to change without notice. Prices do not include sales taxes, which will be charged (if applicable) based on your state or country of residence. Canadian residents will be charged applicable taxes. Offer not valid in Quebec. This offer is limited to one order per household. Books received may not be as shown. Not valid for current subscribers to the Harlequin Special Edition or Harlequin Heartwarming series. All orders subject to approval. Credit or debit balances in a customer's account(s) may be offset by any other outstanding balance owed by or to the customer. Please allow 4 to 6 weeks for delivery. Offer available while quantities last.
Your Privacy—Your information is being collected by Harlequin Enterprises ULC, operating as Harlequin Reader Service. For a complete summary of the information we collect, how we use this information and to whom it is disclosed, please visit our privacy notice located at corporate.harlequin.com/privacy-notice. From time to time we may also exchange your personal information with reputable third parties. If you wish to opt out of this sharing of your personal information, please visit readerservice.com/consumerschoice or call 1-800-873-8635. Notice to California Residents—Under California law, you have specific rights to control and access your data. For more information on these rights and how to exercise them, visit corporate.harlequin.com/california-privacy.
HSEHW22R3

COMING NEXT MONTH FROM

HARLEQUIN

HEARTWARMING

#451 THE COWBOY'S RANCH RESCUE

Bachelor Cowboys • by Lisa Childs

Firefighter paramedic Baker Haven will do right by his orphaned nephews—even keep his distance. He couldn't save his brother, and he can't give his heart to the ranch's beautiful cook, Taye Cooper, either...despite the hope she brings to their home.

#452 HIS PARTNERSHIP PROPOSAL

Polk Island • by Jacquelin Thomas

Aubrie DuGrandpre and Terian LaCroix were rivals in cooking school—and now they're vying for the same restaurant property! When Terian approaches her about a partnership, she agrees. Can a past grudge lead to a lifetime commitment?

#453 A RANCHER WORTH REMEMBERING

Love, Oregon • by Anna Grace

Matchmaker Clara Wallace avoids skeptics—and Jet Broughman, her new client's best friend, is the ultimate nonbeliever. He's also her teenage crush! Now Clara must help Jet's friend find love *without* falling for the gorgeous, stubborn rancher she's never forgotten.

#454 THE OFFICER'S DILEMMA

by Janice Carter

Zanna Winters and Navy Lt. Dominic Kennedy wanted to escape the small town of Lighthouse Cove. But Zanna's surprise announcement might tie them there...and to each other. Can two people who dream of adventure find one with family?